Scar

The Perished Riders MC - Book 2

Nicola Jane

Copyright © 2021 by Nicola Jane

All rights reserved.

No portion of this book may be reproduced in any form without written permission from the publisher or author, except as permitted by U.S. copyright law.

Meet the team

Cover Designer: Charli Childs, Cosmic Letterz Design
Editor: Rebecca Vazquez
Proofreader: Jackie Ziegler
Formatting: Nicola Miller
Publisher: Nicola Jane

Disclaimer:

This book is a work of fiction. The names, characters, places, and incidents are all products of the author's imagination and are not to be construed as real. Any similarities are entirely coincidental.

Spelling:

Please note, this author resides in the United Kingdom and is using British English. Therefore, some words may be viewed as incorrect or spelled incorrectly, however, they are not.

Acknowledgements

I loved writing this book so much. When you meet Scar, you'll probably see why. Thanks for sticking with me and devouring all my books like greedy little book worms. You're the best. xx

Trigger Warning

The material in this book may be viewed as offensive to some readers, including graphic language, sexual situations, murder, violence, and rape (however, the author does not go into detail).

When reading this book, remind yourself it's an MC romance and therefore the above topics are a given.

Scar will not appreciate you taking time to trash him because you didn't read the warning.

Happy reading xx

Contents

Playlist		IX
1.	CHAPTER ONE	1
2.	CHAPTER TWO	11
3.	CHAPTER THREE	19
4.	CHAPTER FOUR	29
5.	CHAPTER FIVE	39
6.	CHAPTER SIX	49
7.	CHAPTER SEVEN	61
8.	CHAPTER EIGHT	71
9.	CHAPTER NINE	81
10.	CHAPTER TEN	91
11.	CHAPTER ELEVEN	103
12.	CHAPTER TWELVE	111
13.	CHAPTER THIRTEEN	123
14.	CHAPTER FOURTEEN	131
15.	CHAPTER FIFTEEN	140
16.	CHAPTER SIXTEEN	149
17.	CHAPTER SEVENTEEN	161
18.	CHAPTER EIGHTEEN	171
19.	CHAPTER NINETEEN	180

20.	CHAPTER TWENTY	195
21.	CHAPTER TWENTY-ONE	203
22.	CHAPTER TWENTY-TWO	213
23.	CHAPTER TWENTY-THREE	223
24.	CHAPTER TWENTY-FOUR	235
A note from me to you		247

Playlist

In Case You Didn't Know - Brett Young
I Found - Amber Run
Til It Happens to You - Lady Gaga
Little Do You Know - Alex & Sierra
Lost Boy - Ruth B.
good 4 u - Olivia Rodrigo
Happier Than Ever - Billie Eilish
Love the Way You Lie - Eminem ft. Rihanna
Rolling in the Deep - Adele
Scars - Lukas Graham
You Signed Up For This - Maisie Peters
She Gets the Flowers - Beth McCarthy
Picking Up the Pieces - Paloma Faith
Lego House - Ed Sheeran
Scars to Your Beautiful - Alessia Cara
Fix You - Coldplay
Helium - Sia
Beauty and the Beast - Ariana Grande & John Legend

CHAPTER ONE

GRACIE

Crawling, that's the only way to describe the feeling across my entire body right now. When did this become me? I glance nervously over my shoulder. I can't see them, but that doesn't mean they aren't coming. Rain pours down, soaking my pale, bruised skin. I must look a state in my dirty, torn vest and far too short denim skirt. The worn canvas shoes I stuffed my feet into as I made a run for it are sopping wet and my toes squish with every step. But it's late, there's not a soul around.

"She must be here somewhere." I jump to life at the sound of the deep, menacing voice I know so well. Ducking behind a car, panic rips through me. I can't stay here, they'll find me, so I drop to my hands and knees and crawl to the next car. I can see a church up ahead. Maybe I can hide amongst the gravestones. "Gracie," he says in a sing-song voice, "come out, come out, wherever you are."

I'm shaking, though I don't know if it's from cold, shock, fear, or the drugs working through my system. I carefully crawl to the next car, then the next. Pushing up onto my feet, I creep closer to the church. I glance back and see three hefty figures a good ten metres away. I keep in the shadows and speed up.

As I step into the church yard, I feel slightly relieved. There're more dark corners to hide in.

Now I'm out of their eye line, I run across the wet, slippery grass, stumbling a few times before reaching the gravestones around the back of the building. An owl hoots, giving the place an eerie feeling. I notice a door to the side of the church is open, where a sliver of light shines like a beacon of hope, so I head for it.

I push my muddy fingers into the gap and slowly open the heavy door, slipping my thin frame into the safety of the church. I'm in a side room, it's small and on a table is a stack of Bibles. The tablecloth touches the floor, so I lift it and slide under the table, curling myself into a tight ball and working hard to steady my rapid breathing.

A few minutes pass before I hear footsteps. They're not heavy, like when the men come, but I still can't control the panic rising in my chest. "I've already seen you, so there's really no point hiding." He sounds amused as he lifts the tablecloth. His black robe and white collar are a sign that maybe, just maybe, I've made it to safety. "Want to tell me why you're hiding under there?" I shake my head. "Okay, but the torch lights outside have gone, so I can only assume the people you ran from have left. How about I get you a blanket and make you a hot drink? You can't stay under that table for the rest of the night."

The vicar's right, I can't stay here. My joints are already screaming in pain from being scrunched up. I slowly slide from under the table. He holds out his hand, and I take it, letting him help me to my feet. He's got to be a good guy, he's a vicar, and what choice do I have?

He gets a soft blanket from a box and hands it to me. I wrap it around my cold, weak body and a stray tear slips down my cheek. It's been so long since I've felt any kind of warmth. I follow him through the main church to another room, which turns out to be an office. He points to a couch, and I sit on the edge, ready to make my escape should I need to. I watch as he turns on a coffee machine and proceeds to make us both a drink. It smells amazing, reminding me of times I spent with friends in coffee shops. It's been so long since I've allowed myself to think back, and my heart fills with sadness.

The vicar hands me a cup, and I wrap my hands around it. It's scalding hot, but I don't care, I'm so happy to feel the heat. "My name's Michael. I've been the vicar here for two years."

"I'm Gracie," I almost whisper.

"Lovely to meet you, Gracie. Do you know where you are?" I shake my head. "You're in London. Hackney, London." My mind races. Did I come here, or was I brought here? I'm so busy working through my thoughts, I don't hear a thing he says until he clears his throat and takes a seat beside me. "Where are you from?" he asks.

"Essex . . . I lived in Essex."

"Not too far then," he says, smiling. "What made you come to Hackney today?" I shrug, confusion hitting me hard. I don't remember coming here. I don't remember any of it.

"Try not to worry about it now. We'll work it all out. I can help you, Gracie."

I shake my head. "I'll drink this and go." The guards will be back soon, I know they won't give up until they find me, so I have to get as far away from here as possible.

"Where will you go?" he asks. "I can keep you safe from whoever you're running from."

"Nowhere is safe," I whisper, repeating *his* words. *Nowhere.*

SCAR

I pull the peak of my baseball cap down over my eyes and pull my hood up. It's raining, but that ain't the only reason I cover my face—I don't want anyone else to see the monster I've become.

My mobile shrills from my kutte pocket, and I pull it out, irritated by the interruption. Mav's name flashes on the screen, and I mutter a few curse words. I've worked my arse off today, clocking off an hour ago, but I'll answer regardless cos he'll only bitch if I don't. I accept the call and press it to my ear. I don't bother with hello, but the Pres doesn't expect me to. He's known me since I was a kid, and he knows I hate talking at the best of times, especially over the phone.

"Scar, I'm sorry to do this, brother, but I need you to do another job. I know you have shit to do, but this is important." I remain silent, waiting for further instruction. If the Pres says it's urgent, of course, I'm gonna drop everything. "Michael called. He's got a girl turned up at the church. She's a mess, brother, and I need you to bring her back to the club. Michael said she's skittish and he thinks she's running from someone, so be on your guard."

I disconnect and throw my leg back over my bike. I take one last look at the house I was about to sit here in the rain staring at, before pulling out into traffic.

∞

I look down at the woman sleeping soundly on the wooden pew. She doesn't look comfortable in the slightest, but judging by the state of her, she's too exhausted to care.

"She sneaked in through the backdoor. She hasn't really said much, but I can sense her pain," explains Michael. I hate these places, they give me the creeps. I glare at him, and he stares back blankly. "You want me to wake her?" he guesses. When I raise a brow, he nods. "Right, of course."

Michael gently shakes the woman, and her eyes shoot open. She sits up fast, scooting away from us. "It's okay, Grace. He's here to help." I keep my head lowered. It's one thing the vicar seeing me—he knows me since he's a patched member of The Perished Riders MC just like me—but this girl doesn't need to be scared any more than she already is. Michael looks at me.

"Should we use your real name? Scar seems a little..." he trails off. "Never mind." He sighs when I don't reply. "This... erm... man... will take you somewhere safe. Another man named Maverick is going to help you."

The girl shakes her head, panic written across her face. I shrug and turn towards the door. The Pres never said anything about begging. I get two steps before the bumbling vicar is getting himself into a flap.

"You can trust me, I promise. He won't ever hurt you. Scar's one of the gentlest giants I know." I freeze at his words.

"Where will he take me?" Her voice is soft and delicate, and I turn to listen better. She's beautiful, and somehow, hearing her speak has me mesmerised.

"Maverick is the President of The Perished Riders MC. We help people like you. There are other women there too, just stay with them until you know what to do. No one will find you there."

She gets to her feet on wobbly legs. I take in the ripped clothes, the dirt and bruises on her pale skin, and ball my fists. Someone did this to her, and I need to find out who.

She reaches me, and I push open the large oak door. It's still raining hard, and she shivers as the cold air rushes in. She's got one of those itchy-looking blankets around her, but she's wearing next to nothing, no wonder she's cold. I glance down at her bare feet and find they're covered in dried mud. The dirty, wet shoes dangling from her hand offer no protection. I adjust my baseball cap again, ensuring it's covering my face before moving towards her. She eyes me warily as I pull on my leather gloves.

Michael steps closer. "Scar doesn't really like skin to skin contact with strangers," he explains, and she frowns as I take her hand in mine. She watches as I place my other arm under her legs, and she allows me to scoop her up. Michael takes her wet shoes, and she places her hands in her lap, careful not to wrap them around my neck, and I smile, appreciative of her consideration.

Outside, I sit her sideways on my bike and reach into the saddlebag, pulling out a plain black leather jacket. She allows me to take the shitty blanket, which I pass to Michael, then she pushes her thin arms into the leather. It buries her small frame, but she'll be grateful for it when we hit the road. I pull out my spare riding boots. They're far too big, but she only needs them to rest her feet against the bars. I show her how to hold on behind her using the sissy bar, which she does.

"Good luck, Grace. I'll come by and visit you soon," Michael says as I climb on the bike in front of her.

GRACIE

I cling to the cold metal bar until my knuckles turn white. I've never been on a motorcycle before, and I'm way too cold to enjoy the experience right now. We ride for ten minutes before stopping outside a pair of tall metal gates. On the other side, a man pops his head out of the gatehouse and shouts something in greeting, but Scar doesn't reply. The gates slide open slowly, we pull in, and I stare up at the building as we come to a stop outside. This place looks like some kind of warehouse.

Scar steps off the bike first. I watch him closely as he removes the heavy, oversized boots from my feet. I haven't yet seen his face, as he keeps it well hidden under a baseball cap and hood. He's careful to keep his chin to his chest as he stores the boots away in a bag hanging over his bike. He taps my leg, and I lift it over so I'm sitting sideways again. It's strange that he communicates in this silent way, and I know exactly what he wants me to do. The rain is still pouring, and I go to shrug the jacket off, but he stops me, placing his gloved hand on my shoulder and shaking his head.

He scoops me into his arms for a second time, carrying me towards the large building and kicking his boot against the heavy wooden door. It opens and another man in a leather jacket pokes his head out. "Brother." He grins, then his eyes assess me, and he frowns.

Scar carries me through the door and marches with purpose through an open-plan room that's filled with tables and couches. There's a bar at one end, a few men in the same jackets seated there. He eventually stops outside a door with a sign that says 'President'. Scar carefully places me on my feet, offering his arm for support as my joints scream in protest. I'm cold to the bone and everything aches. He bangs a fist against the door.

"What?" yells a voice from behind the door. Scar opens it and points for me to go ahead, only, I don't know I want to enter here on my own, so I keep hold of his arm until he relents and leads me inside.

Another large man looks up from his desk. He's scary in a beautiful kind of way. There's no denying he's handsomely rugged. "You must be the girl Michael told me about," he says, and his whole face changes when he smiles, causing me to relax a little. "Thanks, Scar. We'll be okay from here if you want to get back to what you were doing."

But I'm not ready for this man to leave me. Something about him makes me feel safe—not completely but enough that I remain clinging to his arm. He doesn't answer the President, instead remaining by my side with his head slightly bowed and his feet shoulder-width apart, almost like a soldier. The President shrugs, then introduces himself. "Whatever. I'm Maverick."

"I'm Grace, but usually, people call me Gracie," I whisper. My throat is sore and dry, and I'm so tired, my eyes sting.

"Well, Gracie, you're safe here. We'll go over everything tomorrow, after you've had a good rest. I'm sure you'd like a bath and some clean clothes." It sounds like heaven, and I offer a small smile. "Scar, if you'll take Gracie up to the second floor, Rylee and Hadley should be waiting for her in room four."

Without a word, Scar scoops me into his arms and carries me from the office and up some stairs. I don't protest because, quite honestly, I don't think I could walk up a flight of stairs, even with the promise of a bath and clean clothes.

SCAR

I hate human interaction, touching, talking, all of it. But having Gracie cling to my arm like she did in the office, I liked that. It was like a spark left her small, dirty hand and travelled right to my heart. My cold, unloving heart. And for a second, I felt a stirring of life. She needed me, and I wanted her to need me. I liked it.

Hadley, Mav's sister, and Rylee, his ol' lady, are making up the bed in room four as we enter. They both turn and smile warmly, but I'm not ready to share Gracie just yet, so I take her directly to the en-suite bathroom and place her carefully on the sink unit. I plug the bath and turn on the water, removing my gloves so I can check the temperature. I pick up several different fancy-looking bottles and try to read the labels, but it's never been my strong point, and I narrow my eyes in frustration.

"It's the pink one," comes her gentle voice, and my heart stutters again. I pour a good amount into the running water and watch as it takes form, bubbling up.

"I'm Rylee," she introduces as she joins us.

"Gracie."

"Welcome to The Perished Riders MC, Gracie. Do you need any help getting undressed?"

Gracie carefully gets down from the sink unit and winces when her feet touch the ground. "Maybe," she whispers.

Rylee taps me on the shoulder. "That's your cue to leave, big man." Her tap burns, so I shrug it off. I want to tell Gracie I'll be right outside, but the words don't come, so I do as Rylee says and step out.

"Scar," whispers Gracie, and I pause, her gentle voice sending shivers down my spine. I keep my back to her. "Thank you."

CHAPTER TWO

GRACIE

I watch the way Scar's shoulders bunch as he balls his fists. It's like he wants to say something, but just when I think he might, he thinks better of it and leaves, closing the door behind him. "I can't believe Mav sent Scar to get you," says Rylee, shaking her head and laughing. "We have around fifteen other men who would have been so much better, but he sends the scariest motherfucker of them all."

"I didn't think he was scary," I say quietly, and Rylee catches my eyes for a brief second before smiling to herself and gripping my top.

"Lift your arms the best you can, and I'll pull it over your head," she says. I try, but my arms feel so stiff, I get them only a little way before groaning. "Yah know what, this top's not salvageable anyway, let's just cut you out," she suggests, grabbing some scissors from the cabinet and cutting my top off.

Rylee doesn't bat an eyelid at the many bruises littering my torso or the bite marks across my breasts. She pretends she doesn't see the burn marks on my buttocks and legs, and as she offers her arm for support so I can sink into the warm bath, she says, "We'll get you checked over by a doctor in the morning. I'll go and make you a hot drink and a sandwich while you soak here. I'll be back soon."

I let the water envelop me in its warmth and close my eyes. I don't remember the last time I bathed like this.

※

"Stop your fucking crying. It's so irritating." He sneers close to my face, and I flinch. I don't need a reminder of why I need to be quiet, but I'm so sore and cold that I can't stop. One of the other girls nudges my foot with hers and begs me with her eyes to stop. Another bucket of cold water hits my skin, and I cry out. "You wanted a bath, right?" he snaps. Grabbing hold of the hard-bristled scrubbing brush, he loads it up with soap. "Stand up," he orders, and I grip the edge of the tin bath and carefully stand, trying not to collapse from exhaustion. He smirks when he presses the brush against my buttocks, and I flinch. My skin is red raw already, and I know for certain, I'll never ask for a bath again.

"Now, kiss her better," he growls, shoving me towards the other girl sitting naked opposite me. A few cheers from around the room erupt, and the girl grabs my hair and thrusts her tongue into my mouth. It's not what she wants either, but she doesn't have a choice. None of us do.

※

I sit up with a start as the door flies open and Scar stands before me, his breathing rapid. I glance around. I'm in the bath still, and there's water sloshing about from my sudden movements. "You screamed," explains Hadley from behind Scar.

"Oh, sorry. I think I dozed off," I mumble, feeling embarrassed. There were many nights I'd be woken by screams, sometimes my own but other times from the women stuck in hell with me.

Scar takes a large fluffy towel from the heated rail and passes it to Hadley. It's his way of saying he wants me out, and she rolls her eyes as he leaves. "He's worried about you," she says, holding the towel open for me to step into.

"Have I been in here too long?"

Hadley laughs. "Not at all, ten minutes tops. I'd like to tell you why he behaves the way he does, but I have no idea. Scar keeps himself to himself. If he can avoid us all, he will."

"Can't he talk?" I ask as she wraps the towel around my battered body.

"When he chooses to. Meli, my sister, reckons he's a selective mute, but I think he just hates people."

We go into the bedroom, where Scar is sitting by the window in an old rocking chair. I still can't see his face, and I want to, so badly. Rylee returns, placing a hot chocolate and a cheese sandwich on the bedside table. "There's some pyjamas on the bed," explains Hadley. "We'll let you settle." When Scar doesn't move, the women exchange a confused look.

"It's fine, he can stay," I mumble, and they shrug before leaving. It sounds crazy, but I feel comforted having him around. His mysterious behaviour and lack of talking doesn't bother me at all. I've seen much scarier things recently.

I pull the pyjama top over my head and, once it's in place, I release the towel. The top is long enough to cover me, but I know Scar isn't looking anyway. His cap is down, right over his face, and his head is in the direction of the window. I've spent a lot of time being naked around strangers, so this is nothing. I pull on the shorts and climb onto the soft, bouncy bed. It feels like heaven. "I'll be okay," I whisper, "if you have somewhere to be."

He shakes his head once. "Eat," he says, and my breath catches in my throat at the sound of his deep, commanding voice. He spoke. It was only one word, but he spoke to me, and I find myself smiling as I reach for the sandwich and take a small bite.

SCAR
Gracie eats everything on her plate, then drinks the hot chocolate; taking the two painkillers and a sleeping pill I left beside her bed. I keep my eyes downcast, but I hear her every movement, and I know the second she's asleep because she's completely still. I wait for ten minutes before approaching the bed, then I lift my cap slightly so I can get a better look at her beautiful face. She looks peaceful. Her shoulder-length blonde hair fans out around her head on the pillow, and I wrap a tendril around my finger before letting it slide off. Her pink lips twitch slightly, and I brush my thumb over them. They're soft and perfect, just like the rest of her. I shake my head. What the fuck am I doing? What the fuck am I thinking? I touched her lips with my actual thumb. I stare down at it for a few seconds. I touched her skin and it felt nice.

∞

The second I hear her stirring, my eyes shoot open. I adjust my cap to cover my eyes as she pulls herself to sit up. I must have drifted off to sleep. "You stayed all night?" she whispers, and I nod. I didn't want her to wake up alone in a strange place. "Thank you." I point to the glass of water beside her bed and the two painkillers I left there. She takes them with no questions, which I find strange. Shouldn't she at least ask what I'm feeding her?

I nod towards the pile of clothes Meli brought for her to try, and Gracie slowly manoeuvres herself to the edge of the bed, standing on unsteady feet. I resist the urge to rush to her side. She might not want me to touch her.

She slowly heads for the bathroom with clothes in hand. I hate the bruises on her skin. Last night, when I heard her cry out and barged into the bathroom, I saw the bite marks on her breasts and the bruising covering her arms and legs. Some fucker had his hands all over her, hard enough to mark her, and I wanna kill that bastard more than anything.

When Gracie returns wearing a sweater and leggings, she looks comfortable and almost relaxed. Her face is pale and there are dark circles under her eyes, but I remember when Rylee looked like that and she's a picture of health these days. I pull on my gloves and lead her to the door. She needs breakfast, and Rylee is the best cook.

GRACIE

Scar hadn't spoken since last night when he ordered me to eat. I want him to say something again—I want it so badly, it's almost like an addiction—so as he leads me downstairs by hooking one of his gloved fingers around one of my own, I ask him for more information. "Where are we?" He doesn't answer. "What is this place? I don't think I quite took everything in last night."

But he remains quiet, with his head slightly bowed and his shoulders tense like he's waiting for something bad to happen. He opens a door, and I freeze. The kitchen is a hive of activity, and the noise is too much, so I pull back. Scar stops and glances back at me, careful to keep his face in the shadows. "I can't go in there," I whisper. "Everyone will stare."

He seems to think for a minute before shrugging out of his leather jacket, unzipping and removing his grey hooded sweater, and placing it around my shoulders. He pulls the hood up to shade my face, and I bite my lower lip, smiling. I see why he likes it under here—it almost feels safe. It's warm from his body heat and smells of his aftershave. He puts his jacket back in place and takes me by the hand, giving it one gentle squeeze. I squeeze his back twice in response, then we head into the kitchen.

No one bothers to stare. Maybe they're used to people coming and going with so many of them here. I sit in the seat beside Scar and shuffle as close as I can get to his side, careful not to touch him too much, as I sense he doesn't like it. He reaches across the table for a plate of toast and takes a couple of pieces, placing them on my plate before filling his own with bacon. I'm starving, so he doesn't need to tell me to eat this time as I devour the buttery slice. He grabs me some fruit, and I take the time to taste each juicy strawberry and grape. It's been so long since I've eaten anything other than cold, lumpy porridge.

"When you're feeling ready, we can talk," says Rylee, taking the spare seat beside me. "I can go over what we do here and show you around."

"I'd like that," I say, pushing my plate away. Scar pulls it back and nods at the last few strawberries. I smile to myself and finish off my food, too keen to look around and know more. Once I'm done, I look at Scar, and he nods, taking my plate from me.

SCAR

I follow Rylee and Gracie. I wasn't planning on tagging along, but Gracie hooked her finger around mine, and I don't want her to feel alone right now. I feel a responsibility towards her, seeing as I was the first to meet her.

We've looked around the entire clubhouse, the place where I grew up since my dad joined The Perished Riders MC way before my brother, Ghost, and I came along. Now, we're both fully patched members, me being one of the club's Enforcers and Ghost being the shadow around the club. You want a job done, he'll be the one to case it out. He can follow someone from half a mile without their knowledge. He's good at computers too, can hack any system. We're close, and he ain't just my brother but my best friend too, so when he slaps me on the back, I unhook my finger from Gracie's and shove my hands in my pockets.

"You good, brother?" he asks, and I nod. He glances under the peak of my cap to catch my eye, and when I nod again, he gives a satisfied smile.

"Gracie, this is Ghost. He's Scar's real blood brother as opposed to just a club brother," Rylee explains. Gracie smiles sweetly at Ghost as he kisses the back of her hand. I scowl even though neither can see my expression.

"You need anything, just give me a shout," says Ghost, winking at her and heading out of the club.

After the grand tour, we settle in Mav's office. Gracie doesn't attempt to hook our fingers again, and I miss it. I rest my elbows on my knees and keep my head lowered while Mav explains the rules of the club.

"No outsiders," Mav adds. "We don't let people walk through our gates without knowing who they are, which leads me to my next question. Your full name. I need to run a background check. It's standard."

"Grace Stone," she whispers. "No other names."

Mav writes it down. "What was your last address?"

"Address?" she repeats, sounding confused.

"Where did you live before we found you?"

She knots her fingers together in her lap. "Erm . . . well . . . I don't know."

"You don't know your address?" asks Rylee.

"I remember the one before that," she says, reeling off an address to a place in Essex. "But I haven't been there for some time. I'm not sure how long exactly."

"Right," mutters Mav. "Where exactly have you been staying, with whom?"

"I don't know," she repeats, and Mav sighs. He's confused, and so am I, but Gracie sounds scared. I reach over and place my gloved hand over hers, squeezing it once. She squeezes twice in reply and relaxes slightly. Sucking in a deep breath, she says, "I was taken . . . from a party. Since then, I've been kept in a prison."

"Like a real prison?" asks Rylee.

"No. One that was run by men. Men I didn't know."

"Let me get this straight," says Mav, and I can sense him pinching the bridge of his nose in that way he does when he's confused. "You lived in Essex, you went to a party, then you were taken by someone you didn't know and kept prisoner in a place you don't remember by men you don't know?" Gracie nods. "So, you're effectively missing, and you have no idea how long you've been gone?"

"I remember when the party was," says Gracie quietly. "It was my friend's birthday. June twentieth."

Rylee gasps. "We're in October."

"Twenty-twenty," adds Gracie.

"Fuck," mutters Mav. I'm so tense, my arms hurt. "Shit, Gracie, it's twenty-twenty-one."

A sob escapes her, and she clasps her hands over her mouth to stop it. I don't think as I pull her to stand and wrap my arms around her tightly. She sniffles into my chest, and I grip the back of her head, desperately wondering how her hair would feel gripped in my bare hand right now.

"Mav, we have to call the cops," says Rylee.

"No," hisses Grace, turning to Mav. "No. No police. I can't risk them ever finding me again."

Mav nods and shrugs at Rylee, whose eyes bug out of her head. "We won't do anything you're not ready for," he explains.

CHAPTER THREE

GRACIE

The rest of the morning goes by in a blur. I've been gone for over a year—sixteen months, to be precise—and I can't get my head around that. It felt like a long time, but when you're crammed into a cage only fit for dogs, every minute feels like an hour. We were kept mainly in the dark, so after the first few nights, I lost track of night and day. Eventually, it was always night.

Scar had to leave. Maverick sent him out with Ghost, and without him, I feel lost.

Rylee joins me on the couch, where I've been sitting for the last hour in a daydream . . . or nightmare, depending on how you look at it. "How are you feeling?" she asks.

I shrug. "Numb. Confused. Sad. Relieved. Why are you helping me?"

Rylee smiles. "Everyone needs a helping hand at some point in their lives. Mav helped me too, and he wanted to keep on helping people. He set up bedrooms for women and men who suffer domestic abuse. You're the second person the club's helped."

"I can't believe my luck. I used to dream of escaping, so now that I have, why do I feel so lost?"

"It's a process. You're gonna feel all types of messed up for a while. I still do and I've been safe for months. But trust me, each day gets a little easier."

"What happens next?" I ask because it's been weighing on my mind. I have nothing. No way of getting home or even knowing if I still have a home.

"Mav will do things at your pace. Give yourself some time to settle. You've been through a lot. The place where they kept you prisoner, were you the only woman there?" Sadness fills me and tears immediately cloud my eyes as I remember them, all of them. I shake my head. "Shit, Gracie, we have to find out who they are. They're still suffering, and we need to get them out." I cry harder, feeling tremendous guilt for leaving them behind, but I had no choice. I had an opportunity, and I took it, like we always agreed we would.

A shadow falls over me, and I'm suddenly scooped up against Scar's body. I instantly relax in his arms. "She's fine, Scar. We were just talking about things," explains Rylee. I feel relieved he's back and press into him harder. As if sensing what I need, he hooks his finger around mine and leads me to the stairs.

Scar doesn't stop until we're in my new bedroom. "Rest," he mutters, and my heart beats a little faster.

"Will you stay?" I whisper, and he nods once.

I climb into bed, and he takes his usual seat in the rocking chair beside it. Lying on my stomach, I tuck my hands under the soft pillow, turning my head towards him. "I wish you'd talk more. Your voice makes me feel safe." When he doesn't respond, I smile. "And I wish you wouldn't hide your face. I want to know the man who saved my life."

I move my hand out from under the pillow and rest it on the edge of the bed. His gloved hand reaches out and gently brushes back and forth over my fingers. My eyes grow too heavy to keep open, and I eventually give in to sleep.

"Hi, my name is Braydon." The fancy-looking guy in the expensive suit holds out his hand and I take it, giggling like a damn teenager. Jen's party is all we've talked about for months, and half the people she invited didn't bother to show, which is why we allowed a group of office types on an after-work drink to join the party. Jen has her eyes on one of his friends, but I like this one. He's cheeky-looking and has heartbreak written all over him. Just the type I like, since I'm trying to get over recently being dumped.

"Gracie."

"Pleased to meet you, Grace," he says, and I don't bother to correct him. Grace is my birth name, but nobody ever uses it.

I'm halfway through a glass of wine when I begin to feel a little dizzy. "Are you okay?" he asks, laughing as I grip the table to steady myself. I nod, but my vision is blurry. I can't make sense of it, I only had one glass and I didn't even want that, but Jen insisted I stop being boring.

When I next open my eyes, I'm lying on the back seat of a moving vehicle. I don't remember saying goodbye to anyone at the party. Jen will be mad.

"How much did you give her, man? She's coming round already."

"She ain't going nowhere, stop worrying." The voices belong to men, and they're right, I'm not going anywhere because my hands and feet are tied together. Panic floods me and I pull against my wrist restraints. The man beside me laughs as he comes into focus. "Morning, flower. Nothing to worry about. We're taking you on a little trip."

"It'll be life-changing," says the voice from the front of the car, and they both laugh.

I stare up at Braydon. He doesn't look cute anymore, and he isn't smiling like before. He looks cruel, and his eyes are wild, like he's on drugs. I feel his hand travelling up my skirt, and I thrash around, trying to shake him off. It doesn't stop him.

SCAR

I watch as Gracie thrashes around on the bed. The sheets are twisted around her ankles, and she's sobbing quietly. I don't want to startle her, so I hook my finger around hers and squeeze it gently. She begins to calm down. "There you g-go, Gracie. Be c-c-calm. You're s-safe," I whisper, and she relaxes. The thrashing stops, and eventually, so do her sobs. "Whoever did th-this to y-you, they'll p-pay."

∞

I take a chair next to Ghost. "Brother," he greets.

"We n-n-need to find who d-did it," I mutter, and he waits patiently for me to find my next words. "To Gracie."

"Argh, okay. You caught feelings for the lost little bird already? Brother, she's only been here twenty-four hours." He's laughing, but when I don't join him, it fades. "I'm sure Mav is on the same page. He asked me to check out places around the church where she turned up. He said she was kept as a prisoner and there are more women?" I nod. "Is she okay?" I shake my head.

"Not surprising, really. Fuck knows what they did to her, but I'm sure we have a pretty good idea." I ball my fists. The thought of her being hurt makes me wanna kill people. "Listen, bro, be careful. Chances are, we'll fix her and send her on her way. She had a life before they took her, and I'm sure she'll wanna go back there. She must have people missing her."

I don't reply because I know all this. It's nothing I haven't said to myself, but while she's here, I wanna take care of her. "You'll do what you want, you always do, but I don't wanna see you hurting again, man. Pres got lucky finding Rylee when he did, she didn't have a family or anyone to return home to. Gracie might." Rylee was the first woman we helped escape a domestic violence relationship. She and the Pres fell in love pretty quickly after that, and she's been here at the club since.

Mum joins us. "How are my two favourite boys?" she asks, placing a hand carefully on my shoulder. Diamond, as she's known to the members, is part of the furniture here. She takes care of us all, just like her best friend, Brea, who happens to be Mav's mum.

"We're all good, Ma. We're about to head into church," says Ghost.

"Your father told me about Grace. My heart breaks for her. Well done, Scar, for taking her under your wing. You're a good boy under all that silence." She kisses me on the cheek proudly, and I half smile before following Ghost. We got lucky with our parents. They met when they were young and have spent the best part of thirty years together. They're madly in love, even now.

∞

In church, Mav paces. He's pissed. "Rylee spoke with Gracie. There were other girls there at that prison. It means more women are being hurt right now. We have to find them."

"Not being funny, Pres, but where the fuck do we start?" asks Copper.

"I don't know," he answers, running his hands through his hair. "Ghost is checking out surrounding buildings, but

Michael said she was sopping wet when he found her, like she'd been in that rain for a while. She doesn't remember how she got to the church or what she was doing up until that point. It sounds like they used to drug her a lot. She remembers coming around in a room with a grate in the wall. She pulled it, it came open, and that's how she got out, but they chased her, so they knew she was in this area last. She can't go out until we find these bastards.

"At the moment, Gracie doesn't want to call the police. She's scared, and after our recent experience with the cops, I don't blame her." Rylee's abusive ex was a cop who tried pulling all kinds of strings to get off his charges for hurting her.

"Give her a few days," says Ghost. "She'll begin to remember more when all that shit gets out her system."

"She's dreaming a l-l-lot," I mutter, and everyone stills. They're not used to me having any input in church. "B-b-bad dreams. She'll remember s-soon."

"How do you know she's having dreams?" asks Tatts with a grin. When I don't reply, normal chatter resumes as the brothers move on to other business.

Dogs are good for trauma. I read that once. It's the reason I rode with a small grey puppy tucked away in my kutte across town. If Mav is gonna keep helping these women out, having a dog around the place isn't a bad thing, and if Gracie needs him in the meantime, then it's for a good cause.

I tap on her bedroom door. I've noticed she hides away a lot when I'm not around. She's sitting on her bed, staring out the window with that lost look on her face. I place the Staffordshire bull terrier in her lap, and it brings her out of her daydream. She stares down at it for a long time before finally looking up at me. "I had a dog once," she whispers. I take a seat in the rocking chair and lean across to where she is rubbing the puppy's head as he settles down in Gracie's lap. "He's really cute," she adds. "What's his name?" I hadn't thought that far ahead, so I shrugged. "What about Deuce?" I like it, so I nod.

"Hadley gave me this," she says, holding up a small device. "It's a voice recorder," she explains. "She said I should record things as I remember them, or if I've had a dream." When I don't respond, she sighs. "I had a boyfriend," she mumbles. I keep my head lowered, glad she can't see my face because I hate the words she's just said, and I'm certain my expression will tell her that.

"I stopped myself thinking about him when I was first taken because it was too painful. His name is Edward. Two nights before Jen's birthday party, he dumped me, after two years together. He didn't give me an explanation, and I was so hurt, but I just figured we'd sort things out in time. But then I was taken. Do you think he ever wanted to sort things out? What if he turned up at my flat to make it right and I wasn't there? We could have been married now."

She stares out the window again, lost in her own thoughts. "It's nice talking to you. You're a good listener," she eventually says with a laugh. "I'm glad he dumped me. He'd never be able to move past some of the things that have happened to me. He was the jealous type. Do you have a girlfriend? Or wife?"

I shake my head. "Good thing with the amount of time you're spending with me," she says with a nervous laugh. "Hadley asked me if I wanted to contact my parents." She pauses before adding, "I want to. I missed them so much, but I'm scared. I don't want them to contact the police, and they will, it's the way they are. If the police know about me returning, then the men will know too, and they'll come back for me."

GRACIE

Sixteen months ago...

"*Struggling won't help,*" *whispers the girl from the cell next to me,* "*and if they see you, they'll stick you in the dog cage. Trust me, that's not a place you want to be.*"

"*Where are we?*" *I ask.*

"*In hell. You want some advice? Do what they say, when they say, and exactly how they say, or your life won't be worth living. Not that yah can kill yahself here, trust me, I've tried.*"

"*My friend will alert the police when she sees I'm missing. She knows I wouldn't leave her party without saying goodbye.*"

"*And who'd ya think will come and save us, princess?*" *she spits out angrily.* "*You don't think we all have people out there wondering what the hell happened to us?*"

"*The police,*" *I mutter.*

"*You've got a lot to learn. These men cater to the cops, the high court judges, the millionaire business types. We're every man's dark fantasy, and sometimes their wife's too. By the looks of you, they'll eat you alive.*"

I hold my breath when the gates open and Braydon walks in. I pray he passes my cell, but when he stops and sneers, I know I'm about to find out what the hell this girl's talking about. Another man joins him. He's dressed well and looks older, maybe in his fifties. He peers over the top of his glasses and nods. "*Yes, she's perfect. We'll do a test run now and see how she performs.*"

I'm led from the cell, out the gates, and up some stone steps. Then, a blindfold is placed over my eyes, and I'm guided into a lift. There's a low beat coming from somewhere, and we follow it. It's much louder when we finally stop. I'm pushed to my knees and I'm thankful for the soft, fluffy carpet cushioning them. I've managed to get quite a few scrapes that I have no memory of.

The blindfold is removed, and I gasp. I'm kneeling in the centre of a room, a circle of men surrounding me. All eyes are on me as a woman moves towards me. She cuffs my hands behind my back and then proceeds to undress me. The men look excited, their eyes bright with hunger.

When I'm eventually returned to my cell, I don't mind the damp-smelling, dirty sheets or the thin mattress on the metal bed frame. In fact, I welcome them as I sob myself to sleep.

∞

Present day...

I've spent the last half hour thinking back to those first days after I was taken. The girl in the next cell, Misha, became a good friend. When she didn't return a few weeks before I escaped, I prayed to God she'd managed to get away, but then Braydon made some comment about her taking her last breath with him, and I just knew she'd left the world. It broke my heart.

A soft snore escapes from Scar, and I glance over. He's relaxed, his head to one side. I'm desperate to see what's under that cap. His large, muscled body is possibly created by the gods, and I need to see his face to see if the angels had a hand in his perfection. I know I shouldn't, but curiosity is killing me. I just want one glimpse. I want to remember the man who saved me, before I'm sent home to my parents.

I slide from the bed and carefully creep over. Deuce gives a small whine, like he's warning me not to do it, but I can't stop myself. My heart beats out of my chest, and I hold my breath as I reach out towards him with a shaky hand. The tips of my fingers brush the peak of the cap, and then his hand darts out, taking me by surprise. I yelp as he grabs my wrist and holds it tightly. His chest is heaving like he's just run a marathon.

CHAPTER FOUR

SCAR

I'm not the sort of man you can sneak up on. I've always had this sixth sense that wakes me right at that crucial moment. I release my grip on Gracie, and she stumbles back, landing on her bed. "I'm so sorry," she says quickly. "I just wanted to see you, just one time." She rubs her wrist while she explains herself.

I stand abruptly, and she falls silent, shuffling back on her bed. I gently hold out my hand and wait for her to place her wrist there. As if she can read my mind, she holds it out in front of her, and I take it, inspecting the small red mark I put there. I rub my thumb over it a few times, aware that I don't have my gloves on and I'm not freaking out. The second I grabbed her, I felt it, and I wondered if she did too. The spark that ran from my hand to hers and back again was like a live cable connecting us both with electricity.

"I'm really sorry, Scar. I just wanted to know what you looked like, so when I go home, I'll always remember the man who helped me."

Those words wash over me like a bucket of ice water. What the fuck am I doing? I release her hand and walk out the room, needing to put some distance between us. I have to step away, because eventually, she's going home.

∞

It's been a week since I walked out of Gracie's room and a week since I last stood anywhere near her . . . well, to her knowledge, anyway. Watching her sleep doesn't count. "Are you sure everything's okay?" asks Ghost, and I nod. "It's been a whole week of you acting weird. I can't even say it's down to your silence because you're always fucking silent, but something feels off with you."

I press the binoculars to my eyes again and stare out over the city. Ghost pinpointed some abandoned buildings, and we've spent the last few days watching each one. So far, nothing looks out of place. I don't even know what the hell we're looking for. Men dragging women into buildings kicking and screaming? Carrying them passed out over their shoulders?

Ghost huffs impatiently, he hates just waiting around. "She's gotta remember a detail, anything that can pinpoint where the fuck we should be looking. Do you think she really doesn't remember, or is she just scared?" he asks, and I shrug. "Maybe we should get her hypnotised. I've seen it on television. The mind subconsciously blocks out traumatic shit. Hypnosis can bring it flooding back."

I shake my head. Ain't no way he's doing that to Gracie. If her mind blocked it out, there's a reason for that. I've spent almost every night in that rocking chair, watching her sleep. Ghost would kill me if he ever found out. Creeping around a woman's bedroom is frowned upon, even if I'm doing it for her. Gracie's nightmares are getting worse, but the moment I whisper in her ear, she relaxes.

We give up after another hour of nothing and get back to the club just in time for church. Mav and Grim have their heads together while everyone gets seated. Eventually, they start the meeting. Mav holds up a device, the one Gracie showed me. "Hadley had a brilliant idea. She got Gracie to record things here. I've been listening back and there's some interesting shit. There's also some fucked up, psychotic bullshit there too, but we'll stick to what you need to know," he says. "She describes loud music. Even when she's locked away in a cell, she can hear the bass. It's a constant beat that gets louder at night, so Grim and I were thinking maybe a nightclub?"

"No way, Pres. Someone would have stumbled across her. A load of women locked in cages right under a nightclub?" asks Gears. "Drunk people wander through the wrong doors all the time in those places."

"It would have been heavily guarded," Grim points out.

"So, now what?" asks Ghost. "We case out some nightclubs? There're hundreds in London. Where the fuck do we start?"

Grim lays out a map in the centre of the table. "Here," he says, pointing to the church. "We start here and work outwards."

"This shit will take forever. There are women trapped with these monsters," says Copper.

"What do you suggest we do?" asks Mav.

"I say we go back to where it all started," he says. "We go to the place where her friend had the party. These men are experts at drugging women and taking them. They'll stick to bars they know and watch women for weeks."

"We can't follow every man who takes home a drunk woman," argues Ghost.

"But we could take Gracie back there. She might pick them out for us," replies Copper.

I rise to my feet, shaking my head. There's no way. "N-n-n-" I suck in a breath and try again. "N-n-n-" I growl in frustration.

Ghost stands beside me. "No. Gracie isn't ready for that." I sigh with relief. He always knows the words when I don't.

"You're right," says Mav, paying no attention to my stupid arse stutter. "Of course, she isn't ready, and we agreed we'd never push these women into doing shit they don't want to."

"Speaking of which," adds Grim, "Hadley said Gracie wants to make contact with her parents." I let that news settle in and take my seat again. The thought of her leaving makes me sick to my stomach. "But she isn't ready to leave us just yet. She knows she isn't safe until we find out who did this," he adds, and I sigh with relief. Just knowing she's staying here where she's protected makes me breathe a little easier. "Scar, she asked if you'd take her."

Ghost jumps in before I can answer. "That ain't a good idea, VP. I'll take her. Her parents will have a shit tonne of questions, and Scar . . . well, you know."

"Maybe I'll go with her. Scar, you can come too, but Ghost is right, they'll have questions, and I'll need to make it clear they can't contact the police just yet," agrees Mav.

It's four in the morning when Gracie's crying wakes me. I sit upright. The wooden rocking chair ain't comfy when you've slept in it for a week straight. Moving closer, I whisper, "Shh, y-y-you're okay, Gracie." She doesn't settle like usual, so I gently brush her hair away from her ear and move closer. "It's okay, b-baby, r-r-relax." She sucks in a panicked breath, and as I pull back, her eyes shoot open and she cries out. She's startled for a second, then relief floods her face and she bursts into tears, throwing her arms around my neck. I straighten, and she clings tighter, moving with me and wrapping her legs around my waist. I freeze. I haven't been hugged in . . . well, a fucking long time.

I stare at my hands, splayed out behind her, unsure of where to put them. I don't have my gloves on, but it hasn't burned to touch her before, so I carefully place my hands under her thighs. The skin there is warm and soft, exactly how I imagined it. She's crying hard now, her whole body shaking with gut-wrenching sobs.

Deuce tips his head from side to side, watching us closely. He's the dumbest animal I've ever met, but Gracie seems to adore him. Since I dropped him in her lap, he hasn't left her side.

"I thought you hated me," she cries against my shoulder. "You've been avoiding me." I don't answer. How can I, when I've done exactly that? "I'm sorry for trying to look at you. I shouldn't have done that. If you're not ready, I understand. You've been so kind and patient with me, and I go and do something stupid like that," she wails.

I lower us to the bed, keeping her against me like a baby monkey clinging to its mum. Having her so close is painful, but not in a bad way, not like usual when someone touches me. This feels so intense but good, and I'm struggling to control myself. Her vanilla scent fills my nostrils, and her soft body feels perfect pressed against me like this. I don't ever want to let her go.

I take a deep breath before taking her hand in mine and moving it towards my head. She sits up straighter, her crying subsiding. I let her grip my hood and guide her hand until it falls away. Next, I let her fingers grasp the peak of my cap. My hand drops, leaving hers resting there. She hesitates for a few seconds, and I keep my head bowed. Every fear I've ever had about her finally seeing me, sits heavy on my chest. Slowly, she pulls the cap from my head. The room is deathly silent except for a ringing in my ears.

I hold my breath, waiting for her to scream, or run, or something, but she doesn't. She lays the cap beside me and places both her hands either side of my face. I keep my eyes fixed downwards as she raises my head. And then, she gently kisses my cheek. It's so soft, it takes me a second to register it. My eyes find hers and sadness whirls in those baby blues. I want it to be gone.

"Thank you," she whispers. Then, she does something which takes us both by surprise. She presses her lips against mine. It's a brief second in time, but it engraves itself right into my brain like a giant rubber stamp. And in that second, all my fears slip away. She isn't disgusted or scared, and as her eyes wander over the criss-crossed angry red lines that cover my face, I see acceptance. She doesn't look at them and think of a monster. "Handsome," she mutters as if she heard me. "So handsome." She lays her head against my shoulder and closes her eyes.

I wait for a minute before shuffling farther onto the bed and lying back against her stacked pillows. She stays against me, and I let her. Something about her relaxed breathing makes me feel calm. The constant noise in my head stops, and as I close my eyes, I realise that I feel happy.

GRACIE

I wake with a smile on my face. I don't think that's happened since Jen's party sixteen months ago, when I woke so happy and excited for the upcoming celebrations. Jen, God, I miss her so much. We were so close. I'd known her since we were teenagers.

Scar is beneath me, deep in sleep, which surprises me. The man never seems to sleep unless it's the odd ten minutes dozing in the corner of my room. I run my finger over the deep, red scars that cover the left side of his face, and I wonder how he got them and why he hides them. He opens his eyes, and his expression is blank as we stare at each other. I realise it's a little weird to watch someone sleep, so I sit up and then register that I'm now straddling him, and his morning wood is pressing against my arse.

I jump up quickly, my face burning crimson. I'm not a prude or anything, but I'm sure he's had enough of me pawing him.

Scar lets me see his face and touch him when I'm sure all he wants to do is head to his own room and go back to avoiding me. "I'm sorry for acting weird. Last night and all . . ." I trail off when he frowns. "I practically threw myself at you like an abandoned child and then cried on your shoulder. I don't think I can feel more embarrassed. You must think I'm so strange." He shakes his head, looking amused. Deuce cries at the door, needing to pee, so Scar gets up, grabbing his cap. I catch his wrist, and he stills. "You don't need to wear that, yah know. If you were wondering, which I'm sure you probably weren't, you're hot. The scars just add to that." He smirks but pulls the cap on anyway, then he swoops down, picks Deuce up, and heads out.

∞

Nobody warned me that talking to a complete stranger about my ordeal would be tiring. Rylee arranged for a therapist to come and see me, and I do feel lighter, but I'm so fucking tired that I find myself lying down on the couch in the clubhouse and closing my eyes. Scar's been gone all day and for most of the evening. It's almost eight, and I haven't seen him since he took Deuce out to do his business first thing.

∞

Nine months ago . . .
"You're my favourite, Gracie. I wish I could keep you just for me, but you're in such high demand. Judge Michaelson and his wife are due any time now, and you're not even dressed." I want to scream that it's his fault I'm standing here bleeding and sore. But I don't. It wouldn't be worth the pain I'd suffer. This man and his little circle of special friends are the brains behind my misery and many other girls just like me. He must

be in his fifties, at least. He has an air of importance about him, and the other girls seem to think he's a police officer, but he's never revealed anything about his life to me. The only blessing is, now he's taken a shine to me, I'm not passed around the wardens anymore. No, I'm saved for 'Sir' and his A list guests.

He releases my arms and legs from the cuffs attached to posts and he grins when I fall to my knees. "Stand, Gracie," he says firmly, that cruel look dancing in his eyes. He's almost excited. "Because girls on their knees are only good for one thing." I grip the nearest post and pull myself to stand. He kicks the back of my leg, and I fall down again. He grins, pulling his belt open again. "The judge will have to wait."

∞

Present day . . .
Waking from my nap, I realise Meli and Rosey must be nearby. I hear them talking as I stretch out. I've learnt that Rosey only returned to the club recently, and she and Meli are good friends. "Sleeping beauty is awake," says Meli, smiling.

"Is Scar back?" I ask, and they both grin.

"Not yet. Are you guys . . . yah know?" asks Rosey.

I shake my head and feel my cheeks redden. "No. Nothing like that. I just like having him around."

"He doesn't freaking talk," says Rosey, like I'm crazy for enjoying his company.

"Sometimes words aren't needed," says Meli thoughtfully. "I'm sure after everything you've been through, the quiet is nice."

I nod, relieved that she came up with an explanation. "He rescued you, I get it," says Rosey, shrugging, "but don't get your feelings confused." I wait for her to explain. "Well, you might feel close to him because he was the first guy to be nice to you in a long time. That can make you think stupid thoughts. But at the end of the day, he's still a man and still likely to fuck you over at some point."

"Christ, Rosey," gasps Meli, "talk about man hating! Not all men want to rape and abuse women!"

"That's not what I meant," says Rosey. "Men generally hurt us, especially these kinds of men. Tell me the last relationship you had where you didn't get hurt. A last-minute date cancellation or a snide comment that made you feel crap?"

Meli thinks before also shrugging. "I haven't really had one. One-night stands don't count, right?" They both laugh. "What about you, Gracie? Have you had a relationship before?"

I nod. "Yes. Edward was my boyfriend. He broke up with me right before I was taken."

"See," exclaims Rosey, "he dumped you. A classic example of men hurting women. What was his reason?"

"Erm . . . he didn't give me one." Rosey arches her eyebrow at Meli like she's proved her point.

"Relationships break up all the time, Rosey. You can't never get with a man because you're scared he might dump you or hurt your feelings."

"I'm not scared, who said I was?" asks Rosey defensively. "I'm merely saying, women like us can easily get our feelings confused. We cling on to the nearest good guy because he does a couple of nice things, and then bam," she slaps her hands together, "right outta the blue, they screw you over."

"Well, I feel sorry for you, Rosey. Closing yourself off like that means you might miss your chance of happiness."

Rosey rolls her eyes. "Aren't you listening to me? It doesn't exist. You're gonna spend your life looking for something you'll never find. And, even if you do manage to find something with someone, he'll still make you cry at some point, even if he doesn't mean to."

Meli laughs. "Don't listen to her, Gracie. Scar's a good man."

Rosey rolls her eyes again. "I bet his ex wouldn't agree."

Meli glares at her with a warning in her eyes. "That's enough. You're acting like men can't possibly be victims too."

"Please, if you start whittling on about your stepbrother being a victim, I might scream."

"Crow was a victim of emotional abuse by my dad. And I'm sorry he then made you a victim too, but it's over now and we have to move forward. Crow's gone. My dad's gone. We're a better club for it."

Hadley joins us, and I sigh in relief. Shit was getting heavy there, and I thought for a second they were gonna fight. Hadley looks at us each in turn. "Okay, who died?"

"Rosey's idea of love," says Meli, grinning. Rosey grins too, and just like that, all is forgotten, and they start talking about Rosey's little boy, Ollie, and how she'll raise him to be a better man.

CHAPTER FIVE

SCAR

I take a deep breath. I hate feeling like this, and I can feel my words already twisted in the back of my throat as I press the doorbell. I hear laughter coming from inside and I know she has visitors. When the door swings open and her eyes land on me, her smile fades. "Well, look what the cat dragged in," Katya, my ex and the mother of my child, mutters in that vehement tone she does so well.

I hold out the carefully wrapped gift I spent over two hours choosing. She glares at it like I'm offering her a poisonous apple, then folds her arms over her chest. "What?" she asks, arching her perfectly plucked brow.

I swallow hard as she glares at me, waiting for me to say the words. "A-a-a," I mumble.

She sneers.

"A-a-a," she mimics. "Your daughter's name is August, and if you think you can just come to the door and drop it off, you're fucking wrong. August!" she yells. "August, there's a man at the door for you!"

Moments later, my beautiful fourteen-year-old daughter comes bouncing down the stairs like a lively ball of energy.

She stops when she sees me. I keep my head lowered, a habit I can't break. "Dad," she whispers.

"He's got something for you," mutters Katya in a bored tone, and I hold it out. "Are you going to wish her a happy birthday? I mean, it's the only time you've bothered to show your face," she laughs, "or not."

"It's fine," says August, taking her gift. "Thanks, Dad." I nod and turn to leave. "Actually, we're having some birthday cake. Why don't you stop and have some?" she adds, and I wince. This is what I was afraid of.

"What a great idea," says Katya brightly. "Come in, have a conversation, make some fucking eye contact."

"Mum," hisses August, "stop."

Katya mutters something before storming back inside. August steps out, pulling the door closed behind her. She approaches me carefully, like she's scared I'll take off. "Ignore her. You don't have to come in, I just thought it'd be nice to spend a few minutes together. I see your bike sometimes, well, most nights. You're always outside at ten o'clock, when I'm going to bed. You haven't been there the last couple of weeks, though, and I was worried." She waits for me to respond, and when I don't, she adds, "I think it's your way of saying goodnight?"

I nod, keeping my head low. Since getting out of prison, I make a point of coming over here to be near August around bedtime. I miss tucking her in and saying goodnight, even though at this age, I'm pretty sure she wouldn't let me tuck her in.

But since Gracie arrived, I've been coming here at stupid hours of the night, worried to leave Gracie's side until she's asleep, and sometimes being unable to leave her at all because of her nightmares.

"I haven't told Mum," she adds. "I almost did because I was worried maybe you went back to prison, but here you are." She stands beside me. "Can I open it?" she asks, holding up the present. I nod, and she unwraps the purple paper. "Holy shit," she whispers when the iPhone box becomes visible. "Dad, this is amazing! Thank you!"

I take the box and open it, showing her it's also purple, her favourite colour. She smiles. I then point to the contract details. I wanted to get her something that I could pay for. Katya never accepts money from me for her upkeep. "It's the best present ever, thank you so much."

"Hey," comes Ghost's voice, and August runs at him as he comes through the gate. "Uncle Eric," she cries with delight. They were close when she was small.

"Don't shout too loud. We don't want the witch coming back out," whispers Ghost, and August laughs. "I couldn't let your fourteenth birthday pass by without a gift, although it ain't gonna beat your dad's," he says, grinning. He hands her an envelope stuffed with money. "And this is from your gramps and Ma," he adds, passing her a present from our parents. "It's a diary. Ma said all teens should have one."

"Are you sure I can't tempt you in for some cake?" she asks.

Ghost slaps me on the shoulder. "Nah, kid. It ain't a good idea. But now you have a phone, we'll be able to stay in touch more." He kisses her on the head. "Take care, baby girl." I do the same and watch her head back inside.

We walk towards our bikes. "What the fuck made you come here?" he hisses. "I could have brought the gift over for you." He doesn't know I stop by regularly, even if it is just to watch her close her curtains at night. "Katya wants an excuse to make up more lies, and by coming here, you put yourself at risk," he growls, frustrated by my silence. He peers under my cap. "I can't stand the thought of you going back inside, Hunter." It's serious when he pulls out my real name. "She has some fucking spell on you and keeping away is the best thing for everyone. It's what you agreed to, remember?"

Three years ago . . .

I can't say no. I never can when it comes to Katya. She's the mother of my child, and I desperately need to see my baby girl. The only thing preventing that is her, so if I have to fuck her to see my kid, there's no question I'm gonna do it. I ball my fists as she bounces on my cock, throwing her head back and raking her nails across my chest. She knows I hate it, every touch, every lick, but it's part of her games.

"Put your hands around my throat," she pants, and I grit my teeth. "Now, Hunter," she hisses, taking my hands and guiding them to her throat. I squeeze gently, careful not to press too hard despite wanting to throttle her until she's fucking limp. "I saw the way you were looking at Kelsie," she whispers close to my ear, causing me to shudder. "She's one of my friends. How the fuck can you sit with me and look at her?" It's all bullshit cos I don't make eye contact with no one. And if Kelsie was to stand in a line-up of women, I couldn't pick her out. "How many women have you fucked since we split up?" she asks, rocking against me. I remain silent. Katya smirks. "That many, huh? I fucking hate you." She slaps me, and luckily, it doesn't hurt, because we're in the front seat of her car and she can't get the room to swing her arm. She grips my chin hard between her fingers, digging her nails into the skin and kissing me hard. "Fuck me, damn it, Hunter" she hisses, leaning closer and catching the sensitive skin of my neck in her teeth. I hiss. "Don't you miss the way we used to fuck?" she pants. "We were like animals. This is like fucking my friend. You want to see August, right?" she asks.

Something in me snaps at the mention of our daughter. I open the car door, lifting her out as I stand but keeping us connected. She wraps her legs around my waist, a satisfied smile on her face as I sit her on the hood of the car. I push her to lie back, keeping my hands on her throat. This time I apply more pressure and I hear her gasping as I ram into her hard and fast. She drags her nails down my arm, drawing blood.

"That's it," she cries, kicking her heels against my thigh and catching the skin. I spin her over, keeping her face down so she can't inflict any more damage. I grip her head, pushing her cheek against the car and entering her tight arse. She cries out, coming instantly and reaching behind to dig her nails into my wrist. I pin her still, slamming into her and chasing my own orgasm. I fall over her, breathing heavily. How do we come back to this every damn time? It's toxic.

"You're deluded if you think I'm gonna let you see August," she whispers, and I freeze. "You honestly think a fuck is worth time with her? Please, you're not that good." She shoves me away, pulling her skirt into place. I look around the nightclub car park. It's full of cars but no one's around. "Now, if you'll excuse me, I have a child to get home to." She pulls out her car keys and heads to the driver's side, but I know she's been drinking, so I take them from her. She slaps me hard, catching me off guard. Then she rains blow after blow over my body, like the psychotic bitch she is, punching, slapping, kicking until she has nothing left. She snatches the keys back. "You dumb arse piece of shit," she hisses.

I rush around to the passenger side. The least I can do is make sure she gets home okay. That's the last thing I remember before sirens, blue lights, and the sound of panic surround me.

GRACIE

"It's so frustrating," I groan.

Meli takes my hands in hers. "You're doing amazing," she says. "So, you remember waking up in the room. You remember it being dark. Did you hear anything?"

I think back to the day I escaped. Rosey thought it would be a good idea to try and remember something to see if we could work out where I was. "It was silent," I say, and they exchange a confused look. "Before, there was always music. A thumping beat all the time. But right before I left, there was silence. I couldn't hear anything or anyone, so I don't think

I was in the same place they always kept us. I think I'd been taken somewhere else."

"And the grate in the wall you escaped through, what did it look like?" asks Rosey.

I shrug. "I'm not sure. It was heavy. It opened outwards and was attached at the top to the wall. A bit like a cat flap. It wasn't straight metal bars, it had funny shapes, like something you'd see on a nice gate?"

"We're getting nowhere," sighs Meli.

"You know what might help?" asks Rosey. "If we went back to the church and had a look around?"

Meli shakes her head. "No way. The Pres would freak out."

Rosey looks around. "There's hardly anyone around. Who would know? Look, we want to help catch these fuckers, right? And there might still be women suffering. Gracie's been here for almost two weeks, what the hell could have happened to them in two weeks?"

"She's right," I mutter. "They're trapped, and I can help them." I can see Meli weighing up the options. Eventually, she nods, and Rosey claps her hands together in delight.

"I'll get my car keys."

I grip the handle of the car door like it's a lifeline. "You'll be fine," Rosey reassures me, "I'm a killer. No one will hurt you."

"It's true," says Meli. "She's a man-hater with a gun, what could be more dangerous?"

I smile. "We're just looking, right?" I ask for the third time.

"Yes," they chorus.

I release the handle and follow them across the wet grass towards the church gates. "I went through there," I say, pointing to the back gate. We look around, and I point down the street. "I ran up there. I remember seeing the church when I was hiding behind cars."

"Well, it's a start," says Rosey, leading the way.

As we walk, I look around constantly, trying hard to remember anything familiar. It all seems like a hazy memory. When we come to the end of the street, I look left, then right. "I ran over a little bridge, over a stream maybe?"

"Let's try there," says Meli, taking the lead. We find the bridge just a few yards along the road and cross it. There's a field beyond it, and we make our way through the wet grass.

"I remember running through grass," I say. "It was raining, and I was slipping over."

"That's great. It means we're on the right track," says Rosey.

Meli's phone rings and she winces, "Fuck, that's Grim."

"Answer it, just say we popped to the supermarket," instructs Rosey.

"Hey, Grim," she answers in a super sweet tone, putting him on a loudspeaker.

"Where are you?"

"The supermarket," she lies. "You need anything?"

"Don't fucking lie, Meli, you're not good at it. I've got Scar right next to me, screwing because Gracie isn't in her bedroom. So, I got to thinking, um, I haven't seen Meli or Rosey for at least an hour. What a fucking coincidence. And then I remembered you all talking and looking pretty cosey together."

"Christ, Grim, we just wanted to go for a walk," snaps Meli. "What are you, the fun police?"

"You know how stupid you sound right now?" he yells. "Mav is ready to explode. Get your arses back here."

"We can't do that, Grim," says Rosey.

"The queen of destruction herself," snaps Grim sarcastically. "I'm not asking, Rosey. All of you get back here. That's a fucking order!"

"We're helping Gracie to remember," she explains.

There's a pause before banging and crashing can be heard. "That's the sound of Scar showing how happy he is about that news. Get back here. So help me, God, if I have to come and find you!" The call disconnects.

We all stare at each other before Rosey laughs. "What can they do? We'll only be another ten minutes."

"I don't know, he sounded pretty mad," I mutter.

"We'll cross this field and then head back if you can't remember anything," she says, walking ahead. Meli and I reluctantly follow.

Stopping at the edge of the field, we stare at the industrial units ahead. They stretch on for miles. "I remember this," I gasp. "It was a brewery, and there were some large wooden barrels used to store beer. Oh my god," I whisper, crouching to the ground as I glance back over the field. I feel like I've been punched in the stomach. "I ran out onto this road and a truck almost hit me. The driver screamed at me to watch where I was going, and that's when I saw them chasing me."

"Oh my god, it worked," says Rosey with a grin.

I shake my head. "This isn't where I was kept all the time. I was brought here that night." A sob escapes me as memories assault my brain. "I was blindfolded and given something by injection into my thigh, then I slept. When I woke, I was here. It was a special night, I remember him whispering to me that afternoon. He said he'd got me a special dress and men were lining up to sample me before . . . bidding. They were gonna bid on me, and the judge and his wife were hoping to win."

I dry heave, pressing my fingers into the wet grass and dragging the mud under my nails. The memories are too much, flooding in and assaulting my brain.

Meli crouches beside me and gently rubs my back. "Well done, Gracie, it's a start."

The rumbling of motorbikes fills the air, and Meli stands. "Fuck," she mutters as Rosey waves them down. Mav is the first to march towards us, yanking his helmet off in anger.

"Before you yell," begins Meli, "I just want to point out that we made progress."

"But to what fucking cost?" he growls, pointing to me still dry heaving on the ground. I feel Scar approaching me, his anger radiating off him like a force, and he stands before me with his legs a shoulder-width apart. I can hear every rapid breath, and I hate that he's disappointed in me. "Do you have any idea how fucking dangerous this was?" snaps Mav. "Not only for Grace's mental health but the fact that these fuckers are still out there. You could have all ended up in trouble!"

"Relax," says Rosey with a smile. "We're fine. I had a gun the whole time."

Mav pinches the bridge of his nose. "This was your idea, wasn't it? Part of your little plan to eradicate all men from this planet?"

"Not all," she says with a shrug. "Just the fucked-up ones."

"I can't deal with you right now. All of you, get on a bike. We'll take you back to the car and follow you home."

I stand, but Scar is already on his bike, pulling off. My heart sinks. "You can ride with me," Mav says gently.

CHAPTER SIX

SCAR

I'm a dick, I know that. But for a terrifying hour back there, I thought they might have taken Gracie again. I haven't felt terror like that in years. And now, I'm so fucking mad that I can't touch her or have her near me. Seeing her like that, bent over on the grass like she was in pain and dry heaving, was enough to send me over the edge. What the fuck was she thinking listening to Meli and Rosey? I leave her for one day and this happens.

Grim approaches. "You keep pacing like that and you'll wear a hole in the concrete." I slow down and take a few deep breaths. "She's all good, brother. Mav sent them to their rooms like naughty little school kids. Rosey wasn't happy. He's gonna talk to them tomorrow."

"I th-th-th—" I take a breath. The stammer is worse when I'm upset and angry, or too fucking stressed.

"Take your time, man," encourages Grim.

"Thought she w-w-was g-g-g-gone."

"Yeah, I can imagine that was tough. You caught feelings for her?" I don't reply, and he sits on the nearby wall in front of the clubhouse. "It's not a bad thing, brother. It shows that bitch,

Katya, didn't kill you off completely." I take off my cap and rub my hand over my face, hating the feel of my skin under my touch. "Maybe next, you'll stop wearing that thing." I smirk. "Gracie's nice, Scar. Just be careful. This life might not be for her, yah know, and then what?" He jumps off the wall and heads inside.

∞

I stop outside Gracie's door. Her soft sobs make my heart ache. The only time she didn't cry in her sleep was when she was lying on my chest. Carefully pushing the door open, I'm surprised to see her awake instead of having a nightmare. I take my seat beside her bed, and she watches me as I remove my cap and lay it on the floor by my feet. She holds out her hands for me to see they're caked in mud, like when I first found her.

"They were gonna sell me, Scar." I wait patiently as another round of sobs takes hold of her. "One of the bosses, we had to call him 'Sir', decided he liked me the most. He kept me as his special pet. It wasn't such a bad thing because it meant the guards couldn't have me, and I was glad because they were worse. They'd burn us and take turns to humiliate us." I grit my teeth together to stay calm. "So, when Sir told me I was his, they stopped using me. But it meant I had to see him every day for two hours. And it was two hours of pure hell. Every so often, he'd loan me out to his special circle of friends."

There's a faraway look in her eyes. "They were just faces. I'd shut off and let them do what they needed to do, but there was one man . . ." she pauses, biting on her lip. "He and his wife would pay money to have me for hours. Scar, they'd have dinner parties and put me on the table for the guests." She sobs harder as her memories flood back. "They filmed it," she gasps. "Oh god, they filmed me." I pull her to me, wrapping my arms around her. "They were gonna bid on me too. Sir said they were desperate to have me forever." She breaks down and cries into my chest. Rubbing her back, I fix my eyes to one spot on the wall and picture all the things I'm gonna do to the men that used Gracie. "That's why I was there that night, near the church. They were gonna bid on me."

∞

I wait until Gracie is asleep before transferring her back into her bed and pulling the sheets over her. I head to the bathroom and wet a cloth, using it to clean her muddy fingers. Then I scoop up my cap and head downstairs to see Mav. He looks up from his desk. "She okay?" he asks, and I nod. "Good. Take a seat."

"She r-remembers," I mutter.

"Okay. You want me to talk to her?" I shake my head and take a breath.

"It w-was well o-organised." I take another breath. "Men p-paid the l-leaders." Another breath. "So they c-could do w-what they l-liked."

"You think this was bigger than we first thought?" he asks, and I nod. "Leaders at the top, men paying to fulfil their every desire?" I nod again. "It makes sense for it to be organised. There's money to be made in the sex trade, especially the underground shit."

I nod again. "She t-talked o-of a man she h-h-had to call Sir." I pause to gather my thoughts. "Sh-she was his. H-he let his circle use h-h-h-her."

"Do you think it's organised by men like the mafia, cos I'm sure Arthur can look into it?"

I shake my head. "No. I-important m-men. Men with m-m-money and p-p-power."

Realisation passes over Mav's face. "Jesus. An elite circle of rich fuckers paying above and beyond to carry out their sickest fantasies?" I nod. "No wonder she didn't want us to call the cops."

※

The next day, we fill the men in at church. Ghost draws up another map of the industrial estate and marks out the buildings of interest. Meli said Gracie talked of a brewery, but there's nothing around there that meets that description. There're a few privately rented factories, but as far as we know, they're not being used. It means a few days of watching and waiting to see if we can uncover anything.

"I just want to make it clear," continues Mav, "we're not pouncing on the first man we see entering a building. Even if he's got a passed-out woman in his arms. We have to watch and see what's going on. We know there's a bigger picture, and if they think for one minute we're onto them, they'll shut up shop and move on. Arthur is putting out some feelers." Arthur Taylor is head of a mobster family which The Perished Riders are associated with. "In the meantime, Gracie is beginning to remember a lot more. She's gonna find that hard, so look out for her."

"Any issues with Gracie, take em' to Scar," says Grim. I feel Ghost staring at me. He'll be pissed Grim knows I've caught feelings before I've discussed it properly with him. When the guys clear out, Ghost sticks to me until we get outside.

"Explain," he says, glaring at me. I shrug, and he rolls his eyes. "You fucking managed to explain it to Grim."

"I d-didn't," I mutter. "He g-g-guessed, and I d-didn't deny it . . ."

"You like her. What happened to staying away from her?"

"She needs m-me."

"She needs stability, Scar. She needs safe and she needs not to be dragged into your fucking messed up life with Katya. Have you even told her you have a kid?" I shake my head. "What are you doing, Scar?" he growls.

"It's n-not like t-that."

"Man, she's gonna have to go home. She has a family and people that are missing her. We're gonna sort this out and get her home where she belongs. Then what? You fuck Katya on a rebound? And the cycle starts again." I ball my fists, and he eyes them. "Do it if it makes you feel better, brother!"

"I-i-i—" I sigh, shaking my head. "It's not like th-th-that. I can l-l-l-let her g-g-g-go."

"Let's go help find these fuckers so we can see if you can really let her go, shall we?" He stomps off towards his bike. He's worried. Whenever shit gets hard, somehow, I end up back at Katya's. But since the accident, I haven't. Prison kept me away from her for two years, and since being released six months ago, I've kept my distance. I'm breaking the cycle and I'm sick of him waiting for me to fall.

∞

We sit side by side in silence. It's nothing new for me and Ghost, but he's never usually pissed at me, so I fidget uncomfortably. He's older by two years and he took the role of big brother very seriously growing up. My stutter was ten times worse back then. From three years old, I struggled to string a sentence together, and it became clear that it was always gonna be an issue when after medical intervention, it remained. No one ever ridiculed me, but if they dared, Ghost would knock ten rounds of shit outta them.

When I got to the age of eight, my dad taught me to fight. He was a bare-knuckle champion in his prime, so from then on, I could take care of myself. As I got older, I found it was best not to fucking talk at all if I could help it. The Army had no time for fools, so I withdrew and became known as the nutcase. Most men avoided me, thinking I was crazy.

"I just worry," he eventually mutters. "Seeing how you were in prison killed me, Scar. We lost you for those two years, and I don't think Mum can go through that again."

"Gracie d-doesn't... feel... the same. I just wanna h-h-help her."

"I like her, man. If she decided to stick around and see how things went with you, I'd be over the fucking moon, but I don't think she's gonna. Once she sees her parents and her ex-boyfriend, she'll remember how great her life was and she'll want it all back."

"G-g-good."

"You don't mean that. And we'll have to pick up the pieces. Just promise me one thing, brother." He waits for me to look at him. "Don't go back to Katya. She might finish you off if she gets another chance."

I stare him dead in the eye. "Promise," I say clearly, and he nods, patting me on the shoulder.

"Good to hear, brother. Good to hear."

GRACIE

I like the women here. Although Hadley and Meli are younger than me by around five years, they're mature. Rylee is my age and so is her friend, Nelly. I'm still making up my mind about Rosey. She's fun but a little crazy, and I get the feeling she causes a lot of trouble here at the club.

Mav's spent the last hour talking with Meli in his office about last night. Then, he calls in Rosey, who doesn't look bothered in the slightest. "Next time Rosey gets a crazy idea," Meli hisses as she joins Rylee and me on the couch, "make sure you punch me in the face to knock some sense into me."

Rylee laughs. "Was he really hard on you?"

"No, actually, he wasn't. He pulled the whole disappointed brother routine, and that's fucking worse."

"I'm sorry," I mutter.

"It's not your fault," she says, rubbing my arm. "Rosey has a way of making you think she's got a great idea. I get swept up in her excitement all the time."

"I seem to remember you being just as bad before Rosey came home," Rylee points out. "You were always getting into trouble for sneaking out."

"Hush you," replies Meli playfully. "You've brought out Mav's soft side," she adds. "Years ago, he would have lost the plot if I did something like that." We hear yelling from inside the office. "Never mind, I take it back," she adds, wincing.

"I think Rosey just brings out the worst in him," says Rylee.

"Have you had that conversation yet?" asks Meli, leaning closely. "About him and Rosey's past?"

Rylee blushes and shakes her head. "No. We've only just started seeing each other. I can't start asking about exes."

"They were a thing?" I gasp.

"No, not exactly. Mav loved her, but she was too young for him, so he waited. But then shit happened, and they went their separate ways," Meli explains.

"I thought you and Mav had been together for years the way you are around each other," I say, and Rylee smiles. "You're such a good fit."

"Thanks. He's everything I ever wanted in a man."

Meli sticks her fingers down her throat, and we laugh. "I mean, it's not like they're still a thing. She's returned with our little brother, so it would be weird if he ever went there again."

I gasp louder. "Ollie is your brother?"

Meli laughs. "I know, fucked up, right?"

"Long story," says Rylee. "There's a lot of history in this place and far too many stories to tell."

"What about Scar?" I ask quietly. "It's hard to get to know him when he hardly speaks."

"Are you asking on a romantic level or . . ." begins Meli with a grin.

"No," I almost screech. "Friends."

"Maybe you should just ask him," suggests Rylee. "I don't think he'd like us to discuss him. The guys round here are funny like that."

"Good call," says Grim from behind us, and we jump with fright. "Meli, Brea is looking for you. Rylee, isn't there some dinner to be cooked?" The women jump up and scuttle off, leaving me with Grim. The Vice President of The Perished Riders is a scary motherfucker, scarier than Mav most of the time. He takes a seat and stares at me. I shift uncomfortably, feeling like he's looking into my soul.

"I wasn't prying. I'm interested in getting to know him," I explain, just to fill the silence.

"Scar's had a lot of shit to deal with, just like you have. You'll be back home with your family before you know it, but Scar will still be here. Ghost is worried about how that'll affect him, once you leave. Just think about that before you take things to another level." He walks away, and I'm left wondering what the hell just happened.

I pull my knees to my chest and rest my head there. Mav spoke to me about seeing my family again when I first arrived here. I wasn't ready then, still scared of my own shadow, but I'm starting to feel ready. Mav's waiting on me to make that decision.

I missed my parents more than anyone, and I know they'd have been devastated when they realised I'd gone. My bruises are fading now, and I can hide some of the bad things from them. Mum won't be able to deal with it otherwise.

∞

It's the middle of the night when I wake crying. Scar's by my side in a second, holding me to his chest. What will I do when he's not there to comfort me and chase the shadows away? I hate thinking about that, but Grim's right, I have to go back to my old life, and Scar probably has things he should be doing during the night instead of babysitting me.

"What do you do all day?" I whisper. "You disappear for hours on end. Are you working? What do you do?" He doesn't reply. Instead, he lies me back down and settles back in the rocking chair. "It can't be comfortable," I say. "I don't mind you lying on the bed." I shuffle up, and he stares for a minute before kicking off his boots and climbing beside me. He places his cap on the bedside table and closes his eyes. I lay on my side, staring at his relaxed face. He's so handsome and rugged and the deep scarring doesn't take that away. "I've decided I want to see my parents," I say, and he opens his eyes again, staring straight ahead. "I have to face it some time. Not that it's a bad thing. I love them both so much and I can't wait to see them. I suppose I'm a little scared." His eyes finally land on me. "They'll ask questions. Mum's like that, she's a dog with a bone when she wants answers. I can't just disappear and not expect that, but I'm not ready to talk about it. Not in detail. And then there's the police. Mum will insist on calling them, and that can't happen."

"Why?" he asks, and I smile at the sound of his voice.

"Because there were cops there. Cops, judges, highly respected businessmen." He frowns. "I dream about them, and I feel it in my bones, there were cops there. Important ones. The man and his wife who used me, he was a judge. There were so many important people, and they never let us forget who they were. They said if we went to the police, the case would be shut down.

"They said they had the power to ruin our lives completely and our families' lives. It could have all been empty threats, they never expected anyone to escape, but what if they can do all that? I want to move on. I don't want to ever see them again. If Mum calls the cops, they'll know I'm alive. They'll know where to find me." I begin to panic and my breathing speeds up. Scar wraps a strong arm around me, pulling me to lie on his chest.

"And what will I do when you're not there anymore?" I ask, a sob escaping, because that's scaring me too. Through all the horror, I found Scar, and I don't want to let him go.

"I'm n-n-not," he takes a breath, "g-going anywhere." Hearing him speak warms my heart. His voice is another level of deep. I'm not totally surprised by his stammer. With him avoiding conversation, I sort of guessed at it.

"Grim's right. I have to go back to my life, and you have to carry on with yours."

"Grim?" he repeats.

"He's worried for you. He said you'd been through a lot of shit, just like I have, and eventually, we'll need to go our separate ways. He's right." I glance up, and Scar looks pissed. "Will you come with me to see my parents?" He sighs, looking conflicted. "What is it?" I ask.

"My s-s-s-stammer g-g-g-gets in th-the way."

I smile, gently running my hand down his scarred cheek. "You have a beautiful voice, stammer and all. My parents won't judge you because of the way you sound or look, Scar. When I tell them how wonderful you've been and how you've helped me, they'll think you're amazing, just like I do."

I place a gentle, lingering kiss on the corner of his mouth. I pull away just enough to see his reaction, and when I see his eyes are closed, I place another. He doesn't stop me, so I move my lips to his, hovering for a second before closing the gap. This time, his eyes shoot open, and we stare at each other for a few seconds.

"Wipe their kisses away," I whisper, a tear rolling down my cheek. "Make me forget about it, just for a minute."

Scar's un-gloved hand comes to rest against my cheek, and we press our lips together in a soft, chaste kiss. This time, I don't pause or check his reaction as I deepen the kiss. I've never been so forward with a guy, but this feels right. I need him to make me forget the feel of them.

Before I was taken, there was only Edward, and before that, there were a couple of guys I hooked up with, but they did all the chasing. When I'm with Scar, it feels different from all of them. It's like we're in our own little bubble and the rest of the world and all the bad shit in it, doesn't exist.

As our mouths move together, his other hand cups my cheek, and it only spurs me on as I kiss him hungrily, throwing my leg over him.

CHAPTER SEVEN

SCAR

It's not that I don't want to—in fact, kissing Gracie has been the only thing on my mind the last few days—but as she presses her hands against my chest, I freeze up. She senses the change in my body language and pulls back, staring at me with confusion. Her swollen lips and eyes full of lust taunt me as I lift her from my lap. "Sorry," she whispers, her cheeks turning red.

"N-not y-you," I mutter, getting up and stuffing my feet back in my boots.

"Don't leave," she pleads. I put my cap on and pull it over my eyes. Why do I always fuck it up? I ball my fists. I'm such a fucking freak and a screw-up, just like Katya said. "I won't touch you, I promise," she adds. But touching isn't the only problem. I leave, heading straight downstairs to the bar.

It's the middle of the night, but some of the guys are still milling around. I grab a bottle of tequila and take a seat. I'll never be able to fucking move on from Katya if I allow her into my head like that. Her venomous words replaying over and over in my head like a damn broken record. "Man, you look pissed with the world," says Ghost, joining me. He takes the bottle from me and looks at the label, arching his brow. "And you're drinking, haven't seen you do that for a long time."

"We kissed," I mumble, taking it back, unscrewing the lid, and swagging directly from the bottle.

"Like I said, if you can handle her leaving, then it's fine. But by the looks of this little pity-party you got going on, you ain't handling shit."

"Katya got in m-m-my h-head, r-right as w-w-we were g-getting comfortable."

"She's gonna. She's been wearing you down for a long time, brother. Gracie's nothing like her, though. Not every woman's gonna be a bitch. Some of what Katya did was just plain fucking wrong. And even though you didn't deserve to go to prison like ya did, I'm glad, because it got you away from her. It took that for you to get your head straight."

I nod in agreement. Before prison, I'd always end up back with Katya. She just had to click her fingers, and I'd go running. Mainly for August. She would use our daughter a lot to get me where she wanted me.

Since the accident, things have gotten worse. I wanted to hide myself from the world, and when my stammer became bad again, that urge to slip into the shadows only got stronger. But it meant stepping back from August too.

"You're doing well, Scar. Just think carefully before you throw yourself into something new. I like Gracie, she seems good, but she's suffered too, and you both need to be over all that past shit before you can fully move forward."

I take another drink before screwing the lid back on. I don't like the taste, never have, and usually, I wouldn't drink. But tonight, I needed to take the edge off, and as I march back upstairs, I know I am one hundred percent ready. But I also know that Gracie isn't.

I spend the night in my own bed, tossing and turning. I can't sleep, which isn't unusual, but without Gracie, it's so much harder. By the morning, I'm exhausted and grouchy.

The thought of taking Gracie to see her parents makes me sick to my stomach, not only because I'm like some dumb arse mute but because she might not return to the club with me, and I don't know how to prepare for that.

At breakfast, Gracie isn't at the table, and when she still doesn't appear after I've eaten, I head up to find her. She was so thin when she came here, she can't afford to skip meals.

I tap on the door and enter before she answers, finding her sitting in the window, staring out. She looks more exhausted than me. When she doesn't bother to look at me, I move closer. She turns her head away, resting it on her knees. Without her watching me, I can't communicate properly, and I sigh.

"Breakfast," I say, but Gracie doesn't reply. "Gracie," I say, a little impatiently.

"You must think I'm such a whore," she mutters, "throwing myself at you like that after everything that happened to me. I'm so fucking disgusting. I shouldn't even be thinking like that after everything."

I need her to look at me so she can see it couldn't be further from the truth, but she refuses, shaking my gloved hand away when I try to touch her. "Just leave. I don't blame you for not wanting me. Who will ever want me now, when they know what happened? All those men and . . ." She shudders. "Just go."

Gracie stands to move past me. I take a deep breath before grabbing her by the wrist. I pull her back to me, and she crashes against my chest. I bite the finger of my glove, pulling it off and dropping it on the floor, then I run my hand over her cheek. It's red from her crying, and her eyes are swollen and bloodshot.

"I d-d-didn't leave," I breathe, "b-because of th-that." I grip her hair in my hand and gently tug her head back so we're eye to eye. "You d-don't disgust m-m-me." I swallow hard, concentrating on what I want to tell her and trying not to focus on my stammer. "I'm n-not g-g-good enough," I manage to say.

Gracie's eyes soften. "Why would you say that?"

"I spent y-y-y —" I sigh heavily.

"It's okay," she reassures me. "Take as much time as you need."

"Years being t-t-told I wasn't g-g-g-good enough."

"Whoever told you that was wrong, Scar. So wrong."

"My name is H-h-hunter."

"I like Hunter," she says, smiling. "Why'd ya call yourself Scar when you do so much to hide your face?"

"L-l-long story," I answer. "Another t-t-t-time."

"So, last night," she whispers, glancing away, "I wasn't the reason?"

I shake my head, rubbing my thumb over her cheek. "B-b-but you're not ready. One d-d-d-day at a t-t-time." I place a kiss on her lips. "B-b-big day?"

"My parents," she replies, nodding. "I'm terrified."

"It's g-going to be okay."

GRACIE

Mav decided to come along too. He's worried my parents might call the police and he wants to explain why that might be dangerous right now. I stare at the red door I once painted with my dad. So many happy memories flood me that I feel overwhelmed and I'm not even inside yet. Scar holds my hand in a vice-like grip. "Are you ready?" asks Mav from the driver's seat. I nod. "We can sit here longer if you need to, but a few of the neighbours are curtain twitching." I take a deep, calming breath. This is a happy time, why the hell am I worried?

I knock on the door, something I wouldn't ever have done before. This was my home, but right now, it feels nothing like it. I see the silhouette of my mum through the stained-glass window. Mav and Scar stand behind me, and I wonder briefly how this will look to her. She opens the door without really looking up at first, busy wiping her hands on a towel. When she does catch sight of me, her mouth falls open. She stares at me for a long minute, like she's seeing a ghost.

"Hey, Mum," I say with a small smile. Her eyes immediately fill with tears and her hands cover her mouth. "Can we come in?" I ask with a laugh. Her eyes rake over the two large men behind me and, suddenly, she frowns. "They're good, Mum. They've helped me."

"Carrie, who is it?" I hear Dad shout from the other room. She ushers us inside, still looking at Mav and Scar suspiciously.

Everything is exactly how I remember it. Nothing's changed, and I smile as we pass the framed pictures on the wall of my parents and me over the years. Dad's in the living room, in his usual armchair, reading the newspaper. "Hey, Dad," I say, and he lowers the newspaper, his eyes wide with shock. He throws it to the floor and rushes towards me, almost knocking me off my feet as he scoops me against him and holds me so tight, he crushes my ribs.

"Oh my god," he whispers. "Oh my god." I hear Mum sniffling from somewhere behind us, so I reach my hand back, indicating for her to join us, which she does. We must stay like that for a few minutes before Dad places his hands on my shoulders, holding me at arm's length and taking me in. "Where the hell have you been?"

I wipe my happy tears. "Can we at least get a cup of tea?"

"Of course," says Mum. "Sit yourselves down."

"Sorry, this is Maverick and Scar," I introduce. Dad shakes their hands, but he looks just as unsure as Mum did.

Mav smiles. "Mr. Stone. We're from The Perished Riders MC. We help women in trouble."

"And that's how you met my daughter?" he asks, and Mav nods. "You helped her?" He nods again, and Dad smiles, shaking his hand a second time. "When I saw you, I thought you were going to tell me you'd married my daughter," he says, adding a nervous laugh. My eyes flick to Scar, who's got his cap firmly in place, keeping most of his face hidden.

I place my hand over his gently, and while Dad is distracted talking with Mav, I whisper in his ear, "Take the cap off, Scar. You have nothing to hide." He shakes his head. "Please? I'm not ashamed of you. I want them to see how amazing you are." Mum returns with a tray of tea and sets about handing everyone a china cup. It makes me smile, she only brings her china out for special occasions. It belonged to my grandmother and it's special to her. She holds the cup to Scar, and before he takes it, he removes his cap. I smile proudly, and Mum doesn't bat an eyelid as she pours his tea.

"We found Gracie a couple weeks ago. She'd managed to get herself to a church where the vicar called us," Mav begins.

"A couple weeks?" Mum questions.

"I was in a bad way, Mum," I mutter. "I had to get well again before I came to see you. I didn't want to upset you any more than I knew you'd already be."

"Grace, we were out of our minds with worry. When the police told us they were stopping the search, we gathered everyone we knew and began our own. But there was no trace, nothing," she says. "We never gave up hope. We knew you hadn't run away. We told them you'd never put us through that."

"I didn't, Mum." Tears fill my eyes again. "I was taken from Jen's party."

"Taken? By whom?" Dad cuts in.

I glance at Mav and let him answer. "We're investigating that, but at the moment, we don't know exactly."

"So, now you're cops?" asks Dad sceptically.

"I know this is going to sound crazy, but right now, we can't trust the cops," he tells them, and Dad scoffs. "I know it's not natural. We have a problem, so they're the first people we should go to, right? But we think some very important people had something to do with Gracie's disappearance, people who pay the cops a lot of money to bury their crimes."

"You're not making any sense," whispers Mum, taking my hand. "Are you saying the police had something to do with this?"

"It's a possibility," says Mav.

"Mum, these men take girls like me by drugging them. They're passed around rich men for their pleasure," I explain. Talking about it as if it didn't happen to me feels easier, but Mum sobs harder.

"Is that what they did to you, Gracie? Did they pass you around?" I nod, and she covers her mouth.

"But I'm gonna be okay, Mum. I got away."

"What did the police say exactly, after she went missing?" Mav asks.

"They told us it was low priority. We had to wait forty-eight hours before they'd even look, and after they'd searched your flat and found your clothes gone, they said you'd probably taken off because of Edward breaking up with you," says Dad.

"My clothes were missing?"

"Yeah, it looked like you'd left in a rush. There was stuff all over the place, and the police said maybe you'd got drunk at the party and decided you'd had enough and left. How could we argue when they were adamant? We never gave up hope, though," says Mum.

"Who do we call? How do we report these bastards?" asks Dad.

"We're working on it," says Mav. "We need some time. But it means you can't tell anyone that you've seen Gracie."

"But everyone's been so worried," says Mum. "What about Jen and Edward?"

"No one can know, or it might put Gracie in danger. They'll want to silence her since she could bring them down."

Dad nods in understanding. "I'm sorry, Dad," I whisper, wiping tears. "I didn't want to put this on you both, but I needed to see you."

"Baby, I'm just happy we have you home. I can keep it a secret forever if you need me to, just as long as I have you back."

"Actually, I can't stay here, not right now."

"We think Gracie will be safer at the club with us," Mav says. "Just for now, until we've worked out if she's still in danger. She'll be able to come home soon, I'm sure."

"How is Jen?" I ask, changing the subject.

"She's great," says Mum, her smile faltering as she glances at Dad. "Actually, she's getting married soon."

"Oh my god, that's amazing. Do I know him?"

"Erm, yeah, very well, in fact. She's marrying Edward."

I choke on my tea, and Scar takes the cup from me and places it on the table. "Sorry, what?"

"They spent a lot of time together looking for you and it just happened. We were really surprised too," Mum explains, "but when we began to think you were never coming back, we took comfort knowing they at least had each other."

I nod. I'd moved on from Edward, though not intentionally. I just stopped thinking about him because it hurt too much when I was living in the pits of hell. And it's not like I expected him to wait around for me for the rest of his life. We'd broken up, after all. But to get with my best friend, well, that kind of stings a little.

Jen knew how much I loved him. I'd bore my friends about how perfect he was for me, and Jen would tell me how she wished she could find a man like him. I guess now she has.

"Are you okay?" Dad asks, and I nod again, not trusting myself to speak.

After a few awkward minutes of silence, I say, "We have to get back. I shouldn't risk being caught here." I stand abruptly, and Mav frowns. We'd agreed I could stay as long as I needed, but suddenly, I feel overwhelmed. "I'm staying here," I say, holding out a piece of paper with the club's address on it. "It's also got my new phone number. You can call and speak to me anytime, and if you want to visit, we can arrange that too," I say, and Mum embraces me. "I'm sorry it's been a short visit, especially when I've just dropped my return on you like this."

"The important thing is you're safe. I'm so happy, Gracie. We love you so much," Mum whispers. Dad joins us again, also telling me how much he loves me. I'm so lucky to have them.

I can't bring myself to speak on the way back to the club. All I can think about is Jen and Edward, and my crazy mind is wondering if it started before I was taken. Is that why he dumped me with no explanation? I don't know why it bothers me, but I can't shake my mood.

The girls are having a little party in the bar, with old school tunes blasting out, and I let Rosey drag me from Scar's side over to their table. She places a shot glass in front of me, and I drink the foul liquid in one go, banging the glass on the table for a refill. She obliges with a grin.

It's not until a few minutes later, when Scar stands before me, with Deuce tucked under his arm and an unimpressed look on his face, that I push the glass away and rise to my feet. He wants me to walk Deuce with him.

The fresh air feels nice against my skin as we step outside. We only walk him around the club's yard, seeing as I can't go out in public. He holds out his arm, and I smile, gently hooking my arm through. It's nice he's letting me touch him so much. "You're u-u-upset about your b-b-boyfriend?"

I shake my head. "He isn't my boyfriend, and I'm not upset, just confused. What if that's why he dumped me because he was seeing Jen? I know it's silly, being upset now when it was over a year ago, almost two, but for me, time kinda stood still. My life didn't move forward, it stood frozen. Will they be happy to see me . . ." I trail off, shrugging.

"You can a-a-ask them s-s-soon."

I sigh. "What would it solve? I should accept it and move on. And I will, I'm just shocked. Take my mind off it, tell me something about you." I like hearing his voice, and I love that he's talking more to me.

CHAPTER EIGHT

SCAR

"I like you," I say in one swift try, and she arches her brows. "Just p-p-putting it out there." I smirk, hoping to God I haven't made a fool of myself.

"I like you too," she says with a small smile. "A lot. But I was hoping for more real talk. Tell me about your love life. How many partners has there been?"

"Shit, that is r-r-r-real."

"I want to make the most of it while you're in a chatty mood," she says.

Gracie makes me want to talk. I feel like she wants to hear what I have to say, not like Katya, who would roll her eyes impatiently whenever I stammered. "Katya," I say, pausing to gather my words, "my ex. T-toxic."

"Is she what Grim was referring to when he said you'd been through some shit?"

I nod. "She wasn't . . . isn't n-n-nice."

"So, how long were you together?"

"I met her w-w-w-when I w-w-w-was twenty-one."

"Wow. And when did you split up?"

"We were on and o-o-off for y-y-years. Last time I w-w-w-was with her was j-j-just over t-t-two years ago."

"So, more than ten years in total?" she asks, looking shocked. We were really off more than we were on, but it's a hard relationship to explain. "Why did you stick around for so long if she wasn't nice?"

"We ha-ha-have a dau—" I take a calming breath. "Daughter."

"Oh." She looks surprised.

"Sorry, I sh-sh-should have s-s-said."

"No, it's fine. You don't owe me an explanation. How old is she?"

"F-f-fourteen. August."

"Nice name. Do you see her a lot?" I shake my head and point to my face as if that explains everything. "You don't see her because of your scars?" I shrug, and Gracie rests her head against my shoulder. "That's so sad."

When I first got out of hospital, August was petrified of me. The scars were all stitched and messy, and she cried every time she looked at me. After that, I made sure to cover up. It didn't help that Katya would taunt me and make fun of the way I looked. It was almost like it pleased her, knowing another woman wouldn't look at me again.

"How did you . . ." Gracie trails off. "Sorry, it's inappropriate."

"My f-f-face?" I ask, and she nods. "Car ac-accident."

"Recently?"

"A few y-y-years ago. My st-st-stammer came b-b-back hard after that."

"So, it wasn't always so bad?" I shake my head. As I grew up, it became less noticeable. I could control it with deep breathing and careful thought. But when things started getting out of control with Katya, it deteriorated, and the accident was the final straw. "Why don't you drink?" she asks, and I frown. "I notice your other brothers drink all the time, but I don't think I've ever seen you with one alcoholic drink."

"I drink. N-not often. Makes m-m-me depressed." I stopped drinking early on in my time with Katya. It caused our already toxic relationship to become unbearable. The nights we went out together always ended in fights, and she'd attack me. Eventually, I had to stay sober to keep my guard up.

"When I was first taken, I missed that the most. I would dream about times I was with friends, drinking a cocktail in a classy bar. That was my go-to place when I needed to distract myself. That, and what I'd do when I got out."

"What was th-that?" I'm starting to relax, and I feel my stammer begin to calm.

"It sounds stupid now, knowing what I know, but the first thing I was gonna do was see Edward and tell him how I loved him and wanted things to be better with us. I was gonna ask him for another shot." A sad look passes over her face. "And all the time, he was screwing my best friend."

"He might ch-change his m-mind when he s-s-sees you again." That thought pisses me the fuck off.

She gives me a shy smile. "I think we've both moved on now. If I was locked in there again, it'd be you I think about," she says, pulling me to stop.

I push my hands into her hair and bring her closer so I can kiss her. It's all I've thought about doing since we left her parents' house.

"I know you think I'm not ready after . . . everything, but I am. I'm ready to forget their hands on me and replace them with good memories." She kisses me and it's hungry, like she's trying to convey how she feels. But it isn't just her I'm worried about. I haven't been with any other woman since Katya, and sex with her was cruel and full of games. I'm not sure how to be when I'm not with Katya. I pull away and smile, placing a gentle kiss on her nose. Disappointment passes over her face for the briefest of seconds. "It's not me, right?" she guesses, and I nod sadly. "It's fine. When you're ready, yeah?" I nod again, and she smiles.

∞

We file into church. Mav looks serious as he waits for us to quiet down. "I've been listening to Gracie's recordings," he announces. He holds up the tape recorder. "Something all the girls in there had in common was they were picked up in the Soho end of London, usually high-end bars, so Grim and I have a plan." He glances at Grim, who stands.

"We set a trap. We send Rosey in and see if they try to pick her up."

"It's a long shot," says Copper. "There'll be hundreds of girls around there, and you said before, they're well organised. Would they choose a random girl without watching her?"

"He's right," says Ghost. "The only way to draw them out would be to use someone they want desperately."

"You mean Gracie?" asks Grim, and Ghost nods.

"No!" I say firmly. They will *not* put her in danger.

"Hear me out," says Ghost. "She'd never be out of our sight. We can place every man within a few feet of her."

"No!" I repeat.

"Brother, we're running out of time. Unless she can remember their names, we have nothing. Girls keep going missing, and that's not even including the ones they already have. We just need her to recognise one man, any of them. We can follow them back to wherever they go and blow the whole thing apart."

Mav nods. "It could work."

"It's not up to any of us. We should ask Gracie. She might not want to do it, and if that's the case, we stick with Rosey. We know she can handle herself," says Grim.

"We could always put Rosey with her. Girls go out with friends, so it wouldn't look odd," suggests Mav.

∞

Gracie is eager to help when Mav talks to her about the plans. "And Rosey will be with me?" she repeats.

Mav nods. "We'd also have men watching your every move." I shake my head in anger. We're not fucking cops, we can't execute this with the same precision. We could end up putting her in serious danger. "I know it's not ideal, brother," says Mav, "but if it helps us find out who did this to Gracie, then we need to give it a shot. Don't you want justice for her?" I feel Gracie's eyes on me, but I can't look at her and I can't see this from Mav's point of view. I know it's selfish, but right now, I don't give a fuck about the other women or even justice. I just want Gracie safe and that means not doing this.

"We'll make our move this weekend, Friday and Saturday night. Wear what you'd normally wear, Gracie. It worked to get their attention last time," says Mav. She nods, placing her hand over mine like it would comfort me. I snatch my hand away and stand abruptly before heading for the exit, hearing Mav tell her to let me cool off.

GRACIE

Scar refused to talk about the plan. After storming out of the clubhouse, he hadn't spoken another word, and when I tried to bring it up, he kissed me into silence. So, I'm surprised when he turns up in my room on Friday evening dressed in jeans and a black tee, his kutte nowhere to be seen. He sits in the rocking chair, and I glance at his reflection through my mirror as I apply my makeup. I haven't worn it since Jen's birthday party, so when Meli brought me a bagful, it took me a while to build up the courage to actually sit in front of the mirror to apply it.

"You're coming?" I ask, and he stares back without a word. I sigh heavily. "I hate that you pick and choose when to talk to me, Scar. A simple yes is fine."

"Yes," he mutters, arching his brow.

"I know you're mad, but I'll be okay. Especially now I know you'll be there."

"I'm n-n-not mad at y-y-you."

"That's not how it feels." Deuce jumps onto Scar's lap, and he gently rubs his head. He's been a great companion, and I'll hate leaving him behind when I go home.

Once my hair and makeup are done, I stand and hear Scar suck in a breath. Good, at least I know he has some feelings as he appraises my body. I was hoping he'd turn up and see the black lace garments Meli brought me to go under the denim dress. I slip my black heels on first to give him the full effect of my toned legs. He grips the arms of the rocking chair, and I smile to myself. I haven't felt beautiful in such a long time and it feels nice.

Once I'm ready to go, we head downstairs. I get to the bottom step, and Scar takes my hand and tugs me back to him. He tips my head back by placing a finger under my chin and then kisses me like I'm his last meal. When he pulls away, I'm short of breath, and he smiles before putting his cap into place.

Mav booked me and Rosey a taxi. Ghost planned out a bar route and made it clear we are to stick to times, so if at any point they lose eyes on us, which they shouldn't, they'll know exactly where we're heading.

The first bar is a modern wine bar with glitzy lights and pumping music. We have to queue to get in, and Ghost and Scar are right behind us. "Come here often?" asks Ghost with a grin, and Rosey rolls her eyes.

"We are so out of your league, don't even try to talk to us," she says, causing me to laugh.

"Out of your league?" repeats Ghost, clearly offended. "I'll have you know, we're a great catch."

"Right," says Rosey, rolling her eyes. "Dumb and dumber."

"I wouldn't come on to you, anyway," he snaps. "I like my balls attached to my body. My type of woman has to be less man hater-ish. I want a lover, not a hater."

"Fucking boring then," says Rosey, and I laugh again. She definitely keeps the guys on their toes.

Inside, we head to the bar, and she orders us each a Coke. "Drink a good mouthful so it looks like you're drinking vodka and Coke," she says as we find a table near the window. "Keep looking around. If you spot anyone, let me know." I nod, glancing around nervously. It's been way too long since I've been in crowds this size and the noise is deafening. When my eyes land on Scar, I relax a little. He's just four tables away, which makes me feel so much safer. "Are you and him a thing or what?" asks Rosey.

I shrug. We haven't spoken about it. "He isn't much of a talker," I say drily, and she laughs.

"What do you do when you're together? If he hardly speaks, it must be hard work."

I think about her question before shaking my head. "Not at all. We're comfortable with silence."

"You know his ex used to hit him, right?" she asks, and I force my face to remain expressionless, like I knew this piece of information. "She was such a bitch, and everyone thought so. She's sadistic. Cruel. And Scar is a gentle giant, he wouldn't ever hurt a woman. I think that's why she did it—she knew he wouldn't hurt her back."

"It's his daughter I feel bad for," I say, hoping she'll tell me more without having to pry too much.

"He only avoids her because she cried when she saw his face. And who could blame her? He was so fucking hot before the accident."

"I think he's still hot," I say, smiling when she playfully hits my arm.

"She made him a nervous wreck. It was hard to watch him go from being so confident and happy to a stuttering mess. Don't get me wrong, he always had a stammer, and sometimes it's not noticeable, but whenever he'd been near her, it was so much worse. If she didn't have August, I'd have killed her by now."

I laugh. "You talk about killing people like it's normal."

"It is in our world. I have never killed anyone who didn't deserve it. When I find the men who took you, I'll smile while I slit their disgusting throats." My smile fades because that thought doesn't repulse me like it should. I want to see them suffer, all of them.

There's nothing odd about this bar. We don't spot any men acting suspiciously, and I don't recognise anyone, so we move on to the next, and then the next.

By the sixth bar, I'm tired and agitated. I thought I'd walk into the first bar and stumble across Braydon. I want so badly to end all this.

SCAR

Having to remove my cap in every bar not only annoys me but also makes it impossible to spy on people secretly. Ghost slaps me on the back. "Mav's outside wanting an update. You okay here?" he asks, and I nod. Dice and Lock are somewhere in here too, so Gracie is safe, and with each new bar, I feel less worried she's gonna disappear.

I check my mobile to make sure she hasn't texted me. I sent her a message in the last bar telling her to let me know when she's had enough. I know Ghost gave her an itinerary to stick to, but fuck that—if she's done, I'm taking her home. By the looks of things, we could spend the next few weekends hanging around in bars until we find something.

"Hunter?" I look up into Katya's crazy blues and my heart stutters in my chest. She looks good, dressed up with a face full of makeup. Not that it works on me these days. "What the hell are you doing in here? You never go to these places."

"Work," I mutter.

"Mav's got you hanging out in bars?" she asks, raising her brow. "Are you sure you're not here because of me?" I shake my head, glancing over her head to check on Gracie. Katya notices and turns to see what I'm looking at. "Wow, Rosey's back at the club," she says, and then she scowls. "Are you and her a thing?" I shake my head, and she looks back to where Rosey and Gracie are laughing together. "And what about the blonde?" When I don't respond, she narrows her eyes. "You're seeing her?" Gracie and I haven't talked about it, but I'd like to think we have something special, seeing as we spend every night in the same bed, and we've kissed more than a few times. "You didn't tell me you'd moved on," Katya hisses, bringing my attention back to her cruel face.

"I'm b-b-busy."

"Too busy to talk to the mother of your fucking child?" she hisses. "Since when?"

I check my watch because Gracie has stood up. It isn't time to move to the next bar, so she must be going to the bathroom. Rosey is at the bar ordering them another Coke. I quash my panic because she's fine in here, we have her covered, and Mav is right outside. Katya takes a seat, and as Gracie passes, she catches my eye. I can't react, mainly because the men could be here watching her and she's supposed to be alone with Rosey, but also because I don't need the argument with Katya, so I lower my eyes.

"How fucking dare you just move on? You've only been out of prison a short time, and you haven't been to talk to me about us."

"T-th-th-there is no u-u-us."

She sneers. "Christ, does she know you talk like a fucking retard? I came to see you in prison. I made the effort to keep your spirits up." I nod in acknowledgement. She did visit me at least once a month, but she refused to bring August. "You think I did that because we were done?" she demands to know.

I glance at the bathroom. There's no sign of Gracie. Katya rubs her hand up my thigh. "Hello, I'm right here, and you're looking for her? You know no one knows you like I do, Hunter. She'll never understand you. What we have is fire, and together, we're so fucking hot. I know we get carried away, but don't give up on us because some virgin-looking Martha has your head turned. She'll never be able to fuck you like I can, or make you come like I do."

Katya moves closer, placing her lips to my ear. I try to pull back, but she nips my ear lobe in her teeth, and I wince. "I miss the way we fuck," she whispers. The second she releases my ear, I pull back, holding her at arm's length.

"T-t-toxic," I whisper, and she narrows her eyes. "F-f-fucking toxic."

CHAPTER NINE

GRACIE

I watch the way the dark-haired beauty leans into Scar and nibbles on his ear lobe. He doesn't tense like I'd expect him to, which makes me think he knows her. When he pulls back, a woman walks right in my view and my attention is pulled to her face. I recognise her. "Jen?" I whisper, and she hears me, even though I said it under my breath.

She stops and turns, and her eyes widen. "Gracie?" she gasps.

"Jen," I repeat, and she throws herself at me.

"Oh my god, what the fuck is going on?"

Panic sets in. I wasn't ready to see her, and when she steps back, she senses the impending panic attack and grabs my hand. She leads me up some stairs and along a quiet corridor, then she opens a door, and we step into a small office. "We've been so worried about you. When the police said you'd run away, I wouldn't believe it, and yet here you are, in the flesh, on a night out?"

I shake my head. "No, I didn't run away. I was taken. Look, Jen, you can't tell anyone about this."

"Are you kidding? You've been gone for almost two years. We've been out of our minds with worry. I visit your parents all the time, and they're heartbroken."

I'm relieved my parents have kept my visit quiet and I decide to do the same. They clearly all still watch out for one another, and I don't want to cause friction between them. "I'll get in touch with them soon. But right now, I'm trying to find the guys who took me. It's really important you don't tell anyone just yet." I grab her hand and feel the large diamond rock on her finger. I raise it to the light and smile. "Oh my god, you're engaged?"

Her expression changes and she pulls her hand away, hiding it behind her back. "Yeah. Long story. Where can I contact you?"

"I'll contact you. Give me your number."

"So you can disappear on me again?" she snaps.

"I won't, I promise. I'm safe now, and people are helping me. I'll be coming home soon enough, then I'll tell you all about it."

SCAR

Katya makes a grab for my cock, and I shove her hand away as she laughs. "You used to like the danger."

Gracie isn't back, and Rosey heads towards me. She spots Katya and scowls. "Look what the devil dragged in," she mutters.

"I always knew you'd end up back at the club," says Katya, sneering. "It's all you're good for, whoring yourself out just like your mother."

"Actually, my mother's dead. And I'm back to help catch evil fuckers like you. Your days are numbered, Kitty Kat." Rosey smiles and turns to me. "She's been gone too long. Call Mav and see if anyone's got eyes on her. I'll go to the bathroom."

I stand, pushing Katya away from me. She growls, glaring at me. I'd cower before when she looked at me that way, because usually, it meant I was in for a night of her screaming and carrying on. But today, I smirk and walk past her like she's nothing. It feels good. I have the power again and I'm not gonna run back into her waiting arms.

After calling Mav, I head towards the bathroom too. Rosey reappears, shaking her head. "She's not there."

My heart is beating wildly in my chest. I look around, praying to God, I spot her somewhere in this place, and when I don't, I ball my fists. My hands itch to touch her, to hold her against me and smell her vanilla scent. I knew this was a bad idea, that I should have kept her safe at the club. Rosey redials Gracie's mobile number over and over, and each time, it goes to the answer message. "We should spread out," suggests Rosey.

There're stairs behind me, right next to the bathroom. It's the only place she could have gone without me seeing her. I head up, taking them two at a time. There's one door at the top, and I shove it hard, letting it crash back against the wall. Gracie spins to face me, looking panicked. Relief floods her expression when she sees it's me.

"Scar," she whispers. I grab her by the wrist and yank her away from the blonde standing beside her. "It's okay," she adds, "this is Jen." I don't give a fuck who it is, I'm so wound up, I can't even see straight. I begin to pull Gracie from the room. "Wait," she hisses, pulling back. I pause, and she turns to the woman. "I'll be in touch, Jen. Remember what I said, keep this to yourself." Jen nods, and I continue on my quest to get Gracie home, where she's safe.

We march past Rosey, who smiles with satisfaction. "I'll call off the search party."

Outside, Mav's entire body sags in relief. "Thank fuck for that. Are you okay?" he asks her, but I don't let her pause to reply. I need to be alone with her.

GRACIE

Scar is focused on getting me the hell out of here. I knew he wasn't comfortable with the idea of me being out in the open, but he's overreacting. Crowds of people are pushing their way towards busy bars as he marches us past Mav and Ghost. They both give me a sympathetic smile, and I figure it's best to let him get us to where he feels calmer, so I tag along behind as he weaves us in and out of people.

As we round the corner towards his bike, I knock my shoulder into someone. Automatically, I look up to apologise, but the words catch in my throat. The man looks just as shocked to see me, and it's almost like time stands still as I lock eyes on Braydon.

I tap Scar on the shoulder, but he ignores me, pulling me towards his bike. "Scar," I hiss, glancing back to see if I can still see him. "Scar," I repeat more urgently as we come to a stop by the bike. "That was him. That was the guy who chatted me up in the bar at Jen's party."

Scar glares at me. "He was going up that way," I say, pointing in the direction we've just come from, "and he saw me. He looked right into my eyes."

Scar looks pissed, and I'm not sure if his murderous expression is because he can't get me out of here like he wanted, or because he knows Braydon is around. He releases his hold on my wrist and takes my hand instead before leading me back the way we've just come. It's no good. By the time we reach Mav and Ghost, I can't see any sign of Braydon. I give a description of what he was wearing to Mav, and they decide to stay and have a look around.

The clubhouse is silent. Almost all the guys are out in Soho looking for Braydon, and I can't help but feel it's where I should be. Diamond smiles from her spot on the couch. "You're back early," she observes. "Good night?"

Scar pulls me past, and I smile apologetically as he leads me upstairs to my bedroom. Once inside, he slams the door and spins to face me. "I get it, you're mad—" I begin, but I'm cut off when his lips crash against my own. My back hits the door, and he takes my wrists, putting them together before pinning them above my head in one of his large hands. His other hand grips the hair at the base of my neck, tugging occasionally as our mouths crash together urgently.

SCAR

The second I laid eyes on her and saw she was safe, this was all I could think about, getting her back here and showing her how much she means to me. I need to be close to her, closer than usual. I want to feel her skin against my own. It's a need I can't ignore as I pull her dress over her head and drop it to the floor. With her hands free to roam, she presses them against my chest and reaches for the buttons of my shirt. I halt her, keeping hold of her wrists as I go back to exploring her mouth. My hunger for her takes over and I move my lips along her cheek, down her neck, and across her collar bone.

"Who were you talking to in the bar?" she asks, her voice breaking the spell. I pause, my lips inches from her skin. "You knew her."

I release her hands and step away, backing up until I'm at the window across the room from her. "You don't have to put distance between us. Was it her . . . Katya?" I hate hearing her name on Gracie's sweet, innocent lips. "Rosey told me about her," she explains. "She said she's evil. Was it her?" I stare at her for a long minute before she sighs heavily. "It's been a really long night, Scar. Seeing Jen and then Braydon, I need to get my head straight."

She picks Deuce up from her bed and passes him to me. "Maybe you should sleep in your own room tonight." And there it is, Katya's poison dripping into my life once again. "It doesn't mean anything," she adds as if to reassure me. "I just need to be alone right now."

Mav is in the bar when I get downstairs. He looks up in surprise when I enter, carrying the pup. "Gracie okay?" he asks, and I nod. "We didn't see him, the guy," he adds. "Ghost is still out there looking, though." I sit down and place Deuce on the ground. "You not keeping an eye on Gracie tonight?" he asks. "Just, I know you spend most nights in her room." I glance up, and he smirks, shrugging. "I'm the club president, man, I know everything."

He sits beside me and swirls whiskey around in a tumbler. The ice cubes clash together. "Hate the stuff," he mutters, tipping the glass towards me. "But the smell, or maybe the sound, makes me feel closer to Dad. I know that's the stupidest shit ever cos he was a dick, but sometimes, when I don't know what the fuck I'm doing, I channel him and it clears my head, yah know?" I nod.

I'm lucky to still have my dad around. Gears was a good friend to Eagle for many years before he died, and although he also began seeing Eagle for his true colours, he still misses his guidance. We all do sometimes.

"You're d-d-doing g-g-good."

He gives me a crooked smile. "Thanks, brother. Means a lot. I thought we had our work cut out when we rescued Rylee from her ex, but this shit with Gracie, it feels well above us. We have no clue where to find any of these guys, and I know she'll remember eventually, but until then, others are suffering."

"Pres," says Ghost, bursting into the club out of breath, "we found him."

GRACIE

I can't sleep. Without Deuce and Scar, I can't settle. It's what I feared, becoming too dependent on them. How will I cope when I return home? Just thinking about it makes me sad. I head downstairs, hoping hot milk or a shot of something strong will help. I'm approaching the room where the guys always disappear to, the room they refer to as church. The door is open, and I can hear voices, but it's hearing my name that causes me to stop. "Gracie s-s-s-said it w-w-was Jen, b-but I didn't look at h-h-her."

"But you think this was her?" asks Mav. "We have to be prepared for the possibility that this guy is now going after Jen."

"Should we watch her?" asks Ghost.

"You said she owns that bar, right?" asks Mav.

"Yeah, I ran a check after Scar said he found Gracie in an office with Jen. She co-owns it with her dad."

"Maybe this guy befriended Jen cos he's looking for Gracie?" suggests Grim.

I step into the room, and they all turn to look at me. Scar stands like he wants to rush me out of there, but I glare at him in warning. "Braydon was with Jen?"

"If it was him," says Ghost, holding up his mobile for me to see a grainy picture. It shows them talking.

I frown. "That's them."

"Did they know each other before?" asks Mav, and I shake my head. "They couldn't have hooked up at her party? They didn't exchange numbers?"

"Not that I know of. I liked him, and she was chatting with his friend. I guess he could have started talking to her and exchanged his number, but she was pretty stuck on pushing him my way. We didn't know them before. We met them in the bar at her party and invited them to join us."

"You'll need to ask Jen about it. In a way that doesn't alert her to the fact this guy is responsible for everything that happened to you," says Mav.

"She gave me her number," I say.

"Call her tomorrow and arrange a meeting. It will need to be away from the club. It's best not to tell her where you're staying right now until we know you can trust her."

"Trust her?" I repeat. "She was my best friend. She would do anything for me."

"Like steal y-y-your b-b-boyfriend?" mutters Scar, and I scowl at him.

"It's for your safety," says Mav.

"Out of interest," says Grim, "what's her dad do for work?"

"He owns a string of nightclubs," I say. He was always working when we were growing up. That's why Jen spent most of her time with me and my family. Her mum died when she was young, so it was always just her and her dad.

"Scar, get her upstairs. We have some shit to get through tonight," Mav mutters.

Scar guides me back upstairs, then hovers in my doorway. "Will you tell me about her, about Katya?" I ask. He thinks for a minute before shaking his head. "Why?" He doesn't answer. Instead, he closes the door and leaves me alone, just like I'd asked him to earlier.

SCAR
Three years ago . . .
"Mr. Anderson, we need to speak to you about the accident," says the police officer from the end of my hospital bed.

"Are you kidding? Look at him," snaps Dad.

"I don't think you understand, sir. Ms. Steele is making some very serious allegations. The sooner we get your son's statement, the sooner we can look into what caused the accident."

"We already told you, she was drinking, you breathalysed her and said she was three times the legal limit," snaps Ghost.

"Yes, but Ms. Steele is claiming there were extremely extenuating facts surrounding how she came to be driving the car."

"The facts are simple, officer. She was drunk and she got in the car and drove. My brother was only in the car to keep an eye on her because he knew she was drunk," Grim argues.

"She claims your brother forced her to drive. She said he sexually assaulted her right before the incident and she was very distressed. Your son isn't answering any of our questions and refuses to speak or give a statement. The accident was three weeks ago, and the nurses said there is no reason why Hunter isn't talking."

"And I've already explained he has a stammer and can't always communicate. Look, officer, if you're going to charge him, then get it over and done with. We'll get his solicitor to give you his written statement."

"If that's the way you want to do it." The officer sighs. "Hunter Anderson, I'm arresting you on suspicion of sexual assault, coercive behaviour, and false imprisonment . . ." The rest of the words blur together.

∞

Present day . . .

I stare out over the London skyline from my seat on my balcony. It's peaceful out here, and as the sun rises, the birds tweet their appreciation for the day. I rub my calloused hands over my tired, wary face. Seeing Katya and then losing sight of Gracie meant I spent the entire night out here thinking shit over. I haven't told Gracie about prison and how I spent two years locked up for something I didn't fucking do, but how do you tell someone who's been through the shit she has, that I was locked up for hurting the mother of my child?

I sigh heavily. I've avoided women for this exact reason. I don't want to explain myself to her, and it's not because I feel guilty, but because I'm fucking terrified she might not believe me. She might see me through the same mistrusting eyes she sees her captors.

At breakfast, I sit a few seats away from Gracie. She pretends not to notice, but I know she does because she stiffens, like I've stuck a knife in her damn chest. A whole night of thinking and all I came up with was to find these fuckers and get her home where she belongs. The sooner that can happen, the better.

CHAPTER TEN

GRACIE

It's been three days since our failed entrapment. The only good thing that came out of it was I saw Braydon, and so now I know he's out there still doing what he does, and that makes me more determined to help The Perished Riders put a stop to it. I tried to call Jen, but she didn't pick up. I left two messages and dropped her a text, but I'm still waiting to hear back.

I stare at the large board in Mav's office. The picture of Jen and Braydon talking is stuck up there with a question mark. "We could look at the Metropolitan Police website," I suggest, and Rylee glances up from the laptop. "I know my mind is blocking it out, but I'd know faces, surely. I knew Braydon's right away. In my dream, I know one of them is a policeman. I just feel it."

Rylee shrugs. "It's worth a shot." She taps away on the keys, then turns it towards me. I take a seat and place it on my lap to begin going through photographs. "I think it's only top dogs on their website," she continues. "How's things with you and Scar? You seem distant from each other."

"He's not ready. He said I'm not, but that's an excuse. He's not."

"Ready for?" she asks.

"Anything," I say. "He's taken a step back and that's okay. Rosey explained about his ex and said he went through a lot, so I'm okay to stay friends." I've spent night after night thinking about it, and I came to the conclusion that I've been so busy thinking about him, I haven't tried hard enough to remember these bastards. All my focus needs to be on these men so I can help the other women they're holding captive. Scar isn't ready to move on from Katya, and I'm okay with that, I just need to keep busy.

Flicking through the pictures, I stop on one of an older man. I sit up a little straighter, and Rylee leans over to see what's caught my attention.

"Chief Constable Chris Guilford," she reads from the title under his picture. I shudder and push the laptop away. "Is that him?" Rylee gasps as I nod. His cruel eyes smirk at me from the screen. I remember his hands on my throat and his breath on my skin. I rub my neck, trying to remove the feeling.

I remember. It all rushes back to me in an instant. "He messed up a sixteen-year-old's rape case. I knew his face before he took me because of that. I'd watched him on the news apologise for his mistake, and I couldn't believe he kept his job. But now, I'm wondering if it was one big cover-up. Did that girl escape like I did?"

Rylee takes my hand. "I guess we'll find out. This is huge, Gracie. If he's the top man, that's massive."

I shake my head. "He isn't. There're others. He's just one of them. The other girls spoke of important men at the top." I wait for my brain to catch up before gasping again. "The judge. The man and his wife who wanted to keep me as their pet, he was a top judge."

"So, we should be able to Google him, right?" asks Rylee, typing away on the laptop. Faces of some of London's top judges fill the screen, and I point to Judge Michaelson straight away. "Holy shit," mutters Rylee. She goes to the office door and shouts for Mav, who must sense the urgency in her voice because he rushes over along with Grim and Scar. "She remembered them. She had the best idea and she's identified two of them. I can't believe we wasted all that time when all along, they were right there at the touch of the keyboard."

The men listen as Rylee fills them in. I remain silent, lost in bad memories. "Well done, Gracie," says Mav. "We can watch these guys and see where they go. We finally have a lead."

"And then I can go home?" I ask, ignoring Scar's eyes burning into me.

"Yes, Gracie, then you can go home," says Grim with a smile.

I push up from my chair. "Good."

I go straight to my bedroom and lie face down on my bed. Why did I say that? Was I expecting a reaction? I certainly didn't get one. I thought I was okay with Scar pulling away, but clearly, I'm not. I close my eyes. I miss him. I miss his stupid ass silence and the way he bows his head slightly to try and hide his scars. I miss his crooked smile, and fuck, I miss his lips on mine. Just the thought of his lips travelling down my neck causes me to sigh out loud, feeling my cheeks flush at the thoughts spinning around my head right now.

A cough interrupts me, and I shoot upright to find Scar staring down at me. "Crap," I whisper hiss, not sure if I'm mad he interrupted me or mad he's smirking like he read my mind. He runs his finger along the blush of my cheek.

"I don't know how t-t-t-to . . ." I wait for him to continue. "S-s-stop myself w-w-wanting you."

My breathing picks up as his finger runs across my chest. "Then don't," I whisper, and his eyes burn with need.

"What if I h-h-hurt y-y-you?"

I frown. "Hurt me? Why would you?"

SCAR

How do I say it? How do I tell her that all I know is hard, rough sex? How do I explain that it gets me off? Pinning her down and fucking her hard is all I can think about, yet I know how much she's been through, so what the fuck does that make me? A monster?

I sit on the edge of the bed and clasp my hands together to stop myself stroking the soft curves of her body. "With K-Katya, it was d-d-different. I don't k-k-know how to be g-g-gentle."

She props herself up on her elbows. "Rosey said Katya was violent."

I nod. It's not a big secret. I'm not ashamed to say I put up with her abuse time and time again, but I did it because I thought I loved her, and I desperately wanted to be a part of my own family. She'd hold that over me a lot. "I n-n-never h-hit her b-back."

Gracie sits, running her hand over my back. I flinch slightly, and she lets her hand drop. "Is that why you hate being caressed?"

I nod. It was easier to keep my distance from Katya. That way, her touch didn't take me by surprise when it turned aggressive, which it often did. Touching became part of her sick games. A stroke here and a punch there, I had to keep my guard up so I avoided it. I used to love the feel of her body.

"Try it," Gracie says quietly. "You might like it. When I first met you, you'd always wear gloves. Now, you don't. You're learning to do things differently already. Let me show you."

I shake my head. She shouldn't be showing me after what she went through. I should be guiding her, and yet here she is, willing to trust me while she shows me how to touch and be touched. She pulls her shirt over her head, and we lock eyes. Gracie gently takes my hand in her own and runs my fingers over her lips. She lies back, keeping hold of my hand as she guides it along her cheek and down her neck. She's soft and warm, and I watch her intake of breath as she runs my fingers across her chest and over the swells of her breasts. Her eyelids flutter closed as she runs my hand across her stomach and back up over her breast. Her nipples pucker under the pink lace material of her bra, and I lean closer until I'm inches away.

I lick over the swollen bud and gently suck it into my mouth. She hisses, arching her back slightly from the bed. I rub the other between my fingers, and she bites her lower lip seductively. I rain kisses over her chest before she reaches behind to unhook her bra. I stare at her perfect breasts. Everything in me is screaming to stay in control as she brings my head down to meet hers and kisses me hungrily.

Gracie holds my face in her hands and smiles up at me. "See, you can be gentle. You're doing it. Will you let me touch you if I go slow?" I know Gracie won't hurt me. She wouldn't ever hit me and she's not into sadist shit, but there's a small part of me that still flinches when she carefully reaches for the buttons on my shirt. She's sitting again, facing me as she carefully unfastens each one, making eye contact the whole time.

As she pushes the shirt from my shoulders, she runs her eyes over the many scars that litter my chest. Some are from the accident, while others from bite marks, burns, scratches, and small cuts. She hesitates before placing her hands there. "Nice and slow," she whispers, running her fingers ever so lightly over my skin. Flashbacks of Katya digging her nails into me assault my brain, and I close my eyes, wincing at the memory. "It's okay," whispers Gracie. "You're with me."

What sort of pussy am I? I can't stand a touch, yet she's had so much worse happen and doesn't even flinch. I pull back in frustration, and she removes her hands straight away, holding them in the air. "It's fine, I'll stop," she says quickly.

I sigh heavily before grabbing her hands and placing them back on my skin. I nod, letting her know it's okay to keep going. Her hands travel down towards my belt, and as she loosens it, she bites on her lower lip like she's wondering if this is a good idea. I lean back, placing my hands behind me on the bed and gripping the sheets to stop me freaking out. Gracie slowly stands, smiling as she shimmies out of her leggings. When she straightens, I take in her perfect breasts and her curved arse encased in lace underwear, committing that perfect image to memory.

She stands before me, placing her hands on my shoulders as she kisses me. I grip her hips, wanting desperately to throw her on the bed and taste every inch of her. When her mouth releases me, I move my lips to her breasts, taking turns to pay each nipple some attention. Her fingers run through my hair as little sighs escape her.

My mobile buzzes from my back jeans pocket, and I ignore it as she hooks her fingers in her panties and lets them drop down her legs. It buzzes again as Gracie kneels, settling between my legs. "I want to see all of you," she says shyly, reaching for my zipper. She tugs my jeans down slightly, and I reach into my pocket to remove my mobile, throwing it beside me on the bed just as another message comes through. August's name flashes, and I make a grab for it. She never messages or calls me.

"My d-d-daughter," I mutter as a way of explanation. Gracie nods, sitting back on her heels while she waits patiently for me to check the messages.

August: Mum is on her way to the club. I didn't tell her you got me a phone and she found it. She's mad.

August: She said you have a new girlfriend and you don't want to see us anymore. Is that true?

August: Call me when you've spoken to Mum. Let me know you're alright. I love you, Dad.

"Everything okay?" asks Gracie.

I shake my head and pull my jeans back into place. "G-g-gotta go," I mutter. She eyes me with confusion. "S-s-sorry."

A bang on the door gets us both up and moving, pulling our clothes back on. "Scar, are you in there?" It's Gears, my dad.

"J-just coming," I say, checking Gracie is decent before I open the door. Deuce rushes in like he's been sitting outside waiting for us to give him entry.

"We have a situation downstairs that needs your urgent attention," Dad says, glancing at Gracie before looking at me.

I nod. "August w-w-warned me."

"What's going on?" asks Gracie.

"S-s-stay h-h-here," I order as I follow Dad downstairs.

Katya is by the bar. She's dressed to impress in a pair of tight-fitted jeans, a low-cut top to show off the breasts I paid for, and a leather jacket *she* got made with 'Scar's Property' sewn on the back. I shake my head at the audacity of this woman. I should have known her discovering me and Gracie would result in unannounced visits and drama.

"You got August a mobile?" she asks accusingly. It's not the reason she's here. She wants to see Gracie so she can cause trouble, but that ain't happening.

"I'm p-paying."

"Damn right you are," she snaps. "Sit down, I want to talk." I remain standing, and she arches a brow, smirking. Knowing how her mind works, I know she'll see this as flirting. "I thought after you were released, you'd come and see me so we could work things out." I remain silent. "But you didn't come, and then you show up on August's birthday with an expensive gift. Is that how it'll always be? You showing up with gifts to outdo me?"

"I owe h-h-her."

"You owe me," she says coldly. I scoff, and Katya narrows her eyes. "I had to raise her on my own. I spent two years visiting you in prison, and you didn't even tell me you got a release date."

"It was y-y-your fault."

"My fault?" she repeats in a low voice, the one she uses before she's about to lose it.

I feel Gracie approach from behind and briefly close my eyes. I told her to stay upstairs. She gently places her hand on my lower back.

"Everything okay?" she asks with a smile.

"Is this the reason?" snaps Katya, looking at Gracie with contempt. "The reason you don't come and see your daughter?"

Gracie keeps her smile in place and holds out her hand. I wince at her naivety. "I'm Gracie. You must be Kathryn . . . Katelyn . . . Kathy?" she asks, frowning, and Katya arches her brow.

"Oh, little lady, I know your game because I'm the queen of them, so stop pretending you haven't heard of me when you clearly know who the fuck I am."

Gracie's hand drops back to her side, but her smile doesn't falter. "That's right . . . Katya. August's mum, right?"

"Katya, Scar's ol' lady."

"Ex," Gracie corrects.

Katya laughs. "You got a fiery one here, Hunter. Not your usual type when it comes to club whores."

"Enough," I mutter.

"Why are you here?" asks Gracie coldly.

"That's none of your business. Club whores don't get to know members' business."

"It's a good job I'm not a whore then."

"If you've not got an old man and you've no bloodline to the club, then you're a whore, sweetheart. You just haven't reached that part in your club journey yet."

"What's she doing here?" snaps Ghost as he enters the club.

Dad steps in front of him. "He can handle it himself, son."

"Maybe we can go somewhere quiet for a chat," Katya suggests to me.

"I'm coming too," says Gracie, and I wonder where the hell this spark came from. She glares at me. "I'm not leaving you alone with her after what she's done."

"What I've done?" screams Katya, her rage finally taking over.

"Stop," I growl in her general direction. I hate my worlds colliding like this, especially when I wasn't prepared. "Gracie, g-go to your r-r-room and wait for m-me."

"You're going with her?" gasps Gracie. She doesn't understand that I have to, that it involves August too.

"Man, don't fucking go with her," groans Ghost.

"Of course, he is, sweetheart," spits Katya. "He fucking loves me," she adds.

"No, he doesn't. You hurt him," snaps Gracie, and Katya laughs harder.

"I hurt him?" she repeats. "Did he not tell you about the time he went to prison for hurting me?" I groan and plead with my eyes for Gracie to go. She's rooted to the spot now, her eyes flicking between me and Katya. "Oh my god, you don't know, do you?"

"Kat, p-p-please," I whisper, and she smirks.

"You know how he got those scars?" asks Katya, gripping my chin before shoving my face away from her, hard. "He raped me over the hood of my car in a nightclub car park, then he forced me to drive him home even though I was three times over the drunk-driving limit. I crashed the car because I was so terrified, I couldn't stop shaking," she hisses.

"Leave it out," yells Ghost. "We all know that's not true!"

"Then why did he serve two years in prison?" she asks.

I stare at Gracie, waiting for her to slap me or spit at me or something. Instead, she smiles kindly, taking my hand and kissing my cheek. "Don't go with her, Scar. Come with me."

"A-a-august," I mutter.

"We'll get you access to August, I'll make sure of it."

"You want to be with a rapist?" yells Katya.

"I've met rapists," snaps Gracie, "and Hunter isn't one. And shame on you for lying. May you never go through it for real." She keeps hold of my hand and leads me away from Katya and back up the stairs. Once inside her bedroom, she throws herself at me, wrapping her arms and legs around me and kissing me hard. "I believe you," she whispers. "I know you wouldn't hurt anyone." My breathing is heavy with emotion as she kisses all over my face and down my neck. "Make me yours, Scar. Make me forget everything else but you."

I walk us to the bed, laying her down and hovering over her. "Th-th-thank you." She smiles. "Are y-you s-sure?" I ask, and she nods.

This time, I take control, pulling her top over her head and tugging her leggings off. I kiss every inch of her soft body until she's practically begging for me. Settling between her legs, I swipe my tongue through her juices. She gasps, shuddering when I do it again. She tastes amazing. Gracie watches as I undress, her eyes widening when my cock springs free. I pull a condom from my wallet. I rip it open and slide it over my erection. "Y-y-you're sure?" I ask again, giving her a last chance to change her mind. She nods again. "W-words," I say, and she grins wide.

"Yes, I'm sure."

I don't think I've ever felt this nervous before. Bracing myself over her, I line my cock up at her opening. It's been a long time since I was with a woman, and as I slowly push inside her, I groan in pleasure. She feels fucking amazing, and as her tight pussy grips my cock, I tense, trying hard not to slam into her and chase that warm sensation I crave. A small gasp escapes her, and I pause, checking she's okay. She smiles shyly. "I'm okay."

I fill her and close my eyes briefly. Keeping control is harder than I thought. She wriggles beneath me, and I groan. "J-just a m-m-minute," I whisper. She giggles, and that sound warms my fucking heart. I slowly withdraw, watching between us, and it's the hottest thing I ever witnessed as I fill her back up again. I keep up the slow pace while she reaches between us, pressing her fingers over her swollen clit. I smirk, knocking her hand away and replacing it with my own. As I apply pressure, she pants, her expression full of concentration. Her body stiffens, then she cries out, shaking below me as her orgasm hits her full force. Her vibrations cause my own orgasm to hit me, and I strain, pushing forward and holding my cock deep inside her as I convulse, grunting with each wave.

I stare down at her beautifully flushed face, the sound of our heavy breathing filling the room. "Are y-y-you okay?" I pant.

"More than," she says, smiling. "Are you?"

I nod, placing a gentle kiss on the tip of her nose. "M-m-more than."

CHAPTER ELEVEN

SCAR

It's the first night of surveillance on Chief Constable Guilford. Rosey and Grim did the day shift but only reported Guilford going into his office at seven in the morning and leaving at five in the afternoon. He's since been at home, and we're three cars away from his house, sitting in Ghost's beat-up BMW.

"Grim got false plates on this thing, but I still think we'll stand out around here," he mutters as a passing dog walker stares in.

"Th-thought you were an e-e-expert at this shit?"

"I am. I'm the best, but I'm not sure if I'm any match for a police constable. If he's any good, he'll spot us."

I sink lower into the seat when Guilford's front door opens, and he steps out, making his way to his own car. We give him a second to drive off before Ghost follows at a distance. We eventually stop outside a bar. "Isn't this the bar Gracie's friend owns?" asks Ghost, and I nod, keeping my eyes fixed on our target as he crosses the street and heads inside. "You can't come in," says Ghost, taking his seatbelt off. "She might recognise you from the other night. Stay here, I'll be back."

I watch helplessly as Ghost heads in after Guilford. A few minutes later, my phone rings and it's Ghost. "You can listen in," he whispers. "I'm gonna sit at the bar near him. He's met with another guy, and they seem to know each other well. Hold on."

I place my phone onto the speaker and relax back. "What can I get you?" I hear the bartender ask.

"Just a Jack and Coke," orders Ghost. "Nice place. You the owner?"

She laughs, and I hear a glass being placed down. "I certainly am. Jenny, co-owner at your service."

"Co-owner?" repeats Ghost, and I know he's grinning, using his flirty smile to get more information. "Impressive. That means my chances are shot, right? If you have a husband to co-own with."

She laughs again, and I roll my eyes at how easy she's fallen for his charm. "Not married, engaged. And my co-owner is right there," she explains. "My father, Doug Harris."

"Jenny Harris," says Ghost. "I like it. It sounds like a bar owner's name. Doug, not so much."

"He's a silent partner, just comes up with the cash every now and then. He's a judge, actually."

"Shit, thought I recognised him," says Ghost, laughing. "Nice speaking with yah." I hear a shuffling, and then he whispers, "Just gonna put you on the table, brother. Not sure if we'll hear anything, but it's the closest table to them."

"That poker game was a fix and you know it," says a man, laughing.

"Any excuse, Guilford." I guess this voice belongs to Harris, Jen's dad. "Speaking of winning, have you heard anything from Michaelson about the next dinner party?" My ears prick up at the mention of Judge Michaelson's name. At least we know we're on the right track.

"Between you and me, since my special friend ran, he's not been the same. I think he had his heart set on her."

"Yes, his dinner parties won't be quite the same without her. I've not tasted anything quite so . . . unique." I clench my fists, pretty certain they're talking about my Gracie. "We need others like her, but that's what I wanted to talk with you about," says Harris, lowering his voice slightly. "Your little friend was spotted a few nights ago. She came here, and Jen spoke with her."

That confirms it. I grip the door handle of the car to stop me rushing in there and shooting them both.

There's silence for a few minutes. "What did she say?" hisses Guilford.

"Nothing about where she'd been. She asked Jen not to tell anyone she'd seen her. Jen called Braydon the second she left in a panic. A man apparently came and removed her, after she told Jen she was being helped," says Harris. He sounds bitter, like just saying the words burns his throat.

"Do you realise how serious this is?" hisses Guilford angrily. "What this could mean if she tells anyone?"

"Of course, I do, that's why I'm telling you now. Braydon and his men are looking for her. They never stopped, but it's like she's disappeared again. Apart from that one sighting, there's nothing," snaps Harris. He sighs heavily, then takes a deep, calming breath. "Let's try not to worry. Maybe she won't remember much, after all the Rohypnol she ingested, and not to mention the GHB, I'd be surprised. We've quashed cases against us before, we'll do it again."

"Just find her, Harris. My wife is already suspicious. Anything like this comes out and she'll believe it. Find the little cunt and take her straight to the judge. He'll fuck her up twice as bad as we ever did. You know he had a special room built just to keep her in? Soundproof and all. He wanted her badly, so let him have her for free, as long as I can fucking watch the light go from her perfect little eyes. I will not let this worthless whore ruin my life," he growls.

"It might be an idea to get some of your officers to pay her parents a visit and remind them to call us if she gets in contact with them," Harris suggests.

"I'll pull up the case tomorrow and see if anything has happened recently. I closed it on the grounds that she's a runaway. I doubt there're any updates."

"Okay. I'll let you know if Braydon finds her. He's hanging at the same clubs to be sure she's not around." He pauses before adding, "We need entertainment to take our minds off this crap. Are you free next Saturday?"

"I can be. What did you have in mind?"

"The usual. My new little pet needs a lesson in manners. You were always good at that side of things."

Guilford laughs. "I'll be sure to have my tools sharpened. See you Saturday at the club."

An hour later, we drive back to the MC in silence. Mav called church after Ghost told him we had some news. I know my words are trapped right now, so once inside, I sit, letting Ghost stand up front to talk. He gives the guys a run-down of the conversation we heard. The men look as pissed as me by the time he's finished. "Jen knows these men. We can't rule out her involvement in any of this."

"Does Gracie know that?" asks Trucker, and Ghost shakes his head.

"Fuck," Trucker utters, shaking his head.

"I could be wrong, but Jen calling Braydon the second Gracie left that night makes it seem pretty dodgy. We should have realised it wasn't a coincidence after they were seen together talking," Grim points out.

CHAPTER ELEVEN

"Someone's gotta break the news to her," says Mav, looking at me. "Do you want me to ask Rylee to do it?" I shake my head and push to my feet. I need to be with her.

I step into her bedroom, where she's curled up on the bed, sleeping with Deuce. His ears prick up, but he doesn't move. I don't blame him—I wouldn't leave her either. I shrug out of my kutte, kick off my boots, and head into the shower.

I'm soaping up when Gracie pulls the glass door open and steps inside. She doesn't even have to say a fucking word and my cock is solid. She smirks, wrapping her hands around it and standing on her tiptoes to kiss me. "I missed you," she whispers, moving her hands back and forth, nice and slow. I lean my head back against the cool tiles, letting the water drizzle down my face and enjoying the feel of her hands around me. After a few minutes, I turn her away so her back is against my front and I pull her against me. Feeling her slippery wet body pressed tightly against mine makes my cock strain harder.

I run my hands over her breasts, transferring some of the soap from me to her. She produces a silver packet, smirking when I take it. I like that she's so prepared and I waste no time putting on the condom. I crouch slightly so my cock nudges at her entrance. She arches her back, giving me easier access, and she's so wet for me, I slip inside her with hardly any effort. Cupping her breasts, I gently pinch her nipples as I massage them. Gracie presses her hands against the tiles, bracing herself as I ease in and out of her.

"Fuck," she hisses, pushing back to meet my thrusts. I pull out and turn her to face me. I need to see her face when she comes apart. She wraps her legs around my waist, crying out as I slam into her. Staring into her eyes, I feel the build-up inside me, swirling in my stomach and rushing down to my balls as I empty myself into the condom, groaning into her neck with relief. I give myself a second to recover before turning the shower off and dropping to my knees. She watches cautiously as I part her legs, guiding one over my shoulder.

"I don't . . . think . . . oh my!" She gasps when I press my mouth to her clit and run my tongue over the soft flesh. Her hands grip my head as I eat her pussy, not stopping until she's shuddering and I taste her sweet juices on my tongue.

We sleep naked, wrapped in each other. I couldn't stand the thought of touch a few months back, but now, I can't stop touching her and having her pressed against me. It's the best feeling in the world. I wake during the night with my erection against her arse. She wriggles, and I see it as an invitation to make love for the third time, only stopping when we're both exhausted and slick with sweat.

By the morning, I realise I've had the best sleep ever. I feel lighter and more refreshed than I have in a long time. I watch Gracie sleeping next to me and smile. I hate that I have to tell her what we know, but keeping it from her won't do any good. I suck her nipple into my mouth, and she smiles, her eyes still closed as she swats me away like an annoying fly. "No more," she whispers.

"Let's g-g-g-go out for the d-d-day."

"I thought I wasn't allowed just yet."

"Nobody w-will s-see us."

She smiles, stretching out. "Okay."

GRACIE

Scar makes me walk up at least ten flights of stairs. We got the lift up the first few flights, but it started making odd noises, so we opted to walk the rest. Apparently, Scar used to hang out in these high-rise buildings when he was a kid. He said he'd throw stones off the roof, not thinking of the consequences. It sounds like he was a typical boy.

When we step out the fire door onto the roof, I gasp aloud. You can see most of London from up here, it's amazing. Scar leans over the edge, and I make a funny squeaking noise in the back of my throat. He looks at me over his shoulder and grins at my obvious panic. He pulls himself to sit on the concrete ledge, and I cringe. One slip and he'd be dead. I shudder at the thought.

"That n-n-night of the ac-accident," he begins, and I take a seat on the floor, looking up at him as he stares out over London, "sh-she said I could see August i-if I h-h-had sex with h-h-her."

"Nice," I mutter sarcastically.

"Sh-she's like th-that. Always a condition when it c-c-comes to seeing August."

"So, you had sex with her, and she lied afterwards to the police?"

He nods. "Our s-s-sex was r-rough. Ag-aggressive. Sh-she had bruises, b-but it was consensual."

"Is that how you like sex?" I ask, wondering if I measure up to his expectations.

He smiles. "I th-thought it was. It's a-all I knew. B-but you showed m-me a b-b-better way."

I'm happy with his answer. "So, you had sex and got in the car?"

"I tr-tried to take the k-keys, but she h-hit me. I th-thought it was best I st-stayed with h-her, b-but she crashed and the c-cops c-came."

"What a bitch," I mutter. "It rocks your faith in the justice system when stories like this come out. The police shouldn't always believe the woman."

"Partly m-my f-fault. I refused to s-s-speak up."

"Why?" I gasp, and he arches a brow in a way that asks if I'm being serious. I laugh. "I don't believe you went to prison just because you didn't want to speak up."

He shakes his head. "W-what was the p-point? Th-that cop summed me u-up the second sh-she c-cried and gave a s-sob story. They n-never w-would have believed a g-guy like m-me."

"Did you ever tell anyone about her and how she was?"

"Y-yeah. I'm n-not ashamed that I d-didn't h-hit her back. I st-stuck around for A-august."

"You must miss her."

"I j-just wanted to g-give her what I had as a k-k-kid, a l-loving family. In p-prison, I h-had time to reflect. I c-can never g-give that to her b-because of K-katya."

"Don't give up, Scar. She's your daughter too. You can get access to her."

He scoffs. "With my r-record? The r-rape charge was dr-dropped before court, but assault, im-imprisonment, th-that all stayed on r-record."

I'm sad for him. No man should go through what he's been through and not be allowed access to his own daughter. I vow to help him, just like he's helped me. There must be a way.

CHAPTER TWELVE

SCAR

"Th-there's something I n-need to tell y-you," I say. "It's a-about Jen."

"She still never returned my calls. Weird, right?"

"N-not really," I mutter. "We found o-out some s-stuff."

Gracie stands and warily moves closer to the edge. She peers over and closes her eyes. "Jesus, it's high up."

"Did y-you know Jen's d-dad?"

"No, not really. He was always working, so Jen spent most of her time at my house. Why?"

"He's a j-judge."

Her face pales slightly. "Right," she mutters, unsure of where this is going. "I thought he owned bars and clubs."

"We f-f-followed Guilford to Jen's b-bar. Her d-d-dad is co-o-o-owner. Ghost and I, we li-listened in. He met with Jen's d-dad. We h-heard them t-talk about y-you. H-Harris told Guilford you'd b-been to see Jen." Her eyes are wide as she takes in what I'm saying. "He s-said Jen called B-braydon after you l-left. Jen knows the man who t-took you."

Gracie's eyes look glassy, like she's holding back a bucket of tears. "What are you saying? That Jen had something to do with it all?"

I shrug. "I d-don't know, b-but it's too m-much of a coincidence to ig-ignore."

"I have to see her," she blurts out.

"No," I say firmly. They still want to find her, and I don't want to scare her any more than she already is by filling her in on their entire conversation. "Sh-she could p-put you in d-danger again. It's not s-safe."

I get off the ledge and pull her to me. "I can't believe she'd do anything to hurt me, Scar. We're best friends. My parents said she went out looking for me. There's no way she knew about any of it." I kiss the top of her head, hoping to God she's right.

Mav adds the photographs of all the new suspects. I smirk at Grim's CSI joke as we all take a seat in church. At the top of the board are Harris, Michaelson, and Guilford. That's just some of the top men we think are running the show. Below them is a picture of Braydon. Gracie referred to him as a guard, but she said there were many others.

"I had Ghost look into all three of these men," says Mav, pointing to the top photographs. "Harris said to Guilford, he'd see him Saturday at the club. We think he was referring to this place," he says, sticking a new picture up. "The Coco Rooms is a nightclub. It's owned by Harris but run by this guy," he adds another new picture. "Kaiden Ratchett. He's got a list as long as your arm for various offences, but Ghost couldn't hack the system to see exactly what some of them were. They'd been hidden, just like those under Braydon's name. These men work for Harris. We think Harris provides the service and the elite clientele pay him good money.

"This man," he adds, pointing to Michaelson's picture, "is one of London's top judges. He and his wife own a mansion in Kensington. To the public eye, they're a very stand-up couple who give to charities and campaign for good causes. Behind the scenes, they're sex addicts who hold dinner parties where girls are forced to have sex with the guests. They share young girls and enjoy inflicting pain. They wanted to buy Gracie and keep her. The judge had a soundproof room built specially to keep her locked away. He still wants her now, and they're determined to find her. Now they know she's alive and well, they want her silenced."

Grim adds a picture of Jenny. "Jen is, or was, Gracie's best friend. They grew up together from teenagers. That's her dad, and he part owns her bar. We know she called Braydon after she saw Gracie, and we think she set Gracie up in the beginning. She can't be trusted. Gracie mentioned making contact with her, but we can't allow that to happen. It'll put her in danger."

"Pres, if these men are all top dogs, how the fuck are we gonna stop them?" asks Lock.

Mav grins. "By bringing in the real top dogs." The brothers glance at each other, confused. "The Taylors. Arthur Taylor is gonna help us bring down their sordid little gang. One by one." The mafia run things around here, so it shouldn't surprise me they're stepping in to help. And if it keeps Gracie safe, I'm all good with accepting their offer. "Arthur has been invited to a dinner party at their house. They've been asking him to attend for a long time, so they were happy he's finally accepted. Rosey will also be going."

"Since when do we involve women in club business?" asks Copper. "Since she wiped out three of our members before we could blink," says Grim.

"I w-want i-in," I mutter, and Grim exchanges a wary look with Mav.

"Not a good idea, brother. Besides, how the fuck would Arthur get you in there?" asks Mav.

"He can say he's his bodyguard," suggests Ghost, and I'm grateful for his support.

"I'll run it by Arthur. That's the best I can do," offers Mav.

As dinner parties go, this one is as boring as I imagine them to be. I'm glad I don't run in these circles, pretending I'm more important than the person next to me. When Arthur agreed for me to come, I wasn't expecting to be standing in the corner of the room watching his every move. I have an earpiece to look the part of bodyguard, but Mav and the others can hear what's going on from a van parked just up the road.

Arthur taps Rosey on the wrist, and she scowls at him. She's pretending to be his submissive, and Arthur is revelling in his ability to annoy her. He arches an eyebrow in warning, and she huffs before lowering her head. He leans in close. "You're not supposed to look around, Red. Your eyes should be downcast at all times."

"Stop calling me Red," she hisses under her breath.

"Oh, Red, I might have to make you kneel if you continue."

"Don't you fucking dare," she mutters.

He catches my eye and grins. He really is enjoying this.

"Arthur, so pleased you could make it," comes a booming voice followed quickly by a large man in a badly fitting suit. He holds out his hand for Arthur to shake before letting his eyes run over Rosey.

"Harry, thanks for the invite. Sorry it's taken me so long to get around to attending. I hear your parties are to die for."

Michaelson laughs and it echoes around the room. "You've clearly been talking to the right people. Who is your guest?"

"This is Red."

"Interesting name. Is she . . . yours?"

Arthur grins, running a finger down Rosey's arm. "For now."

"Come and meet my wife. She loves a man in a suit."

I follow as Michaelson leads us through the room of about fifteen people. A middle-aged blonde smiles in greeting as we approach, and I move to the nearest corner as they make introductions. Michaelson's wife is a little hands-on, constantly touching Arthur's arm or the lapels of his jacket. She's hot for him, and it's clear her husband is turned on just watching the way she is with other men.

A glass is tapped and the room falls silent. "Guests, dinner is served," announces Michaelson, and people move to the dining room, where there's a large table full of silver domed dishes. Arthur sits closest to Michaelson and his wife, with Rosey glued to his side. I stand in the corner closest to Arthur. I'm not out of place, as other bodyguards do the same.

Dinner is fast-paced, almost like it's an inconvenience but a formality they're forced to follow. The starters are quickly followed by the mains, and then people begin to disperse. Michaelson leans in towards Arthur and whispers, "Now for dessert. Are you a dessert kind of man, Arthur?"

"Depends on the treat, Harry," he replies, throwing his napkin on the table. "Sometimes, I like to eat in private."

Michaelson smiles. "I see."

There's a handful of people left in here, while others have moved to another room. I remain rooted to the spot. A door behind Michaelson opens, and two men enter, holding up a woman by her arms. She's not responding, her head lolling to the side and her toes dragging on the carpet as they carry her in. I ball my fists and lower my head, not able to watch this. They lay her on the table before Michaelson. Seconds later, the door opens again, and a woman is brought in handcuffed and gagged. She's fighting hard, and I wince as one of the men slaps her hard. Arthur glances at me, he's not happy either. He stands, pulling Rosey up with him. "Kiss me," he whispers to her.

"Are you fucking kidding me?" she hisses.

"Red, we gotta distract him, get him away from these girls. Trust me and kiss me."

She hesitates before sighing heavily, then she places her hands on his jaw and presses her lips against his. I'm no expert, but the kiss is fire. Even I'm transfixed for a second, but not as transfixed as Michaelson and his wife. Arthur grabs a handful of Rosey's arse, and she moans. He turns to Michaelson, smiling. "Red loves an audience."

"No, Arthur," she whispers, and it takes me a second to realise she's giving them what they want, a vulnerable, scared girl. "Don't make me."

"Now, now, Red. I told you before, you do exactly what I say, when I say. These lovely people fed you, shouldn't you repay them?"

She gives them puppy dog eyes. "What do I have to do?" she whispers.

"Whatever they want you to do. Good or bad."

Michaelson rubs his hands together. "I have a private room if you'd like to go there."

Arthur nods, grabbing Rosey by the hair, gripping it hard. "Lead the way. Mute," he adds, looking in my direction, "bring the fighter."

Michaelson grins, nodding as I make towards the cuffed brunette. She shakes her head, screaming into her gag and trying hard to thrash around as I throw her over my shoulder.

We go down some stairs and along a hall to a door at the end. Michaelson produces a key and unlocks it, then we all move into a tight space as he unlocks another door. It's thick, heavy metal, like that on a safe. Inside is a large four-poster bed, custom-made to allow at least four adults to sleep comfortably. On the wall are chains and various instruments that look fit for torture. Michaelson hangs the key on a hook. I throw the girl on the bed.

Michaelson wastes no time rubbing his hand over Rosey's arse. She keeps her head lowered, and he sniggers, moving his other hand towards her breast. She grabs his wrist, halting his hand mid-air. He eyes her with confusion, then glances at Arthur for an explanation. "What can I say," Arthur drawls with a shrug, "Red is a little crazy."

"My name is not fucking Red," she hisses, glaring at Arthur. She twists Michaelson's arm up his back, forcing him into an awkward position. His wife moves towards them, and Arthur's arm dashes out, stopping her.

"We agreed on a nickname. I thought you'd like it," Arthur says to Rosey.

"We did not agree on it. You said I should choose one, and I didn't. That wasn't an invitation for you to."

"Can someone tell me what the hell is going on?" snaps Michaelson, his face red in anger.

"We're gonna play a game," says Rosey. "Be a darling and lie on the bed."

"Oh," he says, grinning, "you like to take control? I'm okay with that." The stupid bastard still thinks she's gonna fuck him. I roll my eyes as he lies on the bed near the handcuffed girl. Rosey throws her leg over him, rubbing against his crotch. He groans, and she grimaces as she takes the cuffs attached to the wall and slaps them on his wrists. Then, she slides down his body and unbuckles his belt.

"What about us?" his wife whispers to Arthur.

"Maybe you could join us?" asks Rosey, and his wife grins. "There's room for two," she adds, patting the bed.

Once they're both cuffed and half-naked, Rosey gets up from the bed and begins to untie the girl. "It's okay, boys, just leave all the work to me," she mutters sarcastically. The girl dives up, ready to fight. "Relax," says Rosey, "we're here to help. Call us your knights in non-shining armour."

"What's going on?" she asks, backing away from Rosey. She reminds me of how Gracie was when I first met her. "Where the hell am I?"

"We're gonna help you get out of here and move you somewhere safe. I'm Rosey, that's Arthur, and Scar's the moody bastard in the corner."

"What the hell is going on, Arthur? What is she talking about?" yells Michaelson, tugging on his restraints.

Rosey smiles. "I told you, we're playing a game. It's a little like those popular interactive escape rooms that everyone's gone mad on," she pauses, tapping her chin like she's thinking, then she adds, "only there's no escape. Well, not for you at least."

"You need to untie me right now!" he yells.

"That would be cheating. You have to at least try and get out. Make it a little exciting."

"How the fuck do I do that when you have the key?"

Rosey stares at the key in her hand and then grins. "Oh, yeah, silly me. Tell you what, I'll pop it here," she says, placing it on the table a few metres away, "and if you manage to get it and free yourselves, then fine, but if you don't, that's God's way of saying you're no good for this world."

"Do you know who I am?" he growls.

"Yes," says Rosey. "You are a disgusting pig. A man who likes to rape defenceless women. A man who watches his wife rape helpless girls for his own gratification. The world will be a better place without you both in it, and that's the reason I'm going to leave you in here to rot." We head for the door. "And while you're lying here, waiting to die, remember all the women and girls you hurt. Remember each and every one, and I pray that when you get to the gates of hell, they spend eternity haunting you. Remember Gracie."

"Gracie?" he gasps.

Rosey leans closer to his ear. "She sends her love, Judge Harry Michaelson. May you rot in hell."

We lock both doors, wiping any prints we may have left as we go. While we were in there, Ghost snuck up to their bedroom and packed two suitcases with the judge's and his wife's clothes. He took their passports and checked them in online for a flight to Malta. By the time anyone finds their rotting bodies, it'll be too late.

We get back upstairs and find the passed-out girl still on the table. There's a couple nearby, but they're lost in their own passion, and the girl looks untouched as I lift her into my arms.

"What about behind that door?" asks Rosey. I shake my head. Mav is already shouting in my ear to get the hell out and leave the door. Rosey rolls her eyes. "We always have to stick to the plan. It's so boring."

GRACIE

Rosey's little boy, Ollie, is obsessed with Deuce. I watch as he rolls around on the ground with him, giggling. When Rosey bursts in, he rushes at her with enthusiasm, and she swings him around. Mav is close behind her, lecturing her about plans or something, but she doesn't look interested. Scar steps in next, with a woman in his arms. She's asleep, her head resting against his shoulder. It shouldn't bother me, but it does. A jealous pain hits my chest, and I try hard to squash it as he carefully lays her on the couch. He's such a good man, I don't know how I got so lucky.

"I'll call Doc," says Mav, moving towards his office.

I cautiously edge closer. She's pretty, even though she's dirty and bruised and her hair is straggly. "Who is she?"

"L-l-later," mutters Scar, grabbing a blanket and covering her.

Rosey is talking to another girl who looks just as lost and dirty. "This is Gracie. We helped her escape them too," she says, smiling at me.

"You found the place?" I ask, gasping.

"Later," hisses Scar, glaring hard at Rosey.

"No, Scar, now. Did you find the place?" I'm desperate to know if this nightmare is over and the girls are safe.

He growls impatiently and takes me by the hand, pulling me upstairs to my room. "We w-w-went to the j-judge's h-house."

"Judge Michaelson? Holy shit! Why didn't you tell me you were going there?"

"I didn't want y-y-you to w-worry."

"What happened?"

There's a faraway look in his eye as he shrugs. "They won't b-be a p-problem a-again."

"They're dead?" I gasp.

"T-they will be."

I sit on the bed. I'm not sad, or happy, just numb. I wished death on them so many times, but knowing their blood is on the club's hands makes me feel weird. "So, those girls, were they at the party?" He nods. "And they were the dessert, right?" He nods again, this time looking away. Knowing Scar was in that room, the one I used to hate so much, makes me shudder. "Were you there while they hurt the girls?" I whisper, and he scowls angrily. "No, I didn't mean that. I just wondered if . . ." I don't know what I wondered. Did he see what happened to them? Will he look at me differently now, knowing I was laid out on that same table?

Scar pulls me to stand, hooking a finger under my chin and forcing me to look at him. "Don't th-think about them again. They don't d-d-deserve the head-space." He places a gentle kiss on my lips before heading back downstairs.

When Scar doesn't return after an hour, I head down too. I find him on the couch with Ghost and one of the new girls. I go to walk past, not because I'm jealous—I am—but because they look deep in conversation. Not Scar, of course, he's listening, but still. He takes my hand as I pass, stopping me and pulling me onto his lap. I bite my lip to stop the smile. It's the first time he's been so public and open about us in front of the other club members. He entwines our fingers, and Ghost trails off from whatever he is saying. His eyes stare at our joined hands for a second before he smiles. "Interesting."

"Is it?" I ask, grinning.

"Um, seems my brother forgot to have that conversation with me."

"You know how he is, hates to talk and all," I joke, and Ghost rolls his eyes playfully.

"As long as you guys are happy, then I am too." He turns back to the girl. "This is Maddie."

"Hi," I say. "How's your friend?"

"Faith is sleeping. She's hungry and dehydrated," says Maddie quietly.

"Were you there long?" I ask.

"I think so. Rosey said you were there too. How long?"

"Sixteen months," I mutter, and Scar grips my hand tighter. "I escaped."

"Oh my god, you're the girl who ran to the church?" she whispers.

"How do you know?" asks Ghost.

"Oh, the guards were in huge trouble that night. We all heard them being yelled at. You gave us hope," she says with a little smile. "Not that it lasted long. They were extra tight on security after that."

"How come you weren't passed out like the other girl?" Ghost asks.

"They requested someone with spirit, so they hadn't drugged me for days, to keep me conscious. They wanted a girl who would fight."

"So, you saw where you were before Rosey found you?" I ask hopefully.

She shakes her head. "I was blindfolded."

Ghost frowns. "We think we know already," he tells me, and I sit up straighter, eager to hear what he has to say. Scar never mentioned that. "Yeah, we worked out that Harris owns a nightclub."

"Nightclub?" I repeat. It makes sense. There was always music playing somewhere in the building.

"We're gonna find them, Gracie. We just gotta follow the plan and take the motherfuckers out one at a time."

Scar's mobile rings and he pulls it out. I get a glance at Katya's name on the screen as he lifts me from his lap so he can stand. Then, he heads outside.

CHAPTER THIRTEEN

SCAR

"I'd like you to come over," says Katya. I check my watch, it's almost ten in the evening.

"Why?"

"Why else would I be calling you at this time?" she snaps.

"I c-can't," I mutter.

"Can't or won't?" She sighs. "Look, I just want to talk about August. She misses you, and I feel bad. She's seen you once since you got out of prison and that's my fault. Come over here instead, if it's easier, we'll make a plan and try and sort regular contact."

"I'm w-w-with Gracie now," I begin.

"I know, okay. You made it clear. Fuck, bring her if you want."

It isn't right to bring Gracie into my mess with Katya, so I decide against it as I throw my leg over my bike. "On my w-w-way."

Katya opens her front door before I've even knocked. She smiles, which is a warning sign. When she does that, she's plotting. "You didn't bring Gracie?" she asks with mock sadness. I narrow my eyes, and she smiles wider. "I'm kidding. You could have. If she's a part of your life, then she should be in on this too." I follow her inside. "I mean, she is permanent, right?"

"I'm h-here to t-talk about August," I say bluntly.

"Oh, did I touch a nerve? Isn't Gracie in it for the long haul?" She leans against the white, modern kitchen unit, running her red painted nails against it. "You remember when I got this installed?" she asks, grinning. I fucked her over it after she accused me of having an affair with our neighbour's wife. Another drunken row she caused. "We had some hot times, didn't we?"

When I don't reply, she presses her lips together. "Does she like it rough, Scar?"

"Katya," I growl in warning.

"I'm interested. Does she satisfy that hungry need you have?" She steps closer, and I step back. "I miss us, Scar. I miss you fucking me and pinning me down. I miss you making me suck your cock in public places, the thrill of getting caught. I know it wasn't always good, but there were times," she whispers.

I shake my head, pissed at myself for coming here and believing she'd talk about August. "Y-you always use A-a-august," I snap.

She has the audacity to look offended. "It's the only time you'll come to me. Now you've got Miss Goody Two-Shoes, you're not interested. Well, if you want to see August, that's fine with me." Hope builds in my chest, but it's soon stamped out when she sneers. "On the condition you get rid of Gracie."

I shake my head angrily. Who the fuck does she think she is making those kinds of demands after everything she's done to me? "No."

"You're choosing her over our daughter? Unbelievable. Just wait until I tell August."

"I know what y-y-you'll d-d-do. I'll a-a-agree, and you still won't l-l-let me see her. Gracie is right, I n-n-need a court order."

"Oh, please. You don't think I'll lay it on thick about your choice of lifestyle and how you beat me all the time? You watched my performance at your last trial, right? I'll do and say anything to stop you seeing August."

"W-why are you d-d-doing this?"

"Because I can. You think you can get me fucking pregnant and then just go on with your life while I raise her? You don't get to cut me off like I'm nothing. I am the mother of your child, and despite everything, I fucking love you. You let your brother and that damn club get in your head. We were good together, and any problems were because of that club demanding your time. I was sick of coming second."

August comes rushing in and throws herself at me. I breathe through the urge to hold her at arm's length, just like Gracie showed me. "Dad, I thought I heard your voice," she whispers, snuggling against me. I relax a little and wrap my arms around her tighter. "What are you doing here?"

"He's come to see us, baby. We're talking about contact."

"Really?" she cries, looking so happy.

"Really. I was just telling him how much we miss him and want him around, but he doesn't quite feel the same. Do you?"

August looks at me, frowning. "T-that's n-not true," I whisper. "I want t-t-to see you."

"But he wants his new girlfriend more," says Katya.

"Oh," mumbles August, stepping away slightly. I feel the weight of this decision crushing me. "It's fine. You have a life that's separate from us, and I get it."

I look at Katya, pleading with my eyes, but she shrugs. "August or your girlfriend, Hunter. At least tell your daughter to her face if you're gonna walk out of here forever."

A tear rolls down August's face, and I close my eyes briefly. "You, b-b-baby g-girl. A-a-always you," I whisper, swiping her tears away.

She beams so bright, my heart lifts a little, and she hugs me again. "I love you," she whispers.

"Y-y-you too," I whisper back.

"Right, well, off you go to bed. I'll make the arrangements for him to come and get you twice a week. Tuesdays and Thursdays good for you?" she asks, and I nod, hardly believing this is possible after years of her stopping me seeing her. August heads back upstairs, and Katya closes the kitchen door. "On those days, come here at five. We'll have dinner before you take August out, and I'll see you when you drop her off at nine. Don't make me regret this, Hunter."

I nod, and she steps close until her body is against mine. I grit my teeth. "You've made her so happy. I'll see you Tuesday." She rakes her nails over the sensitive skin at the back of my neck and presses her red lips against the corner of my mouth. It's ridiculous that after everything this bitch has done, I still feel that pull to her. "I'll be calling by to make sure you've dumped your little princess."

Reality hits me hard in the stomach as I think about Gracie and breaking her damn heart.

"Where the fuck did you disappear to?" asks Ghost when I get back to the club. Gracie is nowhere to be seen, and he smirks. "Man, she went to bed an hour ago. She said Katya called?"

I nod. "Sh-she wanted to t-talk about August."

"Funny after seeing you with Gracie that she suddenly wants to discuss your daughter. She was never keen before."

"Sh-she said I can h-have contact T-tuesdays and Th-thursdays."

"Wow, brother, if she's serious, that's great," he says sarcastically. "What did you sacrifice?" he adds, keeping his tone dry.

"On th-the condition," I breathe, "that I d-d-dump Gracie."

"Jesus, that bitch is relentless. I hope you told her to fuck herself. We'll go to court and get visitation."

I shake my head, and he groans. "She said she'd p-put on a sh-show and s-say all sorts of c-crap to stop me. It ain't w-worth th-the f-fight."

"Are you shitting me? So, you told her to get fucked, right? In a few years, August will be old enough to come over and see you herself."

"August came down wh-while I w-was there. I c-couldn't ch-choose Gracie over her."

"Fuuuuck," he growls. "How does she always manage to screw you over?"

"It's n-no b-big deal. I've b-been single for y-years. August is wh-what's important."

"You've finally found an amazing woman who's brought out the best in you already, and she's not been around that long. Trust Katya to ruin it." I shrug. Katya always has a way of doing this, trampling my life and pulling me back to her, keeping control. I should have expected it.

GRACIE

Scar never returned after stepping out to take the call from Katya. I ended up going to bed alone, and when I wake in a hot sweat, sobbing and tangled in the sheets, I expect him to come rushing in, but he doesn't. Deuce licks my face, and I ruffle the fur on his head. I'm worried. Knowing how Katya has been in the past makes me scared for him, so I pull on one of his shirts and head downstairs, where I find Ghost.

"Hey," I mutter, and he looks up from his glass of whiskey. "Did Scar come home?"

A pained look passes his face, and he nods. "Yeah. He came home hours ago."

I frown. He always comes to my room. "Oh. Okay." Something is wrong, I can feel it.

"Look, Gracie. There's something you should know about Scar and Katya." He pulls out a stool next to him, and I join him at the bar. "She has this hold over him and . . ." He groans. "I hate her. She's a cruel, vindictive bitch. She's spent years torturing my brother mentally and physically, and I can't stop her. She uses August as a pawn to reel him to her pathetic game of warped love."

"What are you trying to tell me?" I ask, my stomach filling with dread.

"Whatever happens between you two is down to her. Please know that he'd never hurt you. Sometimes, she makes him do things that he doesn't want to, just because she likes to know she has that power, and while ever she has August, she has that power."

"Did something happen between them?"

Scar's shadow falls over us, and Ghost glances back over his shoulder at him, a guilty expression on his face. "Sorry, brother, she came looking for you." I don't want to see Scar's face. For once, I wish he had his cap in place so I could avoid the look of sadness in his eyes. "I'll leave you to it," Ghost adds, leaving the room.

Scar hovers for a few seconds before taking Ghost's vacated seat. He rests his arms on the bar and lowers his head. It reminds me of when we first met and how he avoided looking at me. "You went to see Katya," I begin, and he nods. I sigh when he doesn't continue. "Yah know what, Scar, if you're about to say what I think you are, I'm not going to make it easy for you. If you have something to say, the stage is yours, and I want to hear your words."

He gives me a side glance. "I'm s-s-so sorry."

I bite my lip to stop the tears threatening to fall. "For?"

"I have to s-s-stop seeing you."

"Right. Because of her?"

"She'll l-let me see August i-if I b-b-break it off w-with you."

I laugh, but it's cold and empty. "Scar, don't you see she's just saying that? She's lost control and she's using August to pull you back." He nods. "Then don't give in to her. Fight for what you want."

"It's n-n-not worth it."

I arch my brow. "Thanks. Nice to know."

"I didn't m-m-m-mean . . ." He exhales. "She'll a-a-always find a way."

"It's abuse. What she's doing is abuse. You have to break the cycle."

"And not s-s-see August?"

I hold my head in my hands. "No, of course, not. I know how much you want to see her." I take a breath to gather myself. I can't add to his guilt because he already feels terrible. It's written all over his face. "It's fine. You have to put August first, but I'm gutted, for both of us. I really . . ." I don't finish the sentence. My heart hurts, which is crazy since it's only been a couple of months, but I felt like what we had was real. It was intense and strong and so fucking real. Tears fill my eyes, so I push to stand. "Good luck, Hunter. You'll need it."

CHAPTER FOURTEEN

SCAR

It's been two days since I made the decision to choose August. Two days of not being able to touch Gracie, to bury my nose in her soft hair and breathe in her vanilla scent. Two days of watching her from a distance, not knowing how she's feeling or what she's thinking. Not knowing if she's sleeping well or eating enough. It's killing me inside.

I can't help but watch her. She's with Maddie. They're as thick as thieves these last couple of days. Faith is with them, but she's still got that lost look in her eyes. The drugs are still working out her system, so it's to be expected.

Occasionally, Gracie touches Faith's hand and gives her a reassuring smile. It warms my fucking heart, how she's always thinking of others. She catches my eye and smiles, but I look away. She should hate me, but she's too nice for that. Instead, she smiles at me all the damn time. A bright, happy smile that shatters me. It taunts me and reminds me of what I'm missing.

I read the text message from Katya I received this morning asking me to call round. I know August is at school, but I'm so close to seeing her, I don't wanna risk upsetting Katya by refusing.

When I get there and she answers the door in a silk nightshirt, I inwardly groan. She smiles, grabbing my shirt and tugging me inside. She hasn't even closed the door before her tongue is in my mouth and she's clawing at my kutte. My cock is hard, because it's got a mind of its own when it comes to Katya, and there's nothing I can do to control it.

"August is so excited for tomorrow," she whispers in my ear. I keep my hands by my side as she pulls my kutte from my shoulders, dropping it to the floor. I stare down at it, discarded on the floor like rubbish. She never understood the club or its importance in my life. She pushes a condom into my hand and tugs at my belt.

"K-Kat," I mutter, trying to still her hands.

She glares at me. "What?"

I sigh, because it's not worth the argument. "N-nothing," I mumble, and she grins, pulling my zipper down.

GRACIE

Two days of not having his arms around me. It's breaking me to smile in his direction whenever I catch him watching me, and I catch him a lot. *It's not his fault*, I keep telling myself. Katya is an abusive partner, emotionally bullying him to do exactly what she wants. He feels he has no choice, that he's trapped in a vicious circle. She's screwed his life up so much already, and he's stuck in a rut. That doesn't mean it's not killing me inside to watch.

It's quiet in the club. Most of the guys are out on runs, and a few of the women have gone for a walk around the club grounds. I'm on the couch with Deuce, chatting with Ghost, when Scar comes in. He looks different, sheepish maybe, as he passes us. "You not gonna say hello?" asks Ghost.

Scar pauses, and I see the marks right away, the hickey-type bruising on his neck, the red lipstick on his collar. I bite my lower lip angrily. Two days and he's back in her bed. Ghost must see them too because he laughs, but it's cold and empty of humour. "Really, brother?" Scar keeps his eyes to the ground. "You fucking idiot. I thought this was about August," he growls, standing.

"I-i-it is," he mutters.

Ghost shoves him, and he stumbles back slightly. "Bullshit. You're screwing her again, and we all know how that fucking ends. Should I wait by the gates for the cops to come and arrest you? Because she'll probably call them and make up some bullshit story again." Scar stays quiet, and Ghost shoves him again. I wince, fighting the urge to jump up and protect him, even though Ghost is right. "I will not pick up the pieces this time, brother. I can't do that again." When he shoves him for the third time, I get up and rush for the stairs. I hear Scar call my name, but I don't stop until I'm in the safety of my room.

A few minutes later, Ghost knocks on my door. I wanted it to be Scar, and I can't hide the disappointment showing on my face. "He wanted to come, but I wouldn't let him," explains Ghost. "He doesn't get to comfort you after what he's done."

"It's not his fault. You told me that."

"I've never wanted to kill anyone as much as I want to kill her," Ghost declares. "You're good for him, Gracie, and I'm so pissed he's fucked it up."

"It was always gonna end, you said it yourself, that I'd eventually go back to my life. I should be thankful it ended now and not further down the line."

The door opens suddenly and Scar glares at us. His fists are balled, and he looks pissed. Ghost laughs. "What?" he asks, his voice sounding amused, like he's goading him. "You don't want me here talking to Gracie? You should get used to it, now you don't want her."

I blush, embarrassed. Scar growls, and Ghost stands, ready for a fight. "Please, don't," I mutter, but it's hopeless because they're already squaring up to each other. Deuce grumbles, not happy at the change of mood either.

"You've got Katya, what's the problem? I can make my move on Gracie now you've stepped back. She's fucking hot, brother, I'd be stupid not to go there."

Scar's breathing is heavy, and the way he glares at Ghost makes me want to run and hide. "Don't," he hisses.

"Don't what? Fuck her, date her, have her on the back of my bike?"

"G-g-ghost," Scar growls in warning.

"Please, just leave it," I say, getting between them, trying but failing to push them apart. "This is stupid."

"He needs to realise what he's lost. And if I don't try my luck with you, one of the other brothers will. But Scar knows the rules, don't you, brother? He hasn't claimed you, so you're free."

I shove hard at Ghost's chest, and he steps back once. The motherfucker is solid. "That's enough!" I yell. "I am not free because I'm not on the market. No one is claiming me. This is for the best. Scar needs August more than he does me. She's his daughter, and he has to do whatever to keep her in his life. I get that and I'm okay with it. Soon, this mess will be over, and I can go and live with my parents, then you'll never see me again. Now, get out, both of you!"

Scar runs his finger down my spine, but I shrug him off, keeping my back to them until they leave. Hadley and Rylee are in the doorway watching the exchange. Once the men have left, they come in. "Shit, well done, you," says Rylee. I burst into tears and a look of panic crosses her face. "Oh fuck," she mutters, wrapping me in her arms.

Hadley passes me a tissue, and I wipe my eyes. "Sorry, I don't even know why I'm upset."

"What's going on with you guys?" asks Rylee.

I fill them in on me and Scar. I've not talked to the girls much about us because Scar is a private person, and he isn't the type that'd be happy with us talking about him like that.

"Wow, I knew you'd gotten close, but I just thought it was cos he helped you."

"Maybe that's all it is," I say with a sigh. "An infatuation because he was one of the first people to help me. He was so kind and gentle. I was intrigued by his mysterious ways, and the more time I spent with him, the more he began to trust me. When he let me see him for the first time, and when I first touched him, it was a special moment. But now, when I think about it, maybe it was all in my head. He lets Katya touch him, so it's not special."

"Oh, hunny," says Rylee, squeezing my hand. "Why didn't you come to me?"

"Katya is a cow," states Hadley. "I've always hated her. She was a bitch towards me when she stayed here briefly. She wasted no time getting pregnant, and then she demanded a house with nice things. She wouldn't live here at the club like the other ol' ladies. We thought she was hurting Scar, but no one dared to ask him, and then after the accident, we got to know some things that happened because my legal firm dealt with his case.

"She really played the victim. The only thing she couldn't prove was the rape, so those charges were dropped. But who the fuck does that? Who would stand in court crying about a rape that didn't happen? Scar admitted fully that he was rough, that they'd a fiery relationship and that was how they were in the bedroom. It was hard to prove a rape when she begged to be held down."

Doubt fills my head. Maybe that's why he's gone back to her. I can't give him that side of things because I know without doubt it would trigger me. "Look, he was an end to a means. I needed to have sex with someone patient and kind who knew my history, and he was perfect for that. I won't ever be able to give him what he needs, if he likes that sort of thing. The thought of sex like that . . ." I shudder, and Rylee rubs my arm.

"That's normal to feel like that. And you're right," she says brightly, "you needed him for that, and now, you can move forward. It's just sex, right?"

I nod. "Once I leave here, I'll never tell anyone what happened," I mutter. "Who will understand it?"

"You'll always have us," says Hadley. "We understand and we get it."

∞

The next day, I call Mum. I need to hear her voice, and the second she answers, I smile. "Hey, Mum. It's me."

"It's so good to hear your voice," she whispers. "I miss you so much."

"You, too. How are you both?"

"Good. The police came," she announces, and I frown. "They just asked if we'd heard from you, seeing as you were listed as missing."

"What did you say?"

"I lied like you told me to. I said we hadn't seen or heard from you since the day you went missing. I gave them an earful about how useless they'd all been, and I repeated my belief you were taken and not a runaway." She chuckles. "I don't think they'll come back in a hurry."

I smile. "Mum, did you ever meet Jen's dad?"

"No. He was always busy working, a judge or something, and I think he owns some bars, maybe. He's a busy man, according to Jen. Why?"

"Just asking. I've had a lot of time to think things over and I remembered I'd never actually met him. Have you seen Jen recently?"

"Yes. I went for her last dress fitting," she gushes, then apologies for sounding so excited.

"Don't be sorry. She spent a lot of time with us while we were kids."

"You know, since you went missing, she's been here a lot. She's almost like a second daughter, and your dad and I clung to that. We missed you so much, so it was nice to have someone around, yah know?"

I nod even though she can't see me. "And she's happy with Edward?"

"Very. I was shocked when they told me, but I get it. They spent so much time looking for you, I guess it was a natural progression."

"When's the wedding?"

"It's at the end of the month. They've booked an amazing hotel, The Garlands. It's got the most beautiful scenery. Jen's on her hen weekend this weekend. We're going to a cottage with a hot tub."

"Oh, you're going on the hen weekend?"

She pauses. "Sorry," she utters again.

"Honestly, Mum, stop apologising. I just can't imagine you as the party animal."

"I feel bad for her not having her mum around."

"I hope you have an amazing time. I wish I could be there."

We say our goodbyes, and I promise to call her after the weekend to hear all about the hen night. I stare at my phone for a long time after, trying to remember Jen and our times together growing up.

The door opens, and Scar comes in with some toast. I wish he'd stop doing little things like this, it makes it harder to push him away. The marks on his neck are still visible, and I cringe.

"Y-y-you okay?" he mutters.

"Fine. I don't want breakfast, by the way. That's why I didn't come down and get any."

"Eat," he mutters, keeping his head lowered.

"I don't want to fucking eat," I snap, and he shifts, his stance somehow making him look bigger. I know it's not his fault. I'm not even mad at him, but why the hell does he keep doing sweet shit like making sure I eat? "Get out."

He raises his head slightly and catches my eye. I feel bad, but I can't apologise. I'm angry. I feel like my life has been ripped away, and Jen's just stepped right in there. "Y-y-you wanna t-talk?"

"No, I don't want to talk to you, Scar. I want you to stop turning up in my room and bringing me fucking food that I don't want to eat. Stop trying to take care of me. I don't need you to."

"Y-you're u-upset?"

"Of course, I'm fucking upset. You're back with your ex, you shouldn't be in here with me. Does she know you bring me breakfast?" He doesn't reply, and that just annoys me more. "Why are you even here? Why didn't you spend the night holding her, whispering words in her ear?" *Just like you did with me*, I say in my head.

"I d-d-didn't h-have sex with her. She wanted to, but I c-c-couldn't."

I look away. He's got sadness all over his face, and I can't handle it. I just want to throw myself at him. "You have marks all over your fucking neck. Don't lie to my face. And anyway, it's got nothing to do with me."

"Gracie, I—"

"No, don't explain it. I don't want to hear it. I'm not mad at you, I'm mad at . . ." I pause, *what am I mad at?* "the world. I'm having one of those days where I want to scream 'why me'. Why the fuck me?"

"You want me t-t-t-to call th-the counsellor?"

I shake my head. I already see her once a week, she'll get sick of hearing my pity-party for one. "I'll be fine. I just need a day to feel sad for myself, for the life I've lost."

"Lost?"

"I spoke to my mum. She was telling me about Jen's wedding. She booked the place where I always wanted to get married. The Garlands Hotel was my dream wedding venue, and she's marrying my ex there."

"Shit."

"Maybe what you said," I pause, not wanting to say it out loud, "maybe you were right. Maybe she did want me out the way."

He tries to take my hand and tug me to stand, but I pull away. If he holds me, I'll break, and I can't do that anymore. He isn't mine. "I'm fine. Honestly."

"L-l-let's w-w-walk Deuce."

I shake my head. "Don't take this the wrong way, but I don't want to be around you anymore. Not like that. The truth is, I was really starting to like you, Scar, and I can't pretend I'm not a little gutted. If you keep sticking around, I'll never move on. I know I sound crazy, and you're better off escaping now." I laugh. "I'm not usually so stalker-like, but you made me feel . . ." I sigh. "Never mind. If you need me, if things get too much with Katya and you need help, please come to me. I owe you one after what you've done for me."

"Gracie," he mumbles, his eyes full of pain.

"Give me some space, Scar, please."

He nods once before leaving, and I stare at the closed door. It's for the best. *Totally for the best.*

CHAPTER FIFTEEN

SCAR

It's my second visit with August and it feels good. When I'm with her, I can forget the heartache I've caused Gracie and the mess I'm falling back into with Katya. All my troubles melt away, for a few hours anyway.

August finishes off her ice cream and smiles at me across the table. "I've noticed a change in you," she says. "You're more confident. You don't hide as much and you're talking more." Gracie's image taunts me. *She's the reason. It's because of her.* "And I think I know why." I wait for her to continue. "Because you're not with Mum anymore."

I stare down at my empty container. We always come here for ice cream. Katya cooks dinner at home and we eat together, as a family. So far, it's been okay because August is good at shutting Katya down when she gets to be too much. But I look forward to this part the most, me and my baby girl together and alone, eating her favourite ice cream in her favourite American-style diner.

"You're not good for each other, are you?" I shake my head. "But you look sad again, and I hate that. Is it because of your new girlfriend?"

"I d-don't have a g-girlfriend."

"Because of Mum?" I don't reply. I'd never badmouth her mother to her face, I never have, but now she's older, she can see for herself what's going on. "Did she tell you that you couldn't see me if you had a girlfriend?" I stay silent. "Damn it, Dad," she hisses, and I glare at her for cursing. "I want you to be happy. When Mum said you were making a choice, I thought your girlfriend was pushing you into it."

"I am h-h-happy. Th-things are c-c-complicated with me and y-your mum. Gracie would n-never m-make me ch-choose. She's so k-kind and p-patient."

"Then you should be with her. No one has the right to make you choose. I'll talk to Mum."

I shake my head. It'll do no good, and I don't want August on the receiving end of Katya's temper. "I'm h-happy," I repeat, with a little more conviction this time.

When I drop August home, she goes straight up to bed. Katya opens the door wider for me to go in, but I stay rooted to the spot. "I've got a solution to your little problem," she says, pointing to my cock. She holds up a pack of blue pills, and I snigger. She doesn't get that I can't get hard for her because I hate her guts. Trust me, she's tried everything to get me off, but I just can't anymore. I miss Gracie and the way we were together. "Stop with the wounded puppy look," she snaps.

"I gotta g-g-go," I mutter.

"Back to her?" she hisses, and I roll my eyes. We have this same discussion over and over. I'm not with Gracie, but I'm not with Katya either, and she just can't seem to get it through her head. I begin to walk away, knowing I won't win an argument when she's like this, so there's no point in trying. I'm almost at the gate when she shoves me hard in the back, her fists hitting against me. "If I can't have you, she can't either," she hisses.

I grip her wrists, glancing around to make sure people aren't watching. It happens all the time, they see the size of me and assume I'm hurting her, but that's never the case. I walk her back towards the house and through the door. If I don't get out of sight, someone will call the cops, and that's the last thing I need.

"Calm," I order.

"Fuck you! After everything we've been through. I see it in your eyes, you love her!"

"I d-don't," I mumble, not entirely convinced myself.

"I waited for you while you were in prison."

"I was th-there b-because of y-you."

She slaps me hard, and I feel the burn instantly. Then her nails claw at my cheek, and I know without checking she's drawn blood. I'm so tired of this. "Is this what you want? A fight?" she hisses.

"I d-don't l-love you," I say. It's the first time I've said it to her face. I never bothered before because it would cause endless arguments and fights that I had no energy to deal with. She slaps me again, then makes a grab for my throat. I remove her hands, careful not to mark her skin in case she tries to use it against me later. She falls back against the table, knocking a glass to the floor. It smashes, and she swoops down to grab a jagged piece.

She points it at me. "You're not leaving here tonight."

"Stop th-this," I say with a sigh.

"I mean it, Hunter. If I can't have you, no one can."

"Mum!" screams August from the doorway, and my instant reaction is to stand between them so August doesn't get hurt.

Katya drops the glass and glares at me. "I would never hurt her," she hisses.

"What the hell are you doing?" August demands.

"We were just having a heated discussion. Go back to bed."

"No. This has to stop. Look what you've done," she says, staring at the scratches on my face. "Why do you let her do this to you?" And for the first time, I feel ashamed. I let her do it because my mum raised me to never hit women. "You're both adults. I'm fourteen years old and I can see this is wrong. You have to stop. You're not good together and this ends tonight."

"You're a kid. What do you know about it?" snaps Katya.

"I know if you ever lay a hand on my dad again, I'll run away. You'll never see me again and you'll never be able to use me in your twisted games. Go home, Dad. I'll see you next week for dinner. Maybe we'll go out to eat, give Mum a night off from cooking." Katya tries to object, but August holds her hand up. "I will run away, Mum. I swear it."

I kiss August on the head. "Th-thank you." I feel relieved that she's seen what goes on. I never would have told her and ruined the relationship between them, but now she's seen it for herself. I'm sure Katya will come up with something to stop me seeing her again, but I know for a fact I can't do this anymore. My fight is gone. I don't love her, and she can't pull me back in, especially now our daughter knows. I'm done.

GRACIE

I must have fallen asleep on the couch in the main room because I wake with a start when the door bangs. I sit up and look around, but there's no one except for Scar, who's staring at me like a rabbit in headlights. He's got bloodied scratches on his face and it takes me a second to register he's hurt. Before I have a chance to examine him, he heads for the stairs without a word. I told him I'd be here if he was hurt, and I hate that tired, defeated look in his eyes. There has to be a way we can get him visitation rights to August without him having to go through this.

I take the stairs two at a time and head straight for his room. I tap on the door, but he doesn't bother to answer, so I push it open. He's lying on his bed, staring up at the ceiling. "You're hurt," I say, stepping inside and closing the door.

"So," he mutters, and I smile because at least he responded. It means he wants me here.

"Scratches can cause nasty infections. Dirt from behind the nails can mix with the blood and cause sepsis." It's extreme, but I need a reason to be here in his room.

I go to the bathroom and find a small bowl, antiseptic, and some cotton wool. When I return, his shirt is on the ground and he's lying back on the bed, still staring up at the ceiling. "It might sting a little, but you're a big boy," I say, taking a seat beside him and pressing the wet cotton wool to his wounds. He flinches, and I smile. He deserves a little sting. "If this is what rough sex is like, I'm glad we never tried that," I joke, and he narrows his eyes.

"I don't l-like r-r-rough sex."

"Hate to point it out, but you don't get scratches like that from making love."

He grabs my wrist mid wipe and stares me in the eyes. "I haven't h-had sex with K-katya."

"Oh, I thought . . ." I trail off.

"She w-wanted to, b-but I couldn't. Not s-s-since we . . ." He trails off too.

"Is that why she did this?" I ask, dipping some fresh wool and wiping his face.

"It's done. Me and h-her are d-done. I don't l-love her. I haven't f-for y-y-years. I m-miss you, Gracie. So fucking m-much."

I don't reply as I finish cleaning his face. I miss him too, but what about the next time she clicks her fingers and he has to go running? And there's still that niggling feeling this isn't real. I'm trapped here, and he's all-consuming. When I leave, I might not feel the connection so much. I sigh, knowing that's utter bullshit. I've never liked anyone as much as I like Scar.

I place the bowl on the side table and climb onto the bed beside him. Snuggling against his broad chest, he wraps his strong arm around me. "I don't blame you for stepping back from us so you could see your daughter, and I know things are complicated between you and your ex, but don't ever do that to me again, Scar. I can forgive you once if there was nothing between you and her—"

"N-n-nothing," he confirms.

"It was a blip, a slip-up, but you know she'll do anything to break us up. Don't let her do that again. We'll find a way for you and August but not at the cost of your happiness."

SCAR

I wake with sunlight warming my face and an erection the size of the fucking Eiffel Tower. I glance at Gracie deep in sleep. Needing to resolve this issue before she sees it, I climb from the bed carefully and head for the shower. I step under the hot spray and close my eyes. The feel of Gracie against me all night was torture. I grip the base of my cock and run my hand up, leaking pre-cum onto the shower floor. Suddenly, the door opens and Gracie rushes in, not bothering to look at me as she drops on the toilet.

"Sorry, I needed to pee so ba—" She pauses when she finally glances at me. Her cheeks flush, but she's already peeing, and I still have a handful of cock. She bites her lower lip. "Oh," she gasps.

I turn to face her, bracing myself against the glass door as I move my hand again, staring right at her. She watches, her lips slightly parted and her chest rising and falling faster with each passing second. It's her innocence, the way she blushes, the way her eyes watch me hungrily. Fuck, she's bewitched me and there ain't shit I can do about it. Moving my hand faster, I think of all the times I was buried in her hot, tight pussy and the way her mouth felt when she sucked my cock.

Gracie wipes herself, then kicks off her underwear. It's followed by her top and bra. I think for a second she might join me, but instead, she surprises me by leaning against the sink and moving her hand over her breasts, gently plucking at her erect nipples. She gasps, closing her eyes as her hand travels down to her pussy. I watch her fingers dip into her wetness, and then she rubs circles over her clit, gripping the sink unit for support. It's the hottest thing I've ever watched, but it makes me need her more, so I step out the shower and plant my lips against hers, swiping my tongue into her mouth and biting gently on her lower lip.

I lift her leg, giving me access as I line my cock at her entrance and slam into her. I'm usually slow and gentle, so it catches her off guard and she cries out, grabbing onto my shoulders for support as I continue to fuck her. There's no time for nice, I've missed her too much. She's panting and her wetness coats us both when she orgasms on my cock. I slam into her a few more times before pulling out and gripping my shaft, then I spin her away from me and move my hand back and forth. Seeing her bent over in front of me, her arse up in the air, has me coming hard and I growl until it hurts my throat. My cum drips onto her, and I use my hand to rub it into her soft skin as the last of my orgasm ripples through me.

"That was hot," she whispers, smirking over her shoulder at me. I grin, because damn right it was. I pull her into the shower and hold her against me as the water pours over us. I love the feel of her naked skin against my own.

GRACIE

"I want to go to the wedding," I blurt out, and Scar stiffens. "Not to cause trouble, but I need to see her before she walks down the aisle with Edward. I need to know if she took my life on purpose. I need to know why."

"W-what g-g-good will it do?" He's wrapped around me, completely naked in his bed. It's hard to know which part belongs to each of us, he's so close.

"How can I ignore it? If she was the reason I was taken, I want to know why, what did I do?"

"What if y-y-you see him and it all c-c-comes back?"

I place a gentle kiss on his lips. "It won't. Too much has happened. Besides, he'd never handle what happened to me.

He was jealous like that, and he'd hate the thought of other men . . . well, yah know."

"I hate it t-too," he says, flicking his tongue over my nipple. "But I h-have other ways of d-dealing." He slips a finger inside me, and I close my eyes.

"You don't think I should see her?" I ask.

He presses his erection to my opening. "I th-think we sh-should make sure you're s-s-safe first."

"So, if we get all the bad guys first, you'll come with me?"

He groans softly, and I smile. I love hearing that slight loss of control, knowing I'm doing that to him. "Anything you w-want, b-baby."

CHAPTER SIXTEEN

SCAR

The brothers gather around in church as Mav fills us in on Judge Michaelson and his wife being reported as missing this morning. "That room was so fucking secret, even his staff didn't know about it."

"Or they do and are choosing not to say. Maybe they wanted them dead too," suggests Lock.

"Our next date is the nightclub. Harris owns it," he says, placing a picture of The Coco Rooms Club on the table. "And we think that's where they keep the girls. I had plans of the building sent over. There are tunnels that run all along this area," he says, pointing to it on a map. "No one uses them. They were deemed unsafe years ago by the council. We can access them from any one of these businesses, and that's the plan."

Grim stands. "We're gonna split up into groups. Some of us are gonna go into the caves through this betting shop here. Arthur knows the owner, and he has gated access to the caves from his cellar. We need to grind them open, but then we're good to go. We'll head towards here," he says, using the map again. "If the girls are in there, this is where they'll be."

"The next group," says Mav, "will be in the nightclub. Arthur booked a space in the VIP area. He's sent tickets to London's Gazette courtesy of him for all their coverage of his new restaurant. They've bitten his hand off. It's exposure without us being involved directly, and the journalists will be like dogs with a bone, wanting to get to the bottom of it. The VIP area is right by the door where they'll come up from the cellar."

"What about the Chief Constable? He might get away with it, especially now we're rattling cages, he's gonna have his cover story ready," says Copper.

"We'll get him, don't worry. For now, we just wanna get this story out there. A nightclub full of young people holding up camera phones will blow the internet up. Harris will be arrested, it's his club, and how's he gonna explain it away? We'll deal with Chief Constable Dickhead separately."

"I'm sure he'll be crapping himself, what with the judge gone and Harris being arrested. His days are numbered, and he'll realise that," says Grim. "But that's why we can't expose them ourselves. If we're involved in any way, he'll come for us, and Lord knows he'll be able to pin something on us. We don't need that setback when we're trying to sort this club out."

I find Gracie sitting at the bar and I wrap myself around her. We'd talked all night, about everything that's happened. She's willing to forgive me for hurting her, and as always, she's so goddamn understanding. How the fuck did I get so lucky? But I can't mess up again. She's made that perfectly clear. I push my erection into her lower back, and she laughs. "Seriously?"

"I'm gonna claim y-you, Gracie. I'm gonna f-fill you with babies and t-t-take-care of you f-f-forever."

She looks up at me with a small smile playing on her lips. "Forever is a long time," she says, and I kiss her. I want to have her wrapped in my arms for the rest of our lives, so forever isn't long enough.

Ghost glares at us. I haven't made things right with him since we argued, so I go over to him and hold my hand out. He shakes it reluctantly at first. "S-sorry," I say.

A look of relief passes over his face, and he nods. "Me too. I shouldn't have said that shit."

"K-k-katya is hi-history. August kn-knows e-e-everything. Sh-she saw h-how K-katya was with m-me," I say, pointing to the scratches on my cheek.

He stares at me for a long time before nodding. "I see it," he mutters. "I see it in your eyes. I'm glad, brother. So fucking glad."

"Me t-t-too. I'm gonna s-s-speak to Pres. I'm c-c-claiming Gracie."

"Wow. Quick mover. You sure?" I nod. I've never been so sure about something in my life. "Mum will be over the moon. She loves her."

"Me t-t-too, brother."

∞

Saturday night comes around too quickly. I made sure to spend the day close to Gracie. If it all goes to shit tonight, at least we had today. I shower and dress as she watches me from the bed. "So, you have some big job on, and you can't tell me about it?" she asks, and I nod. I don't want her to worry. I'll tell her the details when we get back. "You look dressed to party," she adds suspiciously. "And the men never all go out together. You always leave someone here to watch us."

"Y-you have Rosey. A-and you c-can call if you n-need me."

"You boys are up to no good, I can tell," she says, grinning. I swat her arse and kiss her on the head.

"S-stay inside. B-b-be g-g-good. Don't let M-meli get you dr-drunk."

∞

The nightclub is packed out. It's hot and I'm glad I wasn't on team rescue mission because I bet those tunnels are fucking boiling. Ghost hands me a drink and we take our seats with Arthur in the VIP area. The newspaper reporters are at the next table, all excited to be here under Arthur's name. I sip my Coke, watching all the while, though nothing seems out of place. Then, I spot Harris. He's shaking hands with men at another table. It's not long before he joins us, greeting Arthur like a long-lost friend.

"You look familiar," he says to Ghost, who shrugs. "Yes, you were chatting my daughter up in her bar a couple of weeks ago."

Ghost grins. "Sounds like me."

"Arthur, there's an after-party this evening. Join us," he adds before walking to the next table.

"Piece of shit," Arthur mutters under his breath. "Do I look like I'm into that sort of shit? First that fat bastard judge and now him, they think I want to force sex on someone, like I can't get it willingly?"

The guys laugh. "Maybe they want to build trust with you, offer business your way," suggests Mav.

"I don't do that kind of business," he mutters.

Mav checks his phone. "When the girls are free, Copper will text us."

GRACIE
Faith pours another glass of wine and hands it to me. "Scar said not to let Meli get me drunk, but he never mentioned you," I say, smiling.

"They can drink at their little boys' night out and you can't?" asks Meli, sounding annoyed.

"Clubbing?" I repeat.

"Yeah. Rylee tracked Mav because he was being so secretive. They're at a nightclub in Soho."

"I thought he looked smartly dressed," I mutter.

"You know, we could always turn up there," Rosey suggests.

"No," snaps Rylee. "Don't even think about it."

"Why do they get all the fun?"

"I agree," says Meli. "They can go out, so why can't we?"

"Because we're keeping Gracie, Faith, and Maddie company," says Rylee.

"I'm good if you girls want to go out. I'll read a book and go to bed," I say.

"I'm happy to stay here too," says Faith, and I smile gratefully.

"The guys will bust a nut if we crash their night," snaps Rylee.

"You don't always have to do what Mav says. You're a free woman now, so you can go where you want. And we could always get the girls wigs if you want us all to stick together," says Rosey. "Gracie, wouldn't you like to go to a nightclub and dance?"

I smile. "It's been a long time since I went clubbing."

"See, she wants to go. We can make her look completely different. No one will know, and the guys will be there if anything bad happens, not that it will. Think about it, why the hell have they gone to all this trouble to keep it a secret? Because they knew we'd insist on going. It's not fair."

Rylee groans, and Meli smiles triumphantly. "All those in, raise your hand."

Everyone puts up their hand apart from Rylee and Hadley. Rosey laughs. "Outnumbered. We're sticking together. Let's go."

∞

I stare at my unrecognisable reflection in the mirror. The short blonde wig and red lipstick make me look like a different person. It's crazy. My low-cut dress isn't ideal and not something I'd usually pick out for myself, but the girls all said it looks amazing. "I don't even think Scar will recognise you," says Rylee.

"Let's hope not in that dress," says Rosey with a grin.

"I have a bad feeling about tonight," mutters Hadley.

"You always have a bad feeling about anything that's fun," Meli retorts.

I hook arms with Hadley and Rylee. "Look, if the guys are mad at us or we're uncomfortable at any point, we'll just leave. No harm done, right?" They nod in agreement.

SCAR

Harris sends over an ice bucket full of beers to the table along with a group of women dressed in next to nothing. "Stay focussed," hisses Mav as girls dance around us.

"Hard to do that with tits in my face," mutters Ghost, and I snigger.

I feel her presence and I pause mid drink, my eyes darting around like a madman trying to figure out why I'd feel Gracie in this place. "You okay, brother?" asks Mav. I nod, scanning the busy club floor.

I see Meli first, waving her arms in the air to the beat of the music and laughing at something Rosey shouts to her from the bar. I scan the group of women, but I don't see Gracie. I shake off the feeling she's nearby and tap Mav, who's staring down at his mobile. "They have the women," he says, looking relieved. I nod towards Meli, and he scowls. "Are you fucking shitting me?" He stands to get a better look. "Oh my god, they're all here!"

I rise to my feet, but I still don't see Gracie. She wouldn't leave the clubhouse anyway, she knows it ain't safe. But then

Mav points. "She's there," he growls, pointing at a blonde. She turns at the right time, and I catch a glimpse of Gracie, face full of bright makeup. Anger burns through me. One of Harris's girls blocks my view when she climbs on the table and begins dancing, thrusting her arse in my face. Then chaos erupts because the door by the VIP area swings open and rescued women begin to step through into the club. They're all similar looking with dirty, straggly hair, pale, and covered in bruises.

"What the hell is going on?" Harris demands. He's staring wide-eyed, hardly daring to believe that his world is about to come crashing down.

Mav shrugs, smirking when the journalists begin snapping photographs. The music cuts and people begin to stare over to the group of women who stand out amongst the party goers. A few women nearby are asking them if they're okay.

Gracie squares her shoulders, and I glare at her, my pleading expression begging her not to get involved, but she can't help herself as she pushes through the crowd. I stand helplessly, waiting for the car crash to unfold. "I'm Gracie," she whispers. "You're safe now."

Harris is trying to explain his way out of things to a journalist, insisting he knows nothing about the women or where they came from. "The caves," says Gracie. "You keep women down there in cages."

"What?" he gasps. "How ridiculous. Do you know who I am?"

"Yes," she says firmly. "I remember your face sneering down at me while you and your friends raped me." There's an audible gasp, and Mav groans from beside me. This wasn't the plan.

"Madam, can we get a story?" asks a journalist.

Mav and I move at the same time, trying to get to her before she answers, but we're too late as she announces, "Yes. I'm Grace Stone, and I've been missing for almost two years." There's a barrage of questions. One of the journalists is holding his phone high to get it all, and I realise he's streaming this live for the world to see.

"Fuck," hisses Mav. "Someone shut her the fuck up before she mentions us."

Everyone's attention, including the live recording, turns to the entrance as police push their way in, ordering everyone to take a seat. I make my move, grabbing Gracie and throwing her over my shoulder. I exit back through the caves, rushing down the stone steps and along a dark passage, with her hissing curse words at my back. There's more steps and another long passage and then we come to an open metal gate. I place Gracie back on her feet.

"What the hell do you think you're doing?" she snaps. She steps through the gate into a dimly lit cave and stumbles, falling onto her arse and letting out a screech as she comes face to face with a dead body. She scrambles back, hitting another dead man. "Oh shit! Shit, shit, shit," she whispers, shaking her hands like she's trying to get something off them. I step over the first body, a bullet wound between his eyes, and swoop down, grip her by the wrists, and pull her to her feet. She presses her back to my front, gripping my shirt in her fists as we move through the room.

We go into the next cave, and it's pitch black. I pull out my mobile and turn on the torch, freezing when I see the cages around the room. They're about big enough for a large dog, each with one dirty blanket inside. My Gracie was kept in here somewhere and it makes me sick to my stomach. She grips me tighter. "I remember this," she whispers. I keep her moving to the next cave, but it's just the same as this one. There's a groaning sound coming from the corner, and I shine the torch on a man sitting against the wall, covering a bullet wound with his hands. "Braydon," whispers Gracie, gripping me tighter. He tries to speak, but nothing comes out, just a gurgling sound followed by blood running down his chin.

"He's th-the guy th-that t-t-took you?" I ask, and she nods. I hand my mobile to her, then reach down, grabbing him by his shirt and pulling him to his feet. He groans louder and blood spills through his fingers. I slam my fist into his face, breaking his nose and cheekbone. If this motherfucker is going to hell, he's gonna be sporting a few black eyes for eternity. I grip him by the throat, and he starts to gasp as I lift his feet from the floor.

"Scar," cries Gracie, hanging on to my arm, "stop." I punch him again and let him fall to the ground before stamping on his leg. He cries out, then slumps down. His breathing is shallow, and I stamp one more time on his stomach. After a few seconds, his breathing stops, and I grab the mobile back from Gracie, take her hand, and pull her through the rest of the tunnels until we find another set of steps. This time, they lead us out into the betting shop, where we find Lock, Copper, and Dice.

"What are you doing here?" asks Copper. I shake my head, too mad to speak. I'm sure Meli and Rosey are behind the women turning up like that, but I didn't think Gracie was stupid enough to follow them again, not after last time. "We're waiting for it to die down a little," he adds as more blue flashing lights fly past the shop.

GRACIE

I can cut the atmosphere with a knife the second we enter the clubhouse. Mav is pacing amongst the couches, where Hadley, Meli, Rosey, and Rylee are seated. He looks up when we enter, and relief floods his face. "Thank fuck. I thought the cops stopped you."

"After her little fucking announcement, Scar could have ended up banged up for kidnapping," mutters Grim. I pull my hand free from Scar, and he looks at me. Folding my arms, I join the women on the couch. I'd never seen a dead body before, and I feel freaked by the entire night. Then to see Scar turn like that, I shudder. He was dead behind the eyes, like he wasn't in the room as he beat Braydon to death. But I'm not sad he's dead, and that makes me question who the hell I've become.

"I don't even know where to start," mutters Mav.

"We were just coming to say hi," says Meli, trying to make light of the situation.

Mav pauses and glares at her. He clearly doesn't appreciate her blasé attitude.

"We had a fucking plan, Amelia, and you lot showing up was not part of it!" he yells, making us all jump.

"We just felt like a night out," adds Rosey.

"And you just happened to turn up in the same club we were in?"

"No, Rylee knew you were there," says Meli, and Rylee kicks her. "Ouch!"

"And how the fuck did you know where I was?" he asks Rylee.

"I might have . . . erm . . . maybe I put . . . look, it wasn't supposed to end in disaster. We thought you'd gone clubbing without us."

He holds out his hand, and she sighs, placing her mobile in it. He stares at it for a few seconds before frowning, "A tracking app?"

She shrugs. "Bad habits are hard to let go of," she mutters, and he hands it back to her.

"We'll talk about that later. Right now, I don't have the words to express how fucking mad I am at the way you all behaved tonight. You're not fucking kids, and turning up like that when three of you are in hiding . . ." He throws his hands up in the air like he's lost for words. "We're trying to help you," he adds, glaring at me.

"We dressed her in disguise," Meli points out.

"Shut up," he snaps, and she presses her lips together. "This isn't a fucking game. These men want to find Gracie, and now we're bringing them down, they'll be even more determined to find her and silence her. Did you think about that when you were playing fucking dress-up?" he yells.

"They're looking for me?" I ask. Scar keeps his head down, and I realise that's something he's kept from me. "I didn't know. I thought they'd given up on me weeks ago."

"If they'd given up, you would be home now with your family," Mav growls.

"Hey," snaps Meli, "we're her family."

I stand. "I'm really sorry, Mav. I didn't know they were actively looking for me. I just thought we were being cautious."

"Well, that's all gone to shit anyway, now you've announced to the world you're alive and well. Christ, Gracie, what were you thinking?"

"The world?" I ask, confused.

"The press was right there, filming your little announcement," Mav says.

I feel sick, lowering back to the couch and digging my fingers into the material. "Oh, crap."

"We need a new plan. You all need to go to bed and stay there until I can bear to look at you again," Mav orders. "Men, we're gonna spend our night in church trying to sort out this fuck-up."

I remain seated as everyone clears out. Scar walks past, and I grab his hand, looking up at him. I need comfort and reassurance that this is all gonna work out, but instead of kissing me or gently touching my cheek like he usually does, he pulls free and heads into church with the others, slamming the door closed behind him.

CHAPTER SEVENTEEN

SCAR

"Well, that was one big fuck-up," says Mav, lounging in his chair at the head of the table. "My fault, I should have left one of you guys behind to watch them, but I thought Meli would have learnt from the last time she took Gracie out of this club."

"She never fucking learns," snaps Grim. "It's her M.O."

"So, now what?" asks Lock."Is it so bad that Gracie announced she's alive?" asks Dice. I roll my eyes at his dumb question.

"It's not ideal," says Grim. "Guilford will be in full panic mode now, and seeing her speak out like that, he might get desperate, and fuck knows what he'll do to silence her."

"What the fuck does it matter? Once they all start talking, he'll be locked up for sure. How can he get out of it with all those victims?" Lock asks.

"What if they don't remember their captors straightaway? It took Gracie a while, and that was because we were pushing her to remember. We have no idea how long some of those women have been there or what drugs they were pumping into their systems," says Mav. "The reason we got the journalists involved was because they could put this story into the world without involving us or Gracie. If we're associated with Gracie after her proud announcement tonight, Guilford will try and pin this shit on us. He could say we were involved."

"Or they could find out about her and Scar and pin the murders of the judge and his wife on him as a revenge killing. His record will back that up. The idea was we rescue the women but distance ourselves from any of it," says Grim.

Mav rubs his forehead and groans angrily. "We have no choice. She's gotta go home to her parents." It's what I expected, Mav has to protect the club, but it doesn't make it an easy pill to swallow. "If she doesn't show up there after her big reveal, people will begin asking questions."

"And we need an urgent plan to get Guilford," adds Grim. "In case any of this traces back to us."

"Maybe Harris will squeal? He won't wanna go down alone for this," Ghost suggests.

"Maybe," mutters Mav. "We'll brainstorm. Scar, do you wanna go and speak to Gracie before we begin?" he asks. I shake my head, feeling too fucking mad to deal with her just yet. "I'll also need a guy at her parents' house all the time. We'll devise a rota system, but we'll have to be real careful not to be seen. It means losing the kutte and maybe even the bikes."

GRACIE

I lie awake for the rest of the night, waiting for Scar to come to me, but as the sun rises, I realise he isn't going to. I slip into some joggers and head downstairs with Deuce. I walk him around the yard, all the while thinking about Scar. "You couldn't sleep either?" asks Rylee from her spot under the tree. I smile sadly, shaking my head as I join her.

"I was waiting for Scar, but he never came to me."

"Mav only came to bed an hour ago. Maybe Scar went to his room, so he didn't disturb you?" I nod, knowing deep down he's avoiding me.

"We really fucked up last night," I mumble.

Rylee sighs. "Don't beat yourself up about it, they'll calm down. We didn't know they were working. They can't stay mad forever."

I sigh. "I hate that Scar's mad at me. He doesn't talk much as it is, and now, he'll completely blank me, and I hate the feeling it gives in the pit of my stomach."

Rylee smiles. "Someone's got it bad."

"Yeah, I didn't realise how bad until he had to stop seeing me for those few days. I was so happy when we made up. Why the hell did I listen to Meli again?"

"She has a way of convincing you she has the best ideas," says Rylee, laughing. "Why don't you come and help with breakfast? It's the way to a man's heart."

I make waffles, the only breakfast I know I'm good at. As the men file in, the usual buzz of chatter and laughter is replaced with silence. I guess most of them were up all night and they're tired. We place the breakfast dishes in the centre of the table. Scar sits in his usual seat, but I hesitate before joining him. I pour us each a coffee as he fills his plate with bacon and waffles. He doesn't pass me my usual slice of toast, so I grab a banana. He hates me only eating fruit for breakfast, so it's a sure way to test how mad he is.

He doesn't bat an eyelid as I peel it and take a bite. "I'm not hungry," I announce, but he doesn't respond, "so I'm just gonna eat this today." He side-eyes me before tucking in to his own breakfast. "I might skip lunch too." He ignores me, and I narrow my eyes. "Your scratches look better today," I say, raising my fingers to touch the deep marks on his cheek. He pulls his head clear of my touch, and my heart twists painfully in my chest.

I watch Rylee getting the same treatment as me and offer a sympathetic smile. At least we're in this together. "I'm gonna have a bath," I announce quietly so only Scar can hear me. That's sure to make him talk to me, because since we started seeing each other, I've never taken a bath alone.

I head up to my room, hungry from eating just a banana, and fill the bath, adding plenty of bubbles. I wait for half an hour, but Scar doesn't appear. When I'm done, I wrap myself in a towel and go to my room, freezing at the sight of him on my bed, looking relaxed and chilled. "This wasn't all my fault," I say, pissed at how he's made me feel this morning. "You didn't tell me they were looking for me." I stare, waiting for his reply, and growl when I don't get one. "If you'd have told me, I wouldn't have left the clubhouse."

"You g-gotta g-go h-home," he says, and my eyes widen.

"Huh?"

"You sh-showed up a-after being m-missing for n-nearly t-two years. Th-the first place y-you'd go is y-your p-parents. It looks s-s-suspicious if y-you don't go b-back."

"Is it safe?"

"Grim will g-g-go with you."

"I don't want Grim to go with me, I want you to."

"I c-can't," he mutters.

"If this is about last night, then I'm sorry. Don't punish me like this."

"It's n-not l-like that."

"It feels like it is," I snap.

He rises to his feet, standing close. "Y-you f-fucked up. If I sh-show at y-your house with you, the c-cops will t-try and pin those bodies in th-the caves on me," he hisses angrily. "A-and M-michaelson."

"Why?"

"Because I h-have a r-record as l-long as your a-a-arm."

I frown. "How many times have you been to prison?" I ask. He looks away, and my eyes widen. "Scar?"

"A c-couple. And I'm not r-r-ready to go away f-for m-murder. I've got access to A-august now. I c-can't go b-back inside."

"You didn't tell me the men were still looking for me. You didn't say you were at the club to get Jen's dad, and you told me you went to prison once. How much have you kept from me, Scar?"

"M-maybe you sh-should have a-asked me b-before you l-let me f-fuck you," he snaps, and I recoil. He's never spoken to me like that before, and I don't like it.

I take a breath and pull the towel around me tighter. "Yeah, you're right. I should get my whore-like behaviour in check. Thanks."

He groans. "Gracie—"

"Forget it. Maybe I'm just desperately clinging to the man who saved me. Maybe these feelings, all this," I pause and look away, pain ripping through me, "shit I feel in here," I say, rubbing my chest, "isn't real at all. I know what you guys are like, sex is sex, and I'm not complaining because I needed it. I needed to forget their hands all over me and replace them with someone else's. You did that for me, and I'm sure the next guy will do the same. And suddenly, going home seems like a great idea." I turn my back to him and stare out the window. "I'll get my shit together and be right down. Let Grim know to be ready."

I wait for the door to open and close before letting thick, wet tears fall down my cheeks.

○○

Ten minutes later, I place my bag by the door. Most of my belongings were not actually mine, so I've left a lot behind. I did steal one of Scar's shirts, because I need something to know this was all real and not a dream.

The girls line up and hug me one by one. "I'm so sorry," whispers Meli, wiping her eyes. "This is all my fault."

"I'm a big girl, and I have my own mind. Besides, they should have told us what they were doing, then we wouldn't have gone there. We're not totally to blame."

"Once this all blows over, we'll be in touch," says Rylee, kissing my cheek.

I smile, knowing it won't happen. This could take months to blow over, and Mav's already made it clear I can't be involved with the club right now. Mav wraps me in his large arms, and I melt against him. So thankful for everything he's done, I have no words.

"Take care of yourself. Like Rylee said, once we have a plan, we'll be in touch."

"Thank you so much for everything, Mav. You've done so much for me and the other girls. You've changed their lives. I owe you one."

There's no sign of Scar, and as I say my last goodbye, I follow Grim outside to the car with a heavy heart. I hear Deuce bark and look around as he bounds toward me. I kneel and let him jump around me, barking and licking. "I'm gonna miss you, even though you took up most of the bed." When I rise to my feet, Scar is staring down at me.

"Y-you're wrong," he mutters, hooking his little finger around mine and staring into my eyes. "It was r-real. A-all of it." I smile sadly as he places a gentle kiss on my head. "W-we're n-not d-done, Gracie. Y-you are m-mine. W-we're j-just on hold."

I turn my back, getting into the car. It feels like we're done.

Grim stops the car at the top of my parents' street. We'd already done a drive-by, and Mav was right, there are two photographers waiting outside. "Will you be okay?" he asks.

I nod, wiping my eyes. I haven't stopped crying since I left the club, feeling like my heart has been ripped out of my chest and stomped on. "I'm gonna climb over the back wall. I can't face the questions today."

"Any plans on what you'll say?" I shake my head. Mav talked to me about possibilities, and we came up with a few lies. Either I had only escaped recently and was too scared to face home in case they were angry, or I'd temporarily lost my memory and only just remembered stuff, or I'd found an old friend and I'd been hiding out, too scared to come forward. All of it seems too sketchy, so for now, the best thing to do is say nothing.

"You know, I'm not one for gossip or girly talk, but Scar really likes you, Gracie. I've never seen him like this before, and it's killing him that you've had to leave the club and he's got to stay away from you. But it's not forever. You'll find a way to make it work once the dust settles."

"Just look after him for me. Don't let him go back to her," I mutter. I don't even need to say her name. Grim nods and kisses me on the cheek.

I throw my bag over the garden wall. It's a terraced house, which means all the houses are so close together, it's impossible to sneak around without the neighbours seeing, so I'm not surprised when a few curtains twitch as I heave myself over the five-foot wall and drop down into my parents' back garden. Pushing the back door open, I step into the kitchen, letting the familiar smell of my childhood envelope me once more. I smile as I drop the bag by the door. It's something I've done a hundred times over, but this time, it feels special. I'm finally home.

"Mum? Dad?" I shout. As I move towards the living room, I hear voices.

Inside, I find Jen with my parents. She's crying, her make-up running from her eyes, and my mum is comforting her. Thoughts of her dad leering over me make me shudder. "Gracie," gasps Mum, rushing to me and hugging me. Dad follows. "The police just left an hour ago," she adds.

"The police?" I ask.

"Yes, after what you said," screeches Jen.

My dad places an arm around her, and I stare at it like it's poison. "I don't understand," I say.

"It's been all over the internet," explains Mum. "There's footage all over social media. People are horrified about the girls in the caves, and then you show up like that."

"Oh," I mutter. Mav said the journalists were there, but I didn't think of others filming the incident. Nothing was reported on the news, but Mav said that's because the police would have asked them to hold off so as not to ruin any investigations.

"My dad's been arrested," sobs Jen. "A few days before my wedding!"

"They say he's involved in the girls being held there," adds Mum.

"It's all lies. He doesn't know anything about them," snaps Jen, and Mum pats her hands, whispering words of comfort. I remain silent. I have so many questions, but she's clearly hysterical right now, and I'm exhausted. "I'm gonna go," she adds, grabbing her coat, and relief floods me.

"You don't have to go," says Dad, and I narrow my eyes. No, she really does.

"I can't even look at her right now, not after what she said about him. And you guys lied to me. You never said she was back. This could have been avoided." She stomps out, leaving us all in stunned silence.

"So," mutters Dad, "why did you say that?"

Mum glares at him, and I stare in surprise. "Scuse me?"

"What?" he asks. "I'm just having a hard time understanding what the hell is going on right now. You didn't mention Jen's dad was involved when you turned up out the blue the other week."

"Because I didn't know it was him," I mutter. It hurts that he's looking at me the way he is, through mistrusting eyes.

"And at what point did you know?"

"The guys helped me piece it together," I explain, and he rolls his eyes.

"Can we just enjoy having her here?" snaps Mum, pulling me into another hug.

"I'm sorry," he mutters, rubbing his hands over his tired face. "Sorry. It's just a lot to take in."

"I'm back now," I say, quietly, "for good. We've got plenty of time to go over it."

CHAPTER EIGHTEEN

SCAR

Two days of being away from Gracie is tearing me apart inside. It's a physical pain that I can't shake no matter what I do. And now, I'm watching her parents' house because Mav said he was sick of seeing my miserable face. Up until now, he'd avoided putting me on Gracie watch.

I sit up straighter when the front door opens, and she steps out into the early evening sun. There's just one journalist outside her house, and as she passes him, she hands him a cup of tea. Ghost said she hasn't spoken to them yet about what happened, but she always makes them tea.

Gracie turns to walk in my direction, and I suck in a breath. She's stunning in a red dress that hugs her tits and waist, the skirt flaring around her bare legs as she walks. Her hair is curled and falls around her shoulders, and she's got minimal makeup, natural, just how I love her. But she isn't supposed to be out and about alone. As she passes my car, she's too busy looking at her mobile to notice me. I put my cap in place and pull up my hood. I'll follow on foot.

She walks for around ten minutes, stopping outside a classy-looking bar. I'm gonna stand out like a sore thumb, so I wait outside, occasionally peering through the window. She waits at the bar, and it occurs to me she might be on a date, but I soon shut that idea down when my heart beats faster and my fists clench. I can't watch her with another man without storming in there and letting her know exactly who she belongs to. When I next look in, she's with a guy, and everything stops. They're tightly embracing, and for way too long. Seconds later, I'm at the bar, not caring about the funny looks I get as I take a seat beside them. Gracie doesn't spot me straightaway.

"I can't believe it," the man gushes, placing his hands on her shoulders to get a good look at her. "You're still fucking beautiful," he adds, and she blushes. I scowl. She blushed like that when I kissed her the first time, and she has no fucking right doing it here for this muppet. He's not even her type with his floppy blonde hair and his preppy college boy looks.

As if she senses me, Gracie looks back and our eyes connect. She's thrown, and for a second, the guy looks confused before hooking a finger under her chin and pulling her to look at him again. She smiles awkwardly, shaking her head and apologising. I watch from under my cap as he leads her to a side table.

GRACIE

I'm shaking as I take a seat opposite Edward. What the fuck is Scar doing here? I've not seen any of The Perished Riders since being back home because they're damn good at their job and hang back in the shadows. So good, I sometimes forget they're there. Trust Scar to make himself seen.

The waitress brings our drinks over. Two glasses of red wine. I take a large gulp and wince. *Did I actually use to enjoy this stuff?*

"I was surprised when you called me," I say. He and Jen are yet to find out that I know about them, and since Jen walked out when I returned, I've heard nothing from her.

"I was surprised when I watched my ex-girlfriend show up on the internet telling the world she'd been taken and wasn't actually a runaway like we all thought."

"Surprise," I mutter drily.

"What the fuck, Gracie?" He sounds exasperated.

"It was Jen's party," I explain. I pause, letting the memories flood my mind. "I was so sad," I whisper, "and I was thinking of calling you, but then Jen invited these guys to join the party. She said I needed a distraction. I guess I did. They got us a drink, and even though I wasn't drinking, Jen nagged me, accused me of being boring."

"Jen never mentioned that," he says, frowning.

"You've seen her?" I ask.

His expression falters. "Of course. We looked for you after you went."

"Anyway, next thing I know, I'm in the back of a moving vehicle, and the guy who brought me a drink is leering down on me and . . ." I shake my head, leaving him to guess the rest. "I was locked in a dark room, though I didn't know it was a cave at the time. I was there for about sixteen months, I think, until I escaped."

Edward holds his head in his hands. "This stuff happens in movies, not real life. What the hell? I spent months thinking you'd left because you'd guessed."

"Guessed?" I repeat, and he sighs heavily, not bothering to answer. "Thinking about coming home to you got me through," I say with a small smile, and he visibly pales. "I often wondered if you'd regret it. Would we have worked it out if I'd been around, yah know?"

"Listen, Grace, I—"

I laugh, interrupting him. "I know you didn't wait for two years, Ed. I didn't expect that."

Relief floods his face, and he laughs too. "Right. So, where did you go once you escaped?"

"There was a lot to process," I mutter. "I went to a women's refuge. It wasn't local."

"And this guy, the one who took you—"

"Braydon," I say, trying to gauge if he knows the name.

"Okay, Braydon. He just kept you around all that time? Why?"

"Why do you think? For sex. He wasn't the only one. He worked for a whole host of men who would pass me around. Rich men who paid."

He winces. "It just sounds so . . . far-fetched."

I clench my teeth. He isn't the first one to say it. When I gave my police statement yesterday, the two officers had that same look on their faces, even though they'd interviewed others before me, all saying the same thing. "I guess it's easier to pretend it didn't happen than make people understand," I mutter, and he places his hands over my own.

"I believe you, Grace. It's just crazy. Did you recognise anyone? Were they men you knew?" It's clear he's digging for information for Jen, and that hurts all the more. He isn't here because he's happy I'm back or because he's been out of his mind with worry.

"Actually, funny you should mention it, but yeah, I knew one of the men. I didn't at the time, but it's something I learnt after I escaped. Jen's dad, Doug Harris, was one of them." He fakes shock, and I roll my eyes. "Oh, come on, Edward. I know about you and her. Stop with the bullshit acting."

His body sags in relief, happy he didn't have to tell me and watch me get upset. "Grace, I'm so sorry. It just happened."

"She was my best friend."

Shame washes over him as he nods. "I know, it was a shit thing to do, but I couldn't help it. We just clicked, yah know?"

"Did you click before I went missing or after?"

He bites his bottom lip. I used to find it cute, but now, it's just irritating. "It wasn't like I was hitting on her or anything.

I didn't even like her like that. Then, just out of the blue, she kissed me, and I was hooked."

I arch a brow. "She kissed you when we were together?"

He nods, taking a big swallow of his wine. "It was the night your artwork was hung in the gallery."

I gasp. "*My* night? But we talked about marriage that night? We sat in Waterloo Station for two hours!"

"I know, I know," he groans, covering his face.

"Did you say all that bullshit out of guilt?" He nods, keeping his face covered. "Jesus. What the hell did I ever see in you?"

We fall silent, and I drink my wine, even though I hate the taste. I feel Scar's eyes burning into me, but I refuse to look at him. I can't when it hurts too much. "The thing is, I'm marrying Jen in less than two weeks. She's devastated that her dad might not be there."

"He won't be there, Edward. I'm gonna make sure of it."

"Gracie, come on. This is her dad and her wedding day. She needs him to walk her down the aisle, and you're gonna stop that?"

"He fucking raped me," I hiss, leaning closer. "He held me down and had sex with me, then laughed while the next man did the same. Hours and hours of rape and torture. So excuse me if I don't want to ever see him walk out of prison again."

"It just doesn't sound like Doug," he mutters. "He was a judge before he opened all those businesses," he adds.

"Open your eyes. None of those men went home to their wife and told them what they'd been doing to me all night. They didn't confess to burning me or biting or any of the other sick shit they did. They weren't nobodies, they were men with money. They could afford to pay for their every dirty, dark fantasy to come true."

"But it's a coincidence, isn't it, that you were Jen's friend?"

"Maybe," I mutter, remembering what Mav had said before about Jen setting me up. Edward wouldn't ever believe that, not if he's questioning me about this.

"I love her, Grace. She's my world, and I just want her to have the best day."

My heart aches. Not because I miss him, though maybe some part of me does, but I remember a time when he'd have done anything for me. Hearing him talk like that about the woman who possibly set up my downfall makes me sick to my stomach.

"I'm sorry my terrible ordeal messes up your plans to provide the most amazing day for your bride, but it wasn't just me he hurt. There were others too. He deserves to rot in hell."

He takes my hands again. "She missed you when you were gone. She cried every night for weeks."

"I'm sure you helped ease that," I mutter.

"It was hard without you. We had planned to tell you everything after Jen's birthday, but you disappeared."

"How convenient."

He sighs. "I know it's hard right now, and it must be a shock to know I'm in love with your best friend, but I did love you once and I know you loved me. I'm glad you're safe now. I hope you find happiness."

I nod, glancing at Scar, who has his head low but is watching my every move. "Me too."

"One last thing. Your parents have been amazing supporting us and they're coming to the wedding. I'm politely asking that you stay away. Not because I don't want you there, although that would feel weird, but because Jen's so upset about what you've said."

I laugh, but there's no humour in it. "Fine." I hadn't planned on going to their damn wedding anyway. "Take care."

He leans over the table and places a gentle kiss on my lips. It's sad, almost like a final goodbye, right before he walks out. I press my fingers to my lips and watch him leave.

SCAR

I watch her cry for another man, jealousy burning every fibre of my being. I glance around. The bar is almost empty, so I go over to her table, sliding along the bench until she's pushed into the corner and out of everyone's view. "Don't fucking c-cry over a-another m-man," I grate out.

"Sorry, should I save my tears for you?" she snaps, wiping her eyes on her sleeve.

"I w-wanna k-kill him."

"She literally stole my life. My parents love her, my boyfriend is marrying her . . . what if she did get rid of me so she could take it all?" More tears roll down her cheeks, and I roughly take her face in my hands and use my thumbs to brush them away, smearing them across her pale skin.

"S-stop crying over th-them. Y-you're better o-off without either of th-them." I can't disguise the anger in my voice. He basically accused her of lying. He doesn't deserve her fucking tears. "Y-you n-never said you w-were an artist." It comes out accusingly, and she frowns, sniffling as more tears escape.

"You never asked what I did before." I swipe more tears away. I guess I never did ask her much about who she was before she was found. "It was a piece I did back in university called 'Sadness'. The art gallery snapped it up and displayed it for a few weeks. They were supporting new artists."

"So, th-that was your ma-main j-job?"

She shakes her head. "No. It didn't pay the bills, so I worked in the offices at the art gallery, just doing paperwork."

"One d-day you can sh-show me the p-painting?"

She smiles sadly. "It's hanging in my bedroom at my parents' house. They got my stuff back from my flat after I went missing." She straightens up and wipes her face. "I should get back."

"I m-miss you so f-fucking much," I mutter, and she closes her eyes briefly, like my words hurt her. Moving closer, I'm desperate to taste her kisses, but she moves farther back away from me, until her head is against the wall.

Her rejection stings. I stand so she can make her escape, which she does quickly, wanting to be away from me. I watch her rush from the bar like I'd burned her. I wait a second before following her, and once she's almost home, I head around the back.

The houses overlook one another, so I try the gate and smile when it opens. In the garden, there's a shed, and after a quick look around to make sure no one is watching, I haul my arse up onto the shed roof, then make a jump for the open bathroom window, thankful it's dark enough to hide me a little. I creep carefully along the landing and push open the first door I come to. There's a double bed with a flowery sheet, and I snigger. I'm pretty sure this isn't her room, so I move to the next door. I can hear her downstairs talking to her mum, giving me time to go into the next room.

There's a single bed with a white sheet strewn across it. Gracie's bag is still on the floor unpacked. On the chair next to her bed is one of my shirts, and I smile. I like her wearing my stuff, and the fact she stole my shirt to bring with her gives me hope that she's missing me as much as I'm missing her.

There're some photographs stuck on her wardrobe, and I take my time to run my eyes over each one. She was a happy kid with chubby cheeks and long hair that curled slightly at the ends. As a teenager, she was stunning, and I remind myself that when we have a daughter, I'll need to lock her up. I run my finger over her smiling face in one that was more recent, maybe just before she went missing. She's looking up into the eyes of that arsehole who just made her cry all over again. I take it and fold it in half so I'm only looking at her and then I stuff it into my pocket.

On the opposite wall hangs a painting of a hunched-over man. His hood is pulled up so his face is hidden, but his head hangs like he's got the weight of the world on his shoulders. There's something so heartbreaking and sad about this picture that I can't tear my eyes away from it, even when I hear her enter the room.

"Fuck," she hisses when she sees me. "What the hell? How did you get in here?"

"It's l-like y-you knew me b-before we even m-met," I whisper, nodding to the painting.

"You shouldn't be in here," she mutters.

"I'm d-done being a-apart f-from you, Gracie. I c-can't d-do it." I turn to face her, grabbing her hand and tugging her to me. "Y-you're m-mine. F-forever. And no one's t-taking y-you away from m-me. We'll w-work th-this out somehow."

CHAPTER NINETEEN

GRACIE

It's morning, and I wake in a tangle of bed sheets and legs. Scar is pressed tightly to my back, his light snores filling the room. I can hear my parents moving around in their bedroom, so I gently shake Scar awake. He groans, burying his nose into my hair and inhaling. His morning erection pushes into my back. "You have to go. I can hear my parents getting up." He mumbles something inaudible and proceeds to shift until his erection is pushing into me. I close my eyes. I'm so weak for this man. "Scar, I'm serious. My mum can't find you here."

"Shhh," he whispers as he slowly moves in and out of me. Something about morning sex with Scar is addictive. The way he moves sleepily, nice and slow, savouring each thrilling spark, always brings me to orgasm within minutes. Today is no different as I bury my face into the pillow to muffle my moans. Scar follows, pulling from me and spilling his cum over my arse. I freeze when I hear Mum's voice outside in the hall. I tap Scar, and he moves quickly, rolling from the bed and hiding underneath just as Mum enters the room. I know my face is blazing with embarrassment as I pull the sheets up to my chest. She eyes me suspiciously for a second before smiling. "Tea or coffee?"

"Tea, please." A prod of the mattress from Scar makes me jump. "Coffee," I blurt, and she frowns, though she looks amused. "Sorry, I changed my mind. Coffee, please." Scar hates tea, but I can drink either.

"Are you okay?" asks Mum.

"Yeah. Tired. I didn't sleep too well."

"Is that anything to do with the naked man under your bed?" she asks, trying hard not to laugh as my blush deepens. "So, one tea, one coffee, and I'll see you both downstairs in five minutes . . . fully clothed." I nod as she closes the door, laughing to herself.

Scar slides out looking sheepish. "N-not a very g-g-good hiding p-place?"

"What am I gonna tell them?"

He leans down, placing a kiss on my lips. "That y-y-you're m-my ol' lady."

"And they can't tell anyone, not even the cops, because you killed the men who came for me?"

He shrugs. "M-might be a bit m-much for th-them to t-take but . . ." He grins, and I sigh heavily.

My parents look up as we enter the kitchen. I'm gripping Scar's hand so tight, I'm pretty sure I'm hurting him. "Good morning," Mum says, still smirking. Dad doesn't look as impressed as we take a seat at the table. Scar keeps his head lowered, which probably isn't helping. Dad is a man's man and he'd prefer for a man to come and shake his hand and introduce himself. "You met Scar before. He came here when I first returned," I begin.

"What kind of name is that?" snaps Dad, looking more unimpressed by the second.

"His real name is Hunter, Dad. Scar is his road name."

"What's wrong with him?" he demands to know. "He thinks he can sneak into my home, sleep in my daughter's bed, and then sit at my breakfast table and not even look at me?"

"Dad," I hiss, "you're being rude."

"No, rude is a man sitting here at my table, ignoring me."

I hear Scar sigh before lifting his head. "S-s-sorry, sir. I didn't m-m-mean no di-disrespect."

Dad's chin juts out slightly and he nods in acceptance of Scar's apology. "I didn't want the police or the press to know about us," I say, biting my lower lip. "Scar hasn't got the best track record, and he'd prefer to stay out of the investigation."

Dad scowls. "So, you're dating a criminal?"

"No, the men who took me are criminals. Scar isn't like them, and that's what matters. He's done a lot to help me, more than he should have. I really like him, Dad, and I'd like you to accept that."

"Is a relationship a good idea after everything you went through?" he asks.

"Scar knows everything, Dad. He came to my rescue the night I escaped, and over time, I told him what happened. He still likes me, after knowing all that. When we're not together, it's like I can't breathe."

He stares at me sceptically before sighing and nodding. "Fine. You're an adult, you know what you want. I guess it could be worse. He could have a kid too," he mutters.

Mum notices my expression and jumps in to rescue me. "So, Scar, do you live locally? Are your parents around here?"

"I live j-just t-ten minutes a-away, with The P-perished R-riders club. M-my p-parents are also c-club members."

"I can't wait to see this club. I'm so intrigued," she says excitedly.

She serves breakfast, and we sit in silence. Eventually, I can't take it anymore, so I break the ice. "I saw Edward last night." It wasn't the best topic of conversation. Scar stiffens, Dad almost chokes on his eggs, and Mum stares wide-eyed, waiting for me to continue. "I'm not invited to the wedding. He politely told me to stay away. Shocker."

"What did he say?" Mum asks.

"He just told me that they fell in love, and I'm okay with that. As long as they're happy. He wanted me to drop the complaint against Doug Harris so he could walk Jen down the aisle."

"Oh. What did you tell him?" she asks.

"I said no. That man deserves to be in prison. I hope he rots there."

Mum nods, rubbing my knee. "Me too, sweetheart."

"Actually, since you brought it up. Jen called us last night. She asked if I would walk her down the aisle if her dad isn't released by then," says Dad casually. I eye him over my cup as I take a sip of tea to distract myself from the thumping of my heart.

"Oh," is all I can manage.

"Your father was put on the spot," explains Mum.

"Exactly," Dad agrees eagerly. "How could I say no? She's heartbroken her dad won't be there, and she was crying when she asked. I had to say yes."

I lower my cup. "Well, you didn't have to, did you?" I mutter. "Don't you find it weird? You'll be walking her down the aisle because her dad raped me."

Mum and Dad exchange a worried look. "I know, it's so messed up, but Jen's been lost without you. And finding out you were taken and hurt like that, well, she's not thinking straight, and with the wedding fast approaching, she's trying the best she can to sort everything out as well as run the businesses," Mum explains.

"Poor Jen," I mutter without much sympathy.

"Whatever her dad did, it's not Jen's fault," says Dad sadly. "She's been there for us from the day you left—"

"Was taken," I interrupt.

"Since you were taken," he corrects. "And we've gotten close with her and Edward. We were all so lost after you disappeared. We helped each other."

"You know they were practically together before he dumped me?"

"Edward told us," says Mum. "If it makes a difference, he felt so guilty and blamed himself for you going. He thought you'd found out about the two of them and ran."

I push my breakfast away, my appetite long gone. "Can I come back to the club and stay there?" I ask Scar. I know his answer before he bothers to speak because his eyes tell me it's not possible.

"You kn-know you c-can't, Gracie."

"I'd better shower. Have you made the journalists a cup of tea?" I ask Mum.

"I did, but there's no one out there. They must have bigger fish to fry today."

Scar frowns, pulling his mobile from his pocket and cursing under his breath. "Pres' been t-t-tryin' to c-call." He goes into the living room, closing the door.

"He seems nice," says Mum with a wink.

I smile. "He is. I'm so lucky."

"Look, Gracie, about Jen," begins Dad, but I hold my hand up and shake my head. I don't want to hear about her right now, so I head upstairs to take that shower.

Scar is waiting in my bedroom when I'm done. "Everything okay?"

He nods. "I g-g-gotta take off."

The thought of spending the day without him makes me sad, and my face must show it because he steps towards me and kisses me. "Th-they've found the b-b-bodies of the j-judge and his w-wife."

"Oh," I mutter.

"The cops are g-g-gonna come and t-t-tell you. Look s-s-surprised."

I nod and rest my head against his chest, wrapping my arms around him. "It's all such a mess."

"I'll come b-back s-soon. Your m-m-mum gave me a back d-d-door key."

I smile. "You know, since she saw you naked, she keeps grinning at me."

Scar laughs. "What c-can I s-say?" He presses another kiss to my forehead and smiles sympathetically. "I know it's h-hard with J-jen and your p-p-parents. You've b-been g-gone so l-long, they're just trying to f-f-figure it all out t-t-too."

"I know," I mumble, "I just feel like an outsider, yah know. They've all spent the time getting closer to each other, and I've been in hell. I've come back and messed up their circle."

"It'll w-work out."

SCAR

I arrive late for church and earn a glare from Mav and Grim as I take a seat. "Apparently, the police have a long list of suspects for their murders. It doesn't sound like they're looking in the direction of any of the girls. He was a judge, so he upset people all the time. They think the likelihood is that an old convict has come back for revenge. The only people who might suspect something is Guilford, but he's hardly likely to start screaming about it and risk bringing attention to himself," says Grim.

"If we lie low for a while, he'll think he's gotten away with it. Maybe he'll even begin to think it was pure coincidence that we've taken out his two main players. What we need to watch is that he doesn't begin hiring new men and taking new girls," adds Mav.

"Any news on what the cops plan to do about the girls and Gracie?" asks Ghost.

"Our informant is struggling to get information. I have a bad feeling it's gonna get brushed under the carpet," says Mav.

"Wh-what about th-the p-press?"

"They've been gagged. The police said if they print anything, it might ruin the case, so a gagging order was granted. But get this, it was signed by Michaelson, and we know he couldn't have signed that recently because he's been dead for a couple of weeks. Therefore, they were prepared that this could happen. Who knows what else they had planned!

"Can't we leak the signed document to the press?" asks Ghost.

"No. It might come back on us and then we'd have to explain how we knew he was dead. The important thing is the girls are free and safe. Once we make Guilford pay, we'll walk away."

"Did you watch Gracie overnight?" Grim asks me, and I nod. He smirks. "And?"

"N-n-nothing," I mutter.

"Bullshit. The Pres sent you so you'd end up sorting things out. Don't tell me you actually just watched the house?"

Mav grins, and I roll my eyes. At least his plan worked. "Wh-when this is d-done, I'm c-claiming her b-before any m-more drama h-happens." There're a few laughs from around the room as we clear out.

GRACIE

The days drag. It's been four since Dad told me he was walking Jen down the aisle, and things have been strained between us since. I'm struggling to adjust to their routine. They get up at eight, have lunch at twelve noon, and so on. At the clubhouse, everyone just did what they wanted, and I liked that. I take a small bite of my sandwich. "You haven't seen Scar in a few days," says Mum. "Is everything okay?"

I nod. I know he's busy, but I miss him so badly, and his absence isn't helping things. "Me and your mum were talking, Gracie. We think maybe it's time you looked for a job."

I swallow the bread, but it scratches my throat and I wince. "A job?"

"Yes, it will help distract you. It's not good for you to be brooding over everything that happened."

"And we found a therapist. She's really nice," adds Mum.

"I have a therapist," I snap, annoyed they haven't taken the time to discuss that with me before going ahead and organising it. "And I'm not brooding. I just have to adjust to being out of that place."

"And a job might help you," says Dad.

The door opens and I feel my heart lift, hoping it's Scar. When Jen walks in, I sigh with disappointment. "Good morning." She smiles brightly, scowling when she sees me.

"Is it that time already?" asks Mum, standing. I give her a questioning look, and she grows uncomfortable. "Jen asked me to go to her final dress fitting." I roll my eyes, because of course, she did. "You don't have any jobs at any of your places, do you?" asks Mum thoughtfully.

Jen scoffs. "For Gracie?"

"It's fine. I don't need a job," I snap.

"I do have something, though it doesn't pay great," says Jen with a smirk.

"It's just to get her out the house," says Mum as if I'm not here.

"I need a cleaner. Those men's toilets get disgusting at the club after a weekend."

Mum looks at me with hopeful eyes. "Are you kidding? You want me to clean the toilets of the nightclub where I and other women were held captive?"

"When you put it like that," she mutters.

"People are queuing up to see the club," says Jen with a grin. "We've been packed out every night since word got around about the girls in the caves. People are travelling from far and wide to try and get a glimpse. We had people taking pictures of themselves standing at the door where the girls came through. I'm seriously thinking about opening up the caves as an attraction."

Mum gasps. "Wow, so it's not harmed business? I thought the bad press would keep everyone away."

I stand, hardly believing they're having this conversation. "Maybe I could give tours," I mutter sarcastically. "This is where I was tied to a table and beaten with a hot poker. Follow me into the room where over twenty women were kept in small cages like dogs, only allowed out to shit in a bucket under the watchful eyes of their guards. Oh, and over here is where the girls were blindfolded and led out to a waiting vehicle, then transported to the homes of many rich people, where they would be placed on the dinner table and brutally raped by random guests for hours."

"GRACIE!" yells Dad, his eyes wide.

"Well, we can't waste the opportunity to line the pockets of a man who helped organise the whole fucking thing!" I shout. Taking a deep breath, I scrub my hands over my tired face. "Enjoy your shopping."

I step out to get some fresh air. With the reporters occupied with the deaths of the judge and his wife, I'm being left alone. Leaning on the wall, I watch as a young girl heads my way. She smiles, and I glance around to make sure it's me she's looking at.

"Gracie?" she asks, and I nod. "My name is August."

I look around again, seeing if I can spot any of The Perished Riders, but I can't. "Does your dad know you're here?" I ask.

"No. I was passing by and saw you out, so I thought I'd say hello."

"Oh, erm, how did you know it was me?"

"Dad showed me a picture last night. He said you lived over this way. Sorry, this seems a little stalkerish."

"It's fine. I just don't know if your mum would be happy with you being here, or your dad, come to think of it."

"We don't have to tell them. I wanted to meet you. Dad is so happy when he talks about you, and I needed to see what he meant. But he's right—you're beautiful."

I smile shyly. "Thank you. You could have arranged to meet me through your dad. I'm sure he'd have sorted it."

She shakes her head. "Mum would go crazy. She's looking for any excuse to stop me seeing him." Tears line her lower lids.

"August, is everything okay?"

A tear escapes, and she shakes her head. "Not really. I didn't know where to go, and Dad told me you were really kind and understanding, and about how you've helped him to feel happy again. I need advice. Mum is rubbish at that sort of thing."

"I'm not sure I'd be any better." I have a bad feeling this is gonna annoy Scar, so I reach for my mobile.

"The thing is, I've only just turned fourteen, and I'm pregnant," she mutters, bursting into tears.

My mouth drops open. I stare wide-eyed for a good ten seconds, unable to form the words to reassure her because, basically, she's fucked. When Scar finds out, he'll kill the boy who dared to have sex with his daughter, but I can't tell her that. Instead, I give her a half-grimace, half-smile. "Right, so you thought a complete stranger would know what to do in this situation, a stranger who has no kids?"

"I'm sorry, I shouldn't have come."

I groan, opening my gate and pulling her to me for a hug. "You did the right thing. It's gonna be okay."

A police car slows to a stop and an officer gets out. "Miss Stone," he says, smiling, and I nod. He knows it's me because he came to interview me a few days ago. "We need to tie up some things at the station. Can you spare us ten minutes?"

"Erm, actually, I'm right in the middle of something."

"It really won't take long. She can come too," he suggests.

I look down at August, and she nods. "Right, okay. I'll get this out the way and then we'll talk about what you're gonna do." We get into the back of the police car.

My mobile lights up, and a prospect's name, Daz, appears. "Relax," I say with a smile when I answer, "I'll be right back. They just want me to sort some things down at the station."

"Okay. You want me to stay here and wait?" he asks.

"Let me check," I cover the mouthpiece and lean forward to the cop. "Will you drop us back home or do I need to get a ride?"

He smiles at me through the rear-view mirror. "I can drop you back."

I nod and say to Daz, "I'll be fine. I'll call you when I'm on my way back."

"Okay. Who's the kid?"

"Oh, erm," I pause, glancing at August. If I tell the truth, he'll have to ring Scar and it'll raise questions. "Just my cousin."

I disconnect and smile at August, who's still upset. "How do you think your mum will take the news?" I ask.

"Very bad. She flies off the handle all the time."

"That's what mums do," I say, laughing. "Maybe she won't be as bad as you think. Are you still with the boy?" She shakes her head. "Does he know?" She nods. "So, he's not interested?"

"I lied about my age," she mutters. I glance at the cop, who seems to be distracted.

"How old is he?" I whisper.

"Sixteen."

"Lord Jesus Christ," I hiss. "So, he thought you were sixteen?" She nods. "You know we have to tell your parents, right?"

Panic takes over and she clings to me. "No, please. Can't you take me to have an abortion? They don't ever have to know."

"August, I can't do that without their consent. Do you know what your dad will do to me if I lie to him about this?"

"Imagine what he'll do to me when I tell him," she cries.

I flop back in my seat and look out at the passing cars. I frown, sitting up again. "Hey, where are we going?" I don't recognise this route.

"I just had a message to go to an old police station up the other end of town. I'm not sure why," he answers casually.

"Who was the message from?" I ask.

"We're here," he announces, pulling off the road and into an empty car park. I look around. There's nothing here, not a building, and especially not a police station. He gets out, then opens my door. "This way," he says, and I frown as he points to a van.

"That's not a police station."

He leans in, placing a cuff on my wrist, but I move the other from his reach. "What the hell are you doing?"

"Miss Stone, if you don't come quietly, I'll have to arrest you."

"For what?" I snap as he forcefully grabs my other wrist and cuffs me.

"What's going on?" asks August nervously.

"Follow me," he says sternly, pulling me from the car and leading me to the van.

I struggle to try and free myself, but he's too strong. The back door opens, and three men dressed in dark clothing get out, one grabbing my other arm and helping the officer march me to the van. The other two race across the car park, where I notice August is running away. They take her down and drag her, throwing her in the back with me.

"What's going on?" she whispers.

"I don't know. Stay calm. I'll do everything I can to protect us."

The door opens again, and this time another man gets in with us, seating himself in the corner. The engine starts and the van pulls off.

SCAR

The police station has been a hive of activity since the judge and his wife were found. They'll go all out to find who did that but not bother with what happened to Gracie. I groan, hating all this waiting around.

The Pres calls me. "Where are you?"

"Where I a-always f-f-fucking am," I mutter.

"Has Guilford left the station?"

"No. He n-n-never does. Why?"

"The prospect called. He said a cop car came to get Gracie, and when he called her, she said she was fine and had to go and sort some paperwork. She said he didn't need to follow her, but he did anyway. You need to head towards Hackery Lane, brother. We'll meet you there."

"W-why? What's t-there?"

"Gracie." He doesn't need to ask me twice. I disconnect the call and start the car engine. It's times like this I wish I had my damn bike.

By the time I get there, it's been twenty minutes since Mav called. I find him and my brothers congregating at the end of the road. "Someone t-t-tell me w-what the f-fuck is going on!"

Daz steps forward. "They bundled her and her cousin into a van and drove them here. There's an old police station just up there," he says, pointing to the other end of the street.

"L-let's go g-get her," I growl.

Mav places a hand on my chest to stop me. "We gotta check the area first. We don't know who they are or if there's more of them. And it's daylight, so we can't bust in waving guns about. The cops'll be on us in seconds."

"Fuck th-that," I snarl, trying to move around him.

"Think about it, Scar. There's gonna be cops in there. We think they're waiting for Guilford to show. There's a house abandoned right here," he says, pointing to the house behind me. "We'll break in and wait."

I ball my fists. The panic I feel is making me wanna break something, but what Mav is saying makes sense. The cops don't believe anything as it is, so if we go in there pointing guns in broad daylight, we'll be arrested. They could explain away the fact they have Gracie there, or worse still, kill her so she's not able to speak up. I shudder. Mav is thinking way clearer than me, so I follow them to the empty house.

CHAPTER TWENTY

GRACIE

August is a lot tougher than I'd have been at fourteen. She's not shed one tear since we arrived here and we were thrown into a cell. At least I have a bed this time. There's graffiti on the walls and the place smells of urine and rat droppings. They took our phones and locked us in here, then left us. "What do they want with you?" asks August.

"To silence me," I say. I'd filled her in briefly about what happened before.

"How do you think they plan to do that?"

I shrug, knowing the answer but not wanting to tell her. They'll kill me and probably her. I rub my wrists where the cuffs were to distract me from the anxiety I feel right now. Walking over to the heavy door, I bang on the small plastic window cut out in the centre. "Hello! Is anyone there?" The flap opens, and the cop from earlier stares at me. "What the hell am I doing here?"

"I don't ask questions. I was told to deliver you here and that's what I've done."

"You're a police officer. You're supposed to protect and serve, isn't that your motto?"

"Well, that doesn't pay for the massive mortgage my wife took out on the six-bedroom house we just bought, so . . ." He shrugs.

"Please, I'm begging you to let us go. You don't understand. I was taken and held captive for sixteen months. The people who did that are the ones paying you."

"Like I said, I don't ask questions."

"Well, maybe you should," snaps August, glaring at him from where she sits on the ground. "And you also need to question your morals."

"What's gonna happen next?" I ask.

He checks his watch. "All I know is my time is up in ten minutes. I've got to get out of here, and whoever wants you will be arriving soon after." He slams the window closed, and I slide down the door, sick with worry.

⁂

It's almost an hour later when the door opens. Nobody comes in, it just sort of clicks and then slowly opens. I look nervously over to August. Still, nobody comes in, so I edge towards it. I give it a shove with my foot, and it slams back against the wall, making us both jump. Peering out into the passage, there's no one around. I signal for August to follow, and she grabs hold of my hand. Leading her back through the dark police station and towards the exit, I hardly dare to breathe in case this is some kind of trick. Seconds later, the door flies open, and we both let out surprised screams. It doesn't register it's The Perished Riders until Scar is in my face with a torch, forcing me to blink a few times. "A-are you o-okay?" He runs his hand over my hair and tugs me against his chest. Then, he must shine his torch on August, because he stiffens. "Wh-what th-the f-fuck?"

"Hi, Dad," she whispers. He releases me and stares back and forth between us.

"Long story," I mutter.

"Start f-fucking t-talking."

"It's my fault. I turned up at Gracie's. I just wanted to meet her, but then the cops showed up and I said I'd tag along—" He cuts her off by holding up his hand.

"Wh-why didn't you c-call m-me," he asks, glaring at me.

"I was going to, but then they came and . . . can't you just be happy we're okay?" I squeak.

"You told me it was your cousin," says Daz, and I wince.

"Did I? I don't remember."

Scar grabs August. "Pres, I g-gotta get h-h-her home. Can you s-sort Gracie?" he asks. Of course, he has to sort August, she's his priority, but I can't help feeling a little hurt. I haven't heard from him in days, and now he's here, I just want to stick to his side. Why can't we both take her home?

August gives an apologetic smile. "Sorry," she mouths, and I smile back, telling her it's okay.

SCAR

"Sh-she was with Gracie," I explain to Katya's scowling face.

"She was with you and your girlfriend?" she fumes.

"N-not me. J-just her. I didn't know."

"Bullshit! I made it clear you weren't introducing them without me being there. Who the hell do you think you are?"

"Kat, I d-didn't know."

"He's right, Mum. I turned up at Gracie's. I wanted to meet her," says August from the top of the stairs.

Katya slams the door in my face without another word. It's been a fuck-up of a day and everything in me is pulling me back to Gracie. I need to see she's okay, but I'm mad that she didn't fucking call me when August turned up at hers. She knows things are fragile between me and Katya, and I don't need extra stress. Katya would have blamed me if anything happened to August. I head back to the clubhouse and find Mav in his office.

"Brother, how did it go with Katya?"

I shake my head. She's the last person I want to talk about. "Why'd th-they take them just t-to let th-them g-go?"

"To show they can. Scare tactics. It's Guilford's way of telling her he can get to her. He wants her to back off."

"I'm g-gonna k-kill him," I say firmly. It isn't an empty threat, and Mav knows that.

"We can't get sloppy now, brother. We've managed to get Harris arrested, and we've killed Michaelson and his wife and passed it off as someone wanting vengeance for a past grudge. We'll do the same to Guilford, but if we're sloppy, he'll get away with it."

"Th-then tell me w-what the f-fuck we're g-gonna do, cos I'm o-o-out of p-patience."

"Rosey's gonna take him out," says Mav with a grin. I arch a brow. I don't have anything against women who kill men for fun, each to their own, but seriously, Rosey is a fucking liability. "I know what you're thinking, but she's good at what she does. She took out three men from the club, and we didn't see it coming."

"Don't l-let her g-go rogue on th-this, P-pres. We n-need to know wh-what she's g-gonna do. If sh-she messes it up—"

"Scar, I'm your president, right? I make the decisions, and this is my decision. Don't tell me how to fucking run the club, it's dangerous ground." I nod once. He's right, I shouldn't question him, but I need to know this is gonna run smoothly. "I thought Gracie should come back to the clubhouse," he adds. "I've spoken to her mum and told her to tell people that Gracie is visiting friends and family in Spain. We checked her onto a flight leaving later tonight. If she lays low, no one will know she's here, and if the cops turn up, we'll hide her in the basement. At least she's safe and rogue cops can't pick her up."

"G-gracie is h-here?" He nods, a small smile playing on his lips. "R-right." I back out of the office, unable to control the need to see her any longer.

I go straight to my room, hoping she's waiting for me there, but she isn't. Letting out a frustrated growl, I head for her old room. I push the door, but it's locked, so I knock lightly. "Gracie," I growl. The second the lock clicks, I push the door open. She's been crying, her tear-stained face red and puffy. I grip it between my hands and stare at her. "W-w-hat?"

"It's been a long day," she whispers, another tear escaping and rolling down her cheek. I swipe it away with my thumb.

"W-what do y-you n-need, b-b-baby?"

She shrugs, sniffling helplessly. I pull her against me and lift her, carrying her over to her bed and laying her down. I strip quickly and climb in beside her. She snuggles against my chest, and I gently wrap her hair around my fingers. "I was s-s-so scared t-today. I th-thought I'd l-lost you."

"Me too," she whispers. "And having August there was terrifying. They could have taken her, Scar. That would have been on me." Another round of sobs takes over, and I rub her back.

"It w-wasn't your f-fault. Y-you d-didn't know."

"Everything is such a mess. It's too complicated, bent cops and evil men. I can't cope. I don't know who to trust."

"Tr-trust the cl-club. You're s-safe h-here. Th-the cops aren't l-looking near u-us for the m-murder of the j-judge."

"We can't save everyone, can we? Maybe we should stop now, leave Guilford to it. We've taken half his circle out and we've got the girls. This sort of thing happens all the time. We've done all we can."

I hate she's giving up like this. "Wh-when Mav came b-back to r-run the c-club, I didn't un-understand why he w-wanted to help w-women. It wasn't the c-club's problem. B-but I get it n-n-ow. There sh-should always b-be someone out th-there to help p-people like you, like Rylee, b-because otherwise, the b-b-bad guys w-win." "And you, Scar, people like you.

We're all victims to evil people who use emotions or violence to control us. That's what Katya does to you."

I nod. She's right, but I don't need Mav's help because I have Gracie. "We can't g-give up n-now. Th-they sh-should all p-pay. G-guilford might c-c-carry on. He c-could rebuild his circle."

"I'm just tired," she admits. "Tired of the fight. Men like him will always exist, and we can't get them all."

"No, b-but we c-can try and m-make a difference, even i-if it's s-small."

Gracie sighs heavily. It's been a hectic few months, so I get she's tired. I kiss her again on the head and draw slow circles over her back. "You d-don't have t-to worry anymore, Gracie. I'll worry f-for us b-both. Th-that's why I think we sh-should make it official. Become my ol' lady b-before any m-more drama."

She glances up, smiling. "Really? How do we make it official?"

"Ink."

"A tattoo? Of what?"

"N-names. I g-get yours and you g-get mine." She smiles wider, and I'm glad I decided to use this to distract her. We need something good to happen and this is it. The Perished Riders make a big fuss when a man takes his ol' lady. That shit is serious to us. "I'll t-tell M-mav and the guys in ch-church tomorrow."

She throws her leg over me. "I like the idea of being yours," she whispers, rubbing herself against me. "Forever."

I dig my fingers into her hips, trying to still her before I explode like a fucking teenager. She smirks, biting on that sexy bottom lip and taking my hands in hers. She holds them above my head and frees my erection from my shorts. "Keep your hands where I can see them," she orders, winking playfully. Moving her knickers to one side, she slowly sinks onto my cock, groaning in pleasure as I fill her up. "Why does every time feel like the first time with you?" she whispers, her eyes closed and her breathing rapid.

I remain quiet. I have a strong urge to tell her those three words, but so much rides on them. I don't want to freak her out, and I don't think she gets the seriousness of becoming my ol' lady. She doesn't understand club life and that committing to me is committing to the club. She can't just walk away. But she knows what those three words mean. She knows the seriousness of them. If I say them out loud, it might freak her the fuck out, and I don't want to ruin this moment of calm.

As she moves, she takes my hands and locks our fingers together. I stare into her eyes as we come together. We don't need words, because the way she makes love tells me all I need to know. We love each other. Nothing is going to break us.

CHAPTER TWENTY-ONE

GRACIE

I wake with Scar wrapped around me and smile to myself. I'd missed this. If the last few weeks have shown me anything, it's that I can't be without him. August enters my head and that same sick feeling churns in the pit of my stomach. The same sickness I got when she chose me to confide in. How the hell do I tell Scar? I thought about it last night, but then he distracted me with his announcement to make me his. I know the longer I leave it, the worse it will be.

He's deep in sleep, so I carefully extract myself. When he still doesn't stir, I take his mobile off the bedside table along with my own and head for the bathroom. Sitting on the toilet, I open up his list of contacts, scrolling through until I find August's name. I copy her number into my phone, then sneak back into the room, relieved to see Scar still sleeping.

By mid-morning, the guys all head into church, and I join the women in the main room. Hadley moves closer to me. "I'm so glad to have you back here."

I smile. "Actually, I think it might be more permanent." This gets everyone's attention and my smile gets wider. "We're making it official. He called the tattooist earlier and he's making me his ol' lady."

I'm knocked back into the seat as Hadley and the rest of the women pile on me with excitement. "I'm so happy for you," cries Rylee.

"He's telling the guys now."

"Well, we have to have a celebration," announces Brea, Mav's mum. She looks over to Diamond, who's wiping a tear. "I hope that's a happy tear?"

Diamond nods and takes my hand. "I never thought he'd settle again, not after . . ." she trails off, and I nod in understanding. "I'm so happy for you both." The other women start to talk about party plans while Diamond keeps a hold of my hand. "I really am over the moon," she adds. "Since you came into his life, I've seen a different side to him. He's like the Hunter I knew before the accident. You've made him so happy."

"He's made me happy," I correct, and she shakes her head.

"If you'd have seen the shadow of the man he was after the accident, after she ruined him, you'd see the impact you've had on him. Katya was never right for him, and every time she got her claws back into him, I'd lie awake worrying if that would be the night I got the call to tell me my son was dead. She would have killed my baby and lied her way through it. She'd have had the police believe it was self-defence. Just like before." She takes a deep breath and rubs my hand. "But now, he's got you, and I know you won't give up on him. Because when Katya finds out about this, she'll cause you bother. It's what she does."

I give her a reassuring smile. "Nothing will come between us, I promise. I'll never let her get into his head again."

Diamond hugs me. "Welcome to the family."

My phone beeps and I see August's name pop up. I've been waiting all morning for her to reply after I texted her to ask if she was okay.

August: I'm fine. How are you? I'm really sorry I dropped my problems on you. I shouldn't have done that.

Gracie: As long as you're okay? I can't leave the clubhouse, so I can't come and talk to you about it. Have you made any decisions?

August: No. Please don't tell my dad. Let me work out what to do.

Gracie: I honestly think you should speak to him, or maybe your mum?

August: No. She won't understand. And dad will kill the boy that got me pregnant. But it's my fault. I lied. I'll sort it. They don't need to know.

I stare at the message for a second before replying. She can't expect me not to tell Scar.

Gracie: How will you sort it, what does that mean?

I wait a few minutes, but a reply doesn't come. I'm worried. Worried for August and worried about how Scar will react when he finds out. I step outside and call my mum. She's always great with advice, so she'll know what to do. "Morning, dear, everything okay?" she asks.

"Yes. How are you?"

"Missing you. Maverick called us to say you're staying with him again."

"Yeah, he thinks it's safer for now. What are you up to?"

She pauses, and I hear a door close. "I'm having lunch."

"Oh, lovely. With Dad?"

She hesitates. "No, with Jen."

"Oh." I'm stumped for a second. "That's nice. Have a great time. I'll call you another time."

"No, wait. Are you okay? Did you need me?" she asks quickly.

"No. It's fine. Nothing I can't sort out. Speak soon."

I disconnect and slide down the wall until my arse hits the ground. "That's not a happy face," comes Rylee's voice as she joins me on the ground.

"My mum," I say, holding up the mobile. "She's busy with my ex-best friend."

"This the one who's with your ex-boyfriend too?"

I nod. "I shouldn't be jealous, right? They all supported each other after I went missing. But it's weird. Jen's dad raped me, yet my family is treating her more like a daughter than me." Suddenly, my throat tightens and a sob escapes. Rylee throws an arm around my shoulder.

"I think you have a valid reason to be upset," she reassures me. "I can't be the only one thinking it's weird she's stepped into your life. Your boyfriend, your parents . . ."

I sob harder. "Right?" I agree. She produces a tissue, and I wipe my tears. "My dad's walking her down the aisle, my mum is going to dress fittings with her. It's all too much. What if . . ." I pause, wondering if saying it out loud will make it too real. "What if she set me up?"

Rylee narrows her eyes like she's thinking seriously about my accusation. "You think she knew her dad was taking you?"

I nod. "I think she arranged the whole thing. Was it a coincidence she invited those men into her party? Was it a coincidence that hardly anyone we knew turned up that night? The more I go over it, the more realistic it seems."

"But why would she go to that extent? Your ex admitted he was already with her before you got taken."

I take a deep breath. "She knew something he didn't, something that would have got us back together. I'd confided in her as my best friend." Another sob escapes at how stupid I was not to have seen their relationship. "I was pregnant. I knew once I told my ex, he'd want us to work things out."

"Holy shit," she gasps. "She totally had a motive to get you out of the way!"

I nod. "That's why I know I wasn't drunk that night. I was drinking non-alcoholic wine. I'd had a couple, mainly because Jen nagged me to. When the guy brought me a drink, she insisted I drink it, told me not to be a party pooper, that a couple drinks wouldn't hurt."

"Oh my god, Gracie. Do the guys know about this?"

I shake my head. "It didn't seem important until I really started to think about it all. And now, it's all pointing to her, isn't it?"

Rylee nods. "What happened to the baby?"

"I was on a cocktail of drugs, so I lost it soon after being taken. It never stood a chance."

She hugs me harder. "I'm so sorry, Gracie."

"You don't think I'm over-thinking this? Being slightly crazy?"

She shakes her head again. "No. I think it's one hundred percent realistic to think she wanted you out of the way. And if you're right, that makes her fucked up, and you need to tell Mav and Scar."

SCAR

I can see Gracie's been crying the second I step out of church. The earlier elation from the guys being pumped about me and Gracie is soon forgotten as I pull her against me, staring at Rylee for an explanation. "We should go into the office," she tells Mav.

Once inside, Rylee clears her throat. "Gracie and I think Jen, the ex-best friend, is more involved than we first thought."

"In what way?" asks Mav.

"We think she may have organised for Gracie to be taken." I exchange a look with Mav, and Rylee catches it, narrowing her eyes. "What?" she asks.

"Well, we kind of thought the same thing, only we couldn't work out why."

Rylee looks at Gracie, who sighs heavily. "I was pregnant. Jen knew. I told her the morning of her party. Thinking back now, she was really shocked and maybe a little pissed. I thought it was because she didn't want me to go back to Edward after he'd dumped me without an explanation. I thought she was being a good friend."

"A-and y-you didn't th-think to mention th-this to me before n-now?" I snap. I don't mean to sound so annoyed, but why the fuck didn't she tell me she'd been pregnant?

"It wasn't important. I didn't think anything of it until I really began going over the small details. With her stepping into my life like she has, I thought I was overreacting and seeing things that weren't real. But Rylee agrees, it's weird, right?"

"It certainly gives her a motive," agrees Mav.

"She'll n-never admit it," I mutter.

"I'm going to the wedding," she announces. "I'm going to confront her. I have to know."

"What good will it do?" asks Mav. "Even if she admits it to you, she won't confess to anyone else." "I a-a-agree."

"I have to do it for my own sanity. If she did this, if this whole thing was because of her, then I deserve to know why."

Mav raises his brows and shrugs at me. "Your call, brother. She's your ol' lady now."

I stare at Gracie. She wants this badly, I can see it in her eyes, but putting her in a room with the woman who may have ruined her life, it's a disaster waiting to happen. "If y-you do it, sh-she'll tell your p-parents you're th-th-there to r-ruin her day. She'll t-turn it a-all on y-you."

Gracie nods. "I know. But I want her to know I've worked it out. She needs to know that."

I nod. "F-fine. We'll g-go to the wedding."

She throws her arms around me and hugs me tightly. "Thank you."

CHAPTER TWENTY-ONE

Tatts arrives mid-afternoon. It was safer for him to come here, seeing as we're not letting Gracie leave the clubhouse. Plans to get Rosey closer to Guilford begin this evening, and I'm hoping to God he's out of the way before Jen's wedding.

I have a stencil of Gracie's name in large letters laid out over my heart. It's next to August's, and the second the needle hits my skin, I relax. Having her on my skin forever feels right.

Gracie hasn't had a tattoo before, and although she wants it on her back, I shake my head. I want the world to see she's mine and ain't no fucker seeing her lower back. We agree on her collarbone, and as Tatts sets about his work, Gracie grips my hand so tight, I think she's cut off circulation. Tatts makes a joke about her not being good with pain and that she'll struggle to have a baby, and my mind wanders to her unborn kid. I hate that she didn't tell me something like that. I get it's personal, but I thought she'd told me everything.

She must sense my sudden drop in mood and runs her nails over the back of my neck. "Where'd yah go when you drift off like that?" she asks with a smile.

"P-p-processing shit," I mutter, and she bites her lower lip.

"I didn't keep it from you on purpose. I just didn't think about it. What's the point in thinking about something that didn't amount to anything?"

"B-but I want to know e-everything ab-about you, Gracie."

"We're at the start of our journey," she says. "We have so much time to talk about our pasts. I bet there's loads of things we haven't thought to tell each other." I nod, because she's right about that.

"Don't keep b-b-big things like th-that from me," I say. She looks away, and I frown. "Gracie?"

"I . . . I should maybe—"

"Hurry up, you guys. We want you to come and see the room. Hadley and I have made it look so pretty," shouts Meli.

Tatts rolls his eyes and wipes off the excess ink from Gracie's tattoo. "I'm all done."

I stare at the lettering and smile. 'Hunter' in ink on her tanned skin does shit to me, though I don't think she knows how much this means. I lean in and kiss her.

∞

The women have made the main room look amazing. Gracie is so excited as they rush her off to get her ready for the big night.

Rosey is at the bar, and I join her. "Have y-you come u-up with a plan?" I ask. Mav's letting her lead, which I'm not comfortable with, but he seems to have every confidence she can pull off the punishment of a top-ranking cop.

"What is it that pisses you off more, Scar? The fact Mav trusts me like a brother, or that I'm a woman handling business?"

"Don't s-start all y-your bullshit, Rosey. I j-just wanna k-know you ain't g-gonna fuck th-this up?"

"Yah know, I think I preferred you when you didn't speak. Gracie has a lot to answer for. Have you explained what she's giving up becoming an ol' lady?"

"I p-preferred it w-when you left, b-but here w-we are. Some w-women like m-men, sh-shocker, I know. You m-might wanna be a-alone forever, b-but there's a f-few of us who want to b-be happy t-together."

"A relationship with a biker is like having a relationship with thirty other bikers. The club is life, does she know that?"

"B-bitterness doesn't s-suit you. S-someone w-will choose y-you one d-day." I smirk as she gets up to leave. "K-keep me up to d-date on your p-plan."

When the women finally bring Gracie back to me, she's beautiful in a short black dress and her tattoo on show. I kiss her gently, careful not to mess up her freshly-applied makeup. "Stunning," I whisper against her lips.

"You don't think it's a little too much?" she whispers back, unsure of herself.

"Maybe a l-little too much s-skin, b-but I'll h-handle it," I respond, running my hand down her exposed thigh. "I l-like th-this part," I add, kissing her bare shoulder, right next to where her tattoo ends.

"I'm not sure we had a fair deal. Your tattoo is covered."

"But i-it's right n-next to m-my heart, which only b-beats for you."

She smiles, melting against me. "You win that round."

CHAPTER TWENTY-TWO

GRACIE

The night is perfect, and the girls did great on such short notice. But after hours of dancing and eating great food provided by Rylee, I'm ready to sneak Scar up to the room for some alone time.

He's busy talking to Grim when I wrap my arms around his waist and breathe in his woodsy aftershave scent. Everything about this man calms me. I smile up at him, and it's enough for him to know what I want. He grins, kissing me on the nose. "We'll p-pick th-this up t-tomorrow, G-grim?" he asks, and Grim rolls his eyes.

"Sure, brother, go enjoy your ol' lady."

I smile wider. I love that sentence. We're almost at the stairs when we hear Scar's name screeched from across the room. I look back over my shoulder and see Katya glaring at us. *Great, more drama.*

"Y-you've g-got to be f-fucking kidding me," he mutters quietly.

"It wouldn't be a good night if it didn't end with drama. I'm kinda getting used to it," I say, winking playfully.

Katya takes in the decorations and narrows her eyes on us. "Tell me this is a joke," she hisses.

"Why are you here, Katya?" snaps Diamond angrily.

"I tried calling, you didn't pick up," Katya says directly to Scar, ignoring Diamond.

"I w-w-w-was b-b-b-busy."

I glance at him, seeing his whole expression has changed, and I hate the way his stammer is so much worse when she's around. "Tell us what you want or leave," I say, my patience wearing thin.

Katya smirks, looking me up and down. "Look at you being all brave, claiming your man. Cute."

"You're right, he is my man, and that's why I'm not having this tonight, not on our night. So, leave."

Mav steps forward, taking Katya by her upper arm. "You heard the lady, now leave."

Katya shrugs free, her eyes bugging out of her head. The whole room is silent, waiting for her next venomous sentence. "Will he still be your man when he knows what you know? What you've kept from him?" I feel the colour drain from my face. My heart rate doubles in pace and it suddenly feels too hot and clammy in here. "Not so fucking brave now, are you?"

"Stop this circus, just leave," says Diamond. "Mav, kick her arse out."

"Are you sure about that? It involves your granddaughter," spits Katya.

"August? Wh-wh-what's wrong w-with her?" asks Scar, releasing my hand and stepping closer to her for answers. I feel the loss immediately.

Katya hands Scar a mobile phone, and he stares at it for a few seconds before turning to me. "Wh-what's th-this?" he almost whispers. My mouth opens and then closes again. I don't have the words. "Gracie?" he pushes.

"Not a great start, is it? Not if you've made her your ol' lady, and she's kept something so big from you."

His eyes burn into me. I shake my head, tears filling my eyes. "It's not like that, Scar. I . . . I wanted to tell you, but there was never a good time," I mutter.

"How l-long h-have you known?"

I glance at my feet, knowing this is going to hurt him the most. "That's why she came to see me. She said you told her I was—"

"And y-you didn't t-tell me!" he suddenly roars. I'm so shocked, I take a step back. His face is red with anger and his eyes have that glaze over them. It's like he's a different person.

"Hunter, calm down," says Gears, appearing from nowhere and stepping between us. The fact he even bothers to do that tells me he senses Scar's anger is out of control. All eyes are on us, and I suddenly feel embarrassed. "Let's talk about this."

"N-not h-here," Scar utters, heading for the office. Diamond and Gears follow.

"Just so you know, August is in hospital because of you," Katya hisses as she passes me to follow them. I watch them file into the office, unsure whether to follow, but then Scar turns, his eyes catching mine before he closes the door, making his feelings clear.

"Fuck, Gracie," whispers Rylee, wrapping her arms around me.

"I'd actually like one night where there's no fucking drama," mutters Meli.

"Should I go in there?" I ask. "Explain what happened?"

Rylee shakes her head. "Probably not a good idea."

Minutes later, they step from the office. "Pres, I g-gotta s-step out. I d-don't know w-when I'll be b-b-back, but c-call if anything u-u-urgent comes up."

I wipe my eyes. There's no way he's walking out without speaking to me. "Wait one goddamn minute," I snap, and his eyes settle on me. "You're not walking out without talking to me about this."

"You tell him, girl," I hear Rosey whispering from somewhere behind me.

"Y-you w-wanna bet?"

"Damn right, I do," I yell. "You haven't heard my side. As usual, you've just listened to her, and now, you expect me to sit by while you leave with her?"

"T-this is about my d-daughter," he hisses, stepping closer.

"And you've just made me your ol' lady, which means I'm part of her life too." His face softens slightly. "At least hear me out."

He takes a breath. I see him wavering, but so does Katya and she places a hand on his arm. He shudders, eyeing it like it's poison. Before she can jump in, I smile. "Yah know what, go, be with August. I'll be here when you get home." Katya scowls at me. She wanted the chance to pull the power back, but as I move closer, he shakes Katya's hand off. "Come home to me when you're ready."

I hold his stare for a few more seconds before turning away and heading straight upstairs. The ball is in his court. If he wants to hear me out, he'll see August and return to me. He's been so used to the flight or fight response, and if I want to break that habit, I'll need to be patient and wait for him to come to me. Whenever he's ready.

SCAR

I let Ghost drive me to the hospital. I can't be in a car with Katya, alone, I don't want to hear her poison, and I'm not in any fit state to ride myself. "So?" asks Ghost the second he starts the engine. "Are you gonna tell me what the fuck happened in there or what?"

"Sh-sh-sh-" I pause and take a breath. I can't bring myself to say it aloud, but I have to because this is real. "She's pregnant."

Ghost's head spins to look at me and he almost swerves into the central reservation. After a few curse words, he glares at me. "Katya?"

"No," I snap. "August."

"Fuck!" he yells. "We really should have had this conversation back at the club and not while I'm driving."

"W-well sh-she's in the hospital bleeding, so f-fuck knows if she's still . . . y-yah know."

"Jesus," he mutters, then we drive the rest of the way in complete silence.

The hospital is busy. By the time we're led onto the ward where August is, I'm fit to explode. But the second I see my baby girl lying in that bed with her pale face and puffy, tear-stained cheeks, I melt. "Dad," she whispers and breaks into sobs. I wrap her in my arms and hold her against me, inhaling the strawberry scent of her hair.

A doctor joins us, waiting for me to release her before speaking. "I'm not sure how much August has told you," he begins.

"Fuck all," says Ghost, and the doctor visibly swallows before continuing.

"We know a-about the b-b-baby," I mutter.

"Right, well, she's suffering from an ectopic pregnancy. It means the embryo is forming outside of the womb."

"What the hell does that mean?" snaps Ghost.

"It means the pregnancy is not viable. We'll need to remove the embryo."

"H-how?"

"With an injection to her thigh. This will rid her system of any foreign bodies. The embryo should fall away. We'll need to see her back at the day clinic for the next few days to check her hormone levels are going back to normal, so we know the procedure has worked." August sobs harder, and I sit beside her. "I'm so sorry," she cries.

"Will sh-she b-be okay?"

"Yes," reassures the doctor. "It's quite common and easily treatable because we've caught it so early."

He leaves us, and I keep my arm around August. Katya leans forward. "You need to get talking," she spits.

"What do you want me to say?" August wails.

"For a start, who the hell got you in this state?" asks Ghost.

"Does it matter?" sniffles August.

"Yes," snaps Ghost. "How will I kill him if I don't know who he is?"

"Enough," I growl.

"She's been having sex," hisses Katya. "I can't even look at you right now. How many times have I told you about kids and how they ruin your fucking life?"

"G-get out," I snap.

"Don't tell me to leave. You think because you're here now, you're in charge?" spits Katya.

"L-let m-me t-talk to her," I snap.

Katya takes a breath. "Fine. Maybe it's time for you to deal with her because I am so sick of this bullshit and doing it all on my own." She stomps out, and I feel August relax against me.

"B-baby, h-how are you f-feeling?" I ask gently.

"Tired. I haven't slept well in ages. Is Gracie coming to see me?"

My heart twists as I shake my head. August eyes me suspiciously. "Why?"

"We h-had a d-disagreement," I mutter.

"About me?" she wails, her eyes filling again. "I went to her, Dad, and I begged her to let me sort it out. She said she wanted to tell you, and she tried to get me to tell you, but I begged her. Please, don't be mad at her because of me. You said she was kind and understanding, and I thought she could help me too, like she helped you." She sucks in a deep breath, speaking so fast, it makes her cough. Ghost gives me one of his looks that tells me he agrees with August. I can't help feeling hurt that Gracie didn't tell me right away. She knows how important August is to me. She's fourteen for fuck's sake, just a kid.

"D-don't worry about th-that. Just g-get better."

"I want to live with you, Dad. I can't stay with Mum any more." "B-b-baby, you know I'd l-love that, but y-your mum won't a-allow it."

"She will. I'll talk to her. Just say yes."

I wipe her tears with my thumbs and smile sadly. There's no way Katya will let her live at the club. She's only just agreed to visitation and she doesn't make that easy. "I l-love y-you," I whisper.

"You shouldn't. I let you down."

I shake my head. "Y-you haven't. I sh-should have b-been there f-for you m-more. I p-promise I will be from n-now on."

The next couple days are spent between the hospital and quick shower visits to the clubhouse. I haven't spoken to Gracie, and she hasn't sought me out to explain herself. I'm not sure if that pisses me off more or not. I want to hear what she has to say, but at the same time, it might just make it all worse. She had time to tell me, we laid in bed talking for hours, and she didn't bring it up, and we even agreed to no more secrets.

To top things off, I have an appointment with the social worker this morning. Since Katya walked out of hospital the other night, I haven't seen her. She hasn't come back to see August, and although I know it's just the way she handles shit, the hospital has raised concerns.

I shower, change, and head down to the kitchen to grab some of Rylee's amazing waffles. August loves them, and I know it'll cheer her up. I stop mid-step when I come face-to-face with Gracie. My heart twists, the urge to hold her overwhelming.

"Rylee said you have two waffles, right?" she asks cheerily, holding out a paper bag. I take it, unsure of how to react to her bright mood. I assumed she'd be mad at not hearing from me for two days. "How's August?"

"I-in p-pain."

"Right," she mutters. "Please send her my love. I hope she's okay. If there's anything I can do . . ." She smiles sadly, then moves past me and heads for the door. I'm not comfortable with the way she's acting, like she doesn't know me. Like she hasn't made love to me or got my fucking name on her skin.

"Gracie?" I snap, and she stops with her back to me. It came out sharper than I meant it to. "G-get back here."

She slowly backs up to the same spot. "Yep?"

"I'm m-mad a-at you. It d-doesn't mean we're n-not t-together."

"I know," she says, nodding.

"R-r-right." I'm unsure of what else to say, and she stands waiting patiently. "Aren't y-y-you m-mad at m-me?"

She shakes her head. "No, why would I be?"

I frown. "I h-haven't s-seen you f-for t-t-two days."

"You have a lot on. Worry about August, I'll still be here when you come home to me." She heads out, and I stare in disbelief. She didn't question where the hell I've been or if Katya was still around. She didn't even raise her voice.

∞

"Mr. Anderson, please, come in. I'm Maxim Stewart. Today is nothing to worry about. I'd just like to spend some time getting to know you and August." I watch the social worker from under my cap.

"I'm Deana," says Mum, shaking his hand. "Everyone calls me Diamond." She's nervous as we take a seat.

"Okay, Diamond, great to meet you. You're August's paternal grandmother?"

"Yes. We don't get to see her often, so I can't tell you a lot about her," she mutters.

"Oh," he frowns and makes a note in his book, "why is that?"

Mum glances at me, and I nod. "We have a difficult relationship with her mum. She doesn't make it easy."

"And may I ask where August's mum is right now?"

"We don't know," she admits.

"Hunter?" he pushes.

"He doesn't like to—" Mum begins.

"Sh-sh-she walked o-out," I say, cutting Mum off. This is serious, and I can't let August down by keeping quiet.

"Did she give a reason or a date when she'd return?"

I shake my head. "Sh-she gets l-like this. She n-needs to c-clear her head."

He nods. "I read your record. How's life since you came out of prison?"

"He's a good dad," says Mum. "He loves that girl so much. She's off the rails because her mum doesn't give two craps. She wants to score points against Scar all the damn time."

I place my hand over Mum's to silence her. "Sorry," she whispers.

"Mrs. Anderson, we're not here to score points. We're not even here to remove August from anyone's care. We just want to make sure someone is caring for her and she's happy. I'm not going to judge your son or his relationship with Miss Steele. The fact of the matter is, August is fourteen years old, and she got pregnant while in her mother's care. Now, her mother is nowhere to be seen. You can understand why we're here to check things are okay?"

Mum nods. "We want to work with you to achieve the same outcomes, that August is safe and happy."

"Sh-she's asked if sh-she c-can live w-with me," I say.

"And how do you feel about that?" he asks, making a note.

"I d-don't want to c-c-come between h-her and her mum."

"Because you're worried she'll make up more lies," Mum cuts in.

"No," I say, "b-because sh-she's done a-all the h-hard work."

"But where is she now? When she's really needed," Mum snaps.

"Have you tried calling her?" asks Maxim, politely changing the subject.

I nod. "A-a-a lot. I l-left h-her messages."

"We checked August's birth certificate and you're named there. Technically, if her mum isn't around, the hospital can discharge her into your care."

"Can she come home with us?" asks Mum.

"There's no reason why she can't. If her mum shows up, we'd like to speak to her. But if she doesn't, and August is happy, you can take her home. We'd like to stick around for a while, keep checking in with her. Has she mentioned the father of the baby?"

I shake my head. "What about Gracie?" Mum asks. "Maybe she told her?"

"Gracie?" repeats Maxim.

"My," I pause, "wife," I add. Outsiders don't understand the way our world works, so it's easier to say wife than explain ol' lady.

He makes a note. "We'd also like to speak to her."

CHAPTER TWENTY-THREE

GRACIE

It's the third day of silence from Scar, but I can handle it. I can even handle seeing him come and go from the club. But I can't handle the way he's wearing his stupid cap again and how his hood covers his face. We've moved past that, and I'm frustrated he's gone back there.

"I must say," whispers Rylee, leaning close as she butters a slice of toast. The rest of the room is a hive of activity, like a normal breakfast at the club. "You're handling all this so well." Scar is five seats away from me. He may as well be a hundred because that's how distant he feels. "He just needs time."

"That's what you say whenever I talk about it with you. But how much time are you willing to give?"

"As long as he needs. I'm not going anywhere. He has a right to be mad. I'd be mad. It was a huge secret to keep."

"But you had a lot going on."

"It doesn't matter. August is his number one priority, and I kept him in the dark about something really important."

"You didn't do it to be a bitch." "That's not the point. How would you feel if Mav did that with Ella?"

Scar stands, and I watch as he rounds the table to where I am. "I n-n-need you," he utters, and hope fills my chest as I follow him. We stop in the main room, but he keeps his head lowered. "I n-need a f-favour."

"Anything."

"Th-the social w-w-w-worker wants to meet you," he mutters.

"Are you kidding," says Rosey from where she's sitting on the couch. "You haven't spoken to Gracie in days, and now you want her to play happy family for the social worker?"

"It's fine," I say quickly, "of course."

"Gracie, he hasn't given two shits about you all week. You don't have to do him any favours." "I really don't mind," I hiss, glaring at her to shut the hell up. It's the first time he's spoken to me, and yeah, he wants a favour, but it's the least I can do.

"I've h-h-had to b-be at the h-hospital," he mutters. "I've h-had a l-lot to d-deal with."

"And you don't think she has?" snaps Rosey. "You fucking bikers act like you're the only ones with shit to do. You made her your ol' lady, aren't you supposed to take care of her?"

"Don't listen to Rosey. When do you need me?"

"N-now."

"Do I need to do or say anything?"

"He'll j-j-just ask q-questions."

◦∞◦

It's an hour before Maxim Stewart arrives at the clubhouse looking cool and calm in his casual jeans and shirt with a folder tucked under one arm. He smiles kindly, his eyes assessing the large room where bikers are milling around. "Big place." We take a seat in a quiet corner. "It's nice to meet you," he adds, shaking my hand. Scar's gone to get us tea, leaving us alone. "He only mentioned you yesterday. Have you been together long?"

"A few months.""And you're married?" he asked, sounding surprised.

"Not exactly. We're married in the eyes of the club but not by law."

"Okay." He makes a quick note. "And how's your relationship with August?"

"Erm, okay, I guess. We've only met once, but we have been texting. Her mum isn't the easiest person to get along with."

"Has Hunter had any luck locating Katya yet?" I stare for a few seconds, trying to work out what the hell he's talking about. He smiles awkwardly. "She's not been in contact with Hunter or the hospital in days."

I feel my cheeks redden with embarrassment. "Sorry, I wasn't aware." He makes another note. "He's been so busy looking after August, we haven't had chance to touch base," I add.

"Can I ask something personal?" I nod. "How are things between you and Hunter?"

"Good," I lie. "I mean, it's very early days, but he's amazing. I love him very much."

"Is there a reason you haven't been to the hospital?"

I hesitate. I thought Scar kept me away because of Katya, but to know she hasn't been there makes that a wrong assumption. "I've been busy with work," I lie, "and my best friend is getting married in two days. The wedding prep has been intense. But I have texted August."Scar places a tray of hot drinks on the table. "That's nice, I love a good celebration," says Maxim. "Will you both be going to the wedding?"

"No," I say firmly. Scar catches my eye from under his hood. "It's best if Hunter concentrates on August and finding Katya." I see the way his jaw clenches. He was hoping that piece of information would stay secret from me.

"Hopefully, August will be home by then," says Maxim. "I spoke with the hospital first thing, and if I'm happy with her accommodation here, they'll release her into your care later today," he tells Scar.

"August is coming here?" I ask, surprised.

Maxim frowns. He must be as confused as me. "Didn't you know?"

"Crossed wires," I mutter. "That's fantastic news," I add.

"Maybe you could show me where she'll be sleeping?" he asks, and Scar nods, leading the way. I watch them disappear upstairs before marching over to Diamond.

"Katya has gone?"

She nods. "Didn't Scar say?"

"No. No, he hasn't said anything for days," I snap. "I feel like an idiot. The social worker must have thought I was clueless."

"Sorry, Gracie, I thought he'd have said."

I head up to my room, locking the door. I have no right to be angry, he's well within his rights to keep things from me after what I did, but to ask me to meet the social worker without filling me in was a shitty move. I pull out my mobile and send a text to Rosey, asking her to come up and see me. A few minutes later, there's a knock at the door. I open it, thinking it's her but roll my eyes when it's Scar. I try to slam the door, but he puts his boot there.

"Sorry," he mumbles.

"Yah know what, fuck you, Scar. I've been patient and kind, and I've apologised over and over. And if you don't want to tell me things about your life and what's going on, then don't. It's your choice. But don't expect me to do shit for you like that again."

"I sh-should h-have told you."

"Yeah, you should. Clearly, you don't want me around you right now."

"Y-you're m-my ol' lady, I'll a-always w-want you a-around. I'm just n-not in a g-good place." "Me either, Scar."

Just then, Rosey appears. "Move out of the way," she snaps, and he does.

"I have stuff to do," I mutter as I let her in, then close the door on him.

"Things go okay with the social worker?" she asks, and I shrug. "I hate those people. Always in everyone's business."

"How do you feel about busting me out of this place for a few hours?"

"You know I'm up for an adventure. Where are we going?"

I smile. I love that she doesn't ask any questions or try to talk me out of it. "I need to go and see someone."

I got Jen's new address from Mum, although it took a lot of convincing for her to give it to me. In the end, I told her if I didn't see Jen now, then I'd have no option but to turn up at the wedding. She gave it to me on the condition I didn't tell anyone, especially Jen, where I got it.

Rosey gives a low whistle when we reach the two-story newly built property in Knightsbridge. "Fuck, you didn't say she was loaded," she whispers.

"Trading in the sex industry must be lucrative," I mutter coldly as we climb the white stone steps.

"Are we just going in through the door?" asks Rosey.

"It's how you're supposed to enter a property," I reply.

"I was hoping for a little more drama."

I glare at her as I ring the doorbell. "No drama, Rosey, I mean it. I just need to ask some questions and then we leave. No killing or breaking anything." "You're no fun," she mutters as the door swings open, and Jen's bright smile falls from her face.

"Oh, it's you," she mutters.

"I'd like to talk," I say hopefully.

She sighs heavily but opens the door wider for us to go in. Her house is just as amazing inside as it is from the outside. Everything looks expensive. "I don't have long. I'm going to visit my father . . . in prison."

"It won't take long," I say, adding a smile.

We sit on large white couches, the type you sink into. "Right, well, get on with it."

"I've been thinking about things, a lot of things, actually. Mostly about that night I went missing." Jen eyes me suspiciously. "I remember the guys, and you shouting them over. And I wasn't drinking, can you remember that?" I ask. I find it odd since being back she hasn't asked me about the pregnancy.

"Yes," she mutters, avoiding my eyes.

"And the guys wanted to buy us drinks, and I said no, but you said yes. You told me to stop being boring, that one drink wouldn't hurt, right?"

She nods impatiently. "So?"

"I just want to make sure I remember it right," I explain. "I saw Ed recently, and he told me you'd been seeing each other before we broke up." I wait for her reaction, but she doesn't give one. Instead, she shrugs. "But you told me it started after we broke up, after I went missing."

"What's your point, Gracie?" she snaps impatiently. "So, I'm a shit friend and I screwed your boyfriend behind your back. It was almost two years ago and he's happy with me now."

"What a bitch," mutters Rosey.

"It just feels weird. You were fucking Edward, and then I tell you I'm pregnant." Rosey gasps at that piece of information. "And you knew I was going to tell him, that I was hoping we'd get back together. It's odd that I'm taken before I got to tell him."

"Fuck," hisses Rosey.

"It's just a coincidence, Gracie. What exactly are you trying to say? That I had you taken?" She laughs, and it comes out high-pitched and nervous.

"Yes, I guess I am."

"Don't be ridiculous. I knew Edward wouldn't ever go back to you. He'd told me as much. He said you drove him insane and he was glad he'd dumped you. Telling him about the baby wouldn't have changed that."

"I guess we'll never know, will we? Because I never got the chance to tell him, and I'm sure as hell you didn't tell him." "I didn't see the point. It would have only upset everyone."

"I bet that pissed you off, seeing him upset after I was gone," I mutter.

"He soon got over it."

"I just need to know, Jen. Did you have anything to do with any of it?"

She glances at Rosey, and I realise if I want her to tell me the truth, she doesn't want witnesses. "Rosey, would you give us a minute?" I ask. Rosey must sense it too, because for once, she doesn't argue and leaves the room. "It's just us now, me and you. Tell me the truth. It's not like anyone would believe me. You seem to have them all under your spell."

"I'll tell you the truth if you drop the statement against my dad."

I laugh. "That's not going to happen." She goes over to a cabinet and takes a small device from it. "If you don't drop the statement, I'll send this to every porn website. It will be all over the internet in a matter of days." She holds out the small memory stick. "This shows what a whore you really were during your time away." I feel the colour drain from my face. They recorded me a lot of times. I remember the cameras in my face, even when I was out of it on drugs. Jen smirks. "Maybe I wanted you out of the way, but I didn't know what would happen. I didn't know why they'd take you or what for."

My heart threatens to beat from my chest. "Did you know my drink was spiked?" She nods. "And when I didn't come back, where did you think I was? Why didn't you tell anyone?"

"What was I supposed to say? Your parents were devastated, so when the cops said they thought you'd ran away, it was easier to let them think that."

"Of course, the cops said that. It was all a lie to cover up what they were doing. Your dad, that judge, and the Chief Constable, they were in it together."

"My father was not a part of it. Yes, he got them the girls, but he didn't take part in the rituals." That one word takes me back to my time in captivity, and I shudder. "Some men have desires that the world says are wrong. But who are we to decide that? And if we don't cater to them, they'll go out on the streets and take it anyway. This way, we're controlling those urges, giving them what they want!"

I stare in disbelief. "It's rape, Jen. Those men rape and torture innocent women. I was your best mate."

"I put my dad off you for years. He'd asked me plenty of times, but I told him no. I was your friend and I wasn't going to let him have you, but then . . . well, then I fell in love with Edward and it got out of hand." I press my hand against my stomach, suddenly feeling sick. Rosey comes back in. "Are you okay?" she asks me. I nod before flicking my eyes to the stick in Jen's hand.

Rosey grins, happy to have her moment as she grips Jen's wrist. Jen lets out a scream, but Rosey rips the stick from her hand anyway. "I have copies," she screams.

"I only need the one," I say, standing. "Enjoy the wedding."

SCAR
I take August's hand, and she slowly walks beside me towards the clubhouse. "Will Gracie be here?" she asks, looking so happy.

"Yes."

"You're wearing that cap again. Why?" I don't have a reason to give her, but it just feels right to hide when the world seems so fucking dark.

We enter the clubhouse and are met with the ol' ladies waiting to make a fuss. Every ol' lady but mine. I glance around. "Slight problem," whispers Mum. "She went out."

I narrow my eyes. "With?"

"Rosey. Mav called Rosey, and they're on their way back now. Apparently, they went to see Jen for some answers."

When Gracie walks in five minutes later, she rushes to August and wraps her arms around her. "I'm so glad you're okay," she whispers.

"Thank you. Why didn't you come and see me?"

Gracie doesn't bother to look at me. Instead, she tucks August's long hair behind her ears and smiles. "I'll make up for it, I promise. Maybe we can watch a movie later, if your dad can spare you?" she asks.

August looks at me with hopeful eyes, and I nod. "Maybe we could all watch it together?" she suggests.

"No, let's have some girly time," suggests Gracie quickly before I can reply. "I'm sure your dad has plenty to do, like finding your mum."

Before she can rush off, I grab her wrist. "Wh-what were y-you thinking?"

"That you were busy and I had shit to do."

"Y-you can't l-leave the club without m-m-me."

"Oops. Too late now, though," she says, pulling free and marching off to Mav's office with Rosey. I narrow my eyes. I don't like that she's upset with me. At least with Katya, I knew what to expect, screaming and shouting, but with Gracie, it's a look of sadness and disappointment. It cuts so much deeper.

A few minutes later, Mav comes out and slaps me on the back. "Man, she's one tough cookie."

"Wh-what are y-y-you talking about?"

"She got Jen confessing all, on record. She orchestrated Gracie's kidnapping for her dad." I move towards the office, but he grabs me back, shaking his head. "I wouldn't go in there yet, brother. She's viewing a recording of herself." I stare, waiting for more information, and he shifts uncomfortably. "Jen was going to use it to blackmail her. It's clips of her time with them."

"Mav," shouts Rosey. We both rush to the office. Gracie's crying hard, but the video is paused. "We think you should see this," she mutters, pressing play.

I ball my fists in anger as Gracie comes into view, clearly passed out. She's gagged and hog-tied with thick rope, suspended from a large hook in the ceiling. A naked man comes into view, his back to the camera. He presses something to her skin that makes her jolt, waking her. She begins screaming into the gag, and he laughs, running a finger over her terrified face. He unfastens the gag and then looks at the camera, smirking. Rosey pauses it. "I don't think Jen thought this through," says Rosey, laughing. Chief Constable Guilford is frozen on the screen with his cock in his hand.

"Fuck, we got him," says Mav, his mouth hanging open. "We fucking got him red-handed." I slam the laptop closed and swoop down, scooping Gracie from the couch. She clings to me, burying her face into my neck. "Does this mean I don't get to kill him?" asks Rosey.

"N-no, I d-d-do," I mutter, marching from the room and heading upstairs.

∞

Gracie cries until her throat is hoarse and her eyes are swollen and red. I keep her in my arms, resting against my chest while I stroke her hair and whisper how much I love her. I've missed this.

"I'm so sorry for everything with August," she eventually whispers.

I tip her head back so she's looking at me. "I'm s-s-sorry for ignoring y-y-you all w-w-week. I've b-been an idiot."

"I deserved it," she mutters, which breaks my fucking heart. I'm a complete arse for making her feel like this. I press my lips against hers.

"I d-d-don't know h-how to do th-this. I k-keep messing it up, but I'm trying t-t-to be b-better. W-when I'm angry, I'll try a-and talk a-about it. It's j-just hard to b-break bad h-habits from my r-relationship w-with K-kat."

She smiles sadly. "We'll get there. I knew you needed space, and I was happy to give it to you, but you shut me out completely and that hurt. I want to support you the way you've supported me. I'm never going to argue the way Katya did. I can't scream and shout at you. I'm a talker. I like to talk it through and move on. Is Katya gone for good?"

I shake my head. "She'll t-turn up. M-maxim w-wants to s-speak to her though, and she'll h-hate that. Did A-august tell you who th-the father w-was?"

"No. She told me he was sixteen and she'd lied about her age. Do you want me to talk to her?"

I nod. "You c-can t-try. Maybe sh-she'll open u-up. I'm j-just worried he's s-still sniffing a-a-around her."

"At least with her being under this roof, you can keep an eye on her."

I sigh, and she rests her head against my chest again. "I h-hate it w-when we f-fight," I admit. "A-and what w-w-were y-you thinking s-seeing Jen l-like that?"

"I needed closure," she replies. "I didn't expect her to admit it and I didn't expect the evidence."

"Mav is w-w-working on a p-plan, but I'm gonna k-kill th-that p-piece of shit."

"No, I don't want him to die." She sits up to look at me, removing my cap. "I want him to go to prison. I want him to sit in a cell for the rest of his life and suffer. A cop in prison is the best punishment."

CHAPTER TWENTY-FOUR

GRACIE

Grim calls me into church. Women never get to be in here, so it's a new experience as I enter their sacred place, and also a little intimidating having all the men in one place, all eyes on me. Grim pulls out a chair for me to sit beside Mav. "We've been discussing our next move," explains Mav, "and we wanted to run it past you, seeing as it's about you. Scar said you want Guilford to suffer in prison." I nod. "I'm going to arrange a meeting with the Police Commissioner. I'm going to present all the evidence to him."

"Won't that put you in the frame?" I ask, because Mav wanted to keep the club out of it all.

"If the question arises, I'll say you were sent to stay with us from the women's charity recently because they felt you were in danger. With all this evidence, I doubt they'll be thinking about anything but how to save their own arses once the media get a hold of it."

Grim gently rubs my shoulders. "Have you thought about the media attention, Gracie? Because it's going to be intense."

I nod. I have to do this for all the women they didn't film. They'll never face charges for everyone. And what about the women who never returned to the cages? The women who probably died or were killed to satisfy those sick fuckers. I spoke about it at length with Scar, and we agreed, it's what needed to be done.

"And now we want to know, what you would like us to do with Jen's confession?" asks Mav.

I glance over the table to Scar. We spoke about this also. "I'm going to the wedding tomorrow," I say. "I want to tell everyone what she did. Then the police can do what they want with her."

"Damn, you've spent too much time with Rosey," says Ghost, grinning wide.

"Then let's make a plan she can't wriggle out of," says Mav.

∞

The following day, I stand before the floor-length mirror and check out the pale pink silk dress I bought especially for the wedding. I know Edward asked me to stay away, but I knew deep down, I'd have to get a glimpse of exactly what she stole from me.

Scar enters my bedroom and smiles as I slowly spin to show off my outfit. His three-piece suit looks amazing, and as he pulls me against him, I run my hands over the dark blue waistcoat. "You look handsome." I smile, straightening his pale pink tie.

"I f-f-feel like a t-twat," he says.

I gently run my finger over his scar. It makes him look even more rugged and handsome. "I'm definitely getting a lot of pictures of us like this," I warn him. He rolls his eyes and grabs a handful of my arse.

"You're m-missing the b-b-back of your d-dress," he points out, and I laugh. Although the material falls down to my ankles, the back is open.

"But you get to see my tattoo." I point to the low neckline, showing off my collar bone. He kisses his name.

"A-are y-you sure a-about this?" he asks for the hundredth time, and I nod. I'm more sure than I've ever been. Maverick has a meeting with the commissioner at ten o'clock, and the wedding starts at noon.

∞

There're a lot of people arriving for the wedding, and crowds have gathered at the church. Mum spots me first and her eyes bug out of her head as she makes a beeline for me. "Gracie," she whispers. "Why are you here?"

"My best friend is getting married, where else would I be?" I ask.

"But Edward asked—"

"I know, but I'm sure he didn't mean it. Besides, I'm here now." Guests begin to step inside the church, and Mum looks around panicked, unsure of what to do. "I'll sit at the back, Mum. They'll never know."

She nods, kisses me on the cheek, and rushes off inside. Once everyone's in the church, Scar takes my hand, and we head inside, finding a seat right at the back. "She hired the place I always wanted to get married at," I tell Scar. "The evening event is at The Garlands. I took Jen to look at it once, so she knew it's where I wanted to marry Edward."

Scar kisses me hard, and I smile. "It's t-t-too f-fancy, f-fuck them."

"You shouldn't use that kind of language in a church," I whisper.

"If th-there weren't a-all these p-people here, I'd have you b-bent over this b-bench, fucking you."

I laugh hard, playfully tapping his leg. "You have no morals."

The church doors close and everyone falls silent. I grip Scar's hand tighter and stare at the large white screen at the front of the church. Jen had a montage of her and Edward's journey together made specially to play for the guests before she walks down the aisle. Ghost was especially great at adapting it, and as the screen lights up, I grin to myself. This is gonna be one hell of a show.

A picture of Edward and Jen fills the screen. They're smiling at each other in the perfect Instagram pose. Music begins to play and I roll my eyes as Brett Young's "In Case You Didn't Know" fills the room. The next clip is a video of Edward swinging Jen around on a beach. They look happy, and I feel a small stab of guilt. I'm about to bring down Edward's world, and he doesn't deserve it. He's been tricked too, even if he did cheat on me with my best friend.

The next clip is a short snapshot from the video of me tied to a chair with my head hanging down and my hair covering my face. I couldn't watch the whole thing from the memory stick we took from Jen, but Rosey did. It turns out there wasn't just the one clip on there of me being raped by Guilford. It cuts to a picture of a missing poster showing my face and displaying my parents' contact details. Edward turns towards my mum, who's sitting up front, a puzzled look on his face.

There're a few whispers as a picture of the happy couple flashes up again before cutting to me lying on a table, held by several men, while Guilford burns my thigh with a hot poker. Screams override the music and the guests begin to fidget uncomfortably. The vicar heads towards the back room, but he won't be able to stop the montage because Ghost is back there with three other Perished Riders. Scar kisses me on the cheek before taking his position in front of the large wooden doors. No one is leaving here.

"What the hell is this?" yells Edward.

Various pictures of Edward and Jen flash over the screen, all happy memories created on lies. Edward looks around frantically until he spots me, then he strides over to where I remain seated. He makes a handsome groom. He looks exactly how I pictured he would in his suit. "Gracie, what the fuck?" he hisses.

"She's not who you think she is," I say, and he scoffs. "She's been lying to you, Ed."

"You need to stop this right now. I'm marrying Jen today. I love her. Stop this."

My screams fill the room, and gasps escape from the guests. Edward glances back at the screen, where I'm being bitten over and over. "Gracie, please stop," he mutters, his expression filled with pain. It's the same words I'm crying in the clip, begging my torturer to stop.

The screen goes blank and Edward lets out a sigh of relief. But it isn't over yet, and as Jen's voice fills the church, everyone falls silent again. My conversation with Jen from two days ago plays through the surround sound speakers. As she admits her part in my abduction, Edward's eyes burn into my own. "No," he whispers in disbelief.

"She wanted me out the way so she could have you to herself."

"Pregnant," he repeats. "You were pregnant?"

I nod. "The repeated rapes and torture meant I lost it soon after being taken."

The recording stops and the "Wedding March" music begins. Scar opens the wooden doors and steps to one side. Jen's beaming smile, as she hooks on to my dad's arm, burns itself into my brain. She doesn't seem to register the horror-filled faces in the room as she begins her walk towards the altar. She doesn't even realise Edward isn't at the front until she's almost halfway there.

Her step falters and she glances around, her eyes falling to me and Edward. And suddenly, rage replaces her confusion. She releases my dad's arm and picks up her dress to stop from tripping as she storms towards me. "What the hell are you doing here?" she yells.

"I couldn't miss my best friend's wedding," I say casually. Scar stands behind me, his large frame making her think twice before she steps any closer. "Please, carry on. Don't let me stop the show."

"You're enjoying this," spits Edward.

"Maybe a little. I've had to endure sixteen months of hell, only to return and find my friend living my life. She stole my man, my family, even my fucking ideal wedding. She's crazy."

"What the fuck have you been saying?" she hisses.

"What's going on?" whispers Dad.

"Maybe we should tell the guests to wait outside?" suggests Mum, her eyes red from crying.

Jen spins to face her. "No way! This wedding is happening and no attention-seeking little lying bitch will stop that!"

Her voice recording fills the church again, and I bite my lip to stop me smirking. Jen's face pales. She glares at me, realising I have our whole conversation on record. Edward is staring at her, and Dad's mouth falls open as he hears Jen's confession. I couldn't have pulled this off any better.

"You did this?" whispers Edward.

Jen shakes her head, gripping his arm. "No, it's not how it sounds. My dad made me do it."

"How many girls have you done this to?" he mutters.

"He made me! All of them, he made me lure them to him. I didn't have a choice. I'm a victim too!"

Maverick steps into church, shuddering as he steps through the door. "Hate these places," he grumbles. Two cops appear behind him as he points to the blushing bride.

"You have to be joking," screams Jen. "This is my wedding day!"

Edward loosens his tie. "I don't think so," he mumbles, pulling free of her grip.

"She's lying," Jen shouts as the cop reads her rights. She's led out the church kicking and screaming.

Dad goes to the front of the church. "Sorry, I think the wedding has been cancelled. Please feel free to head over to The Garlands and enjoy the rest of the day." Guests begin to file out of the church until I'm alone with Scar, Mav, my parents, and Edward.

SCAR

Gracie's mum takes her hand, tears rolling down her cheeks. "I am so sorry," she whispers.

"It's fine, Mum. Sorry I ruined the day. I know you were looking forward to it."

"What exactly did I miss?" her dad asks.

"I kind of crashed the video montage," says Gracie. Edward sits with his head in his hands. "Can I have a minute with Edward?" she asks.

Mav leads her parents outside. She waits for me to follow, but I arch my brow, telling her I'm going no fucking where. She shakes her head, rolls her eyes, and moves to sit beside him. "I'm sorry I ruined your day," she says.

"Yah know, Gracie, you could have just come to me and explained what had happened. I didn't deserve that humiliation today."

She nods, looking guilty. "You're right. I wanted to ruin Jen's day and, unfortunately, that meant you got caught in it. I'm sorry for that, but Jen deserved it. She ruined my life for those sixteen months, and God knows how many other girls she led to them."

"I don't understand why she went to those lengths," he mumbles, rubbing at his tired looking face.

"I told her I was pregnant. We'd talked about kids, and I knew it might bring us back together, so I told her that. Obviously, I didn't know you and she were—"

"All along, she wanted you out of the way. I can't believe she sat with me and your parents while we tried to work out what happened to you."

"Her dad is guilty, just like so many other men. There's enough evidence on that memory stick to have them convicted, and the police are headed to your house to look for more evidence. They think her dad gave her files to keep hidden to blackmail important men so he could get out of this."

"It's like a bad fucking film." Edward takes her hands, and I clench my fists, fighting the urge to break his fingers. "I'm sorry, Gracie, I never even suspected her. I can't believe you were pregnant. And you're right, I would have left her for you. Fuck, we could have a kid now and be living happily ever after."

Gracie glances at me and tries not to laugh when she sees the rage on my face. "Everything happens for a reason, Edward. I found Scar and I've never been happier." She stands, and I take her hand in mine, gripping it tightly.

"Can we keep in touch?" asks Edward.

I begin leading her towards the exit. "No," I say firmly. He fucked her best friend, and as far as I'm concerned, none of this would have happened if he hadn't done that.

Her parents are waiting outside. Mav had already filled them in, and her dad wraps her in a hug. "We're so proud of you."

"I'd really like you to come to the clubhouse," says Gracie. "Scar's daughter is staying with us, and I'd love you to meet her and the rest of them."

Mav nods. "Great idea. We should celebrate."

∞

Back at the clubhouse, all eyes are on Gracie as she raises her glass. "To closure," she announces, and everyone repeats it, raising their glasses before cheering loudly. It didn't take long for word to get around about a club party. Everyone is here, even Arthur and his brothers made it with short notice.

"Thanks for today," Gracie says, wrapping her arm around my waist.

"W-when c-can we l-leave?" I ask, and she grins.

"When it finishes." I shake my head, taking her by the hand and pulling her towards Mav's office. "I c-can't wait th-that long," I mutter. She giggles as I lock the door, then press her against it and kiss her. I run my hands over the soft material of her dress and groan when her nipples harden, poking through the silk. "Y-you l-look hot."

"You don't look so bad yourself."

I kiss her, lifting her dress and bunching it around her waist. I glance down and ask, "Where the h-hell is y-your underwear?"

She grins. "I can't have a VPL in this dress. It's silk."

I release my erection from the restraints of the suit pants. "I c-can't b-believe you've been p-pantiless a-a-all d-day. If I'd h-have known . . ."

"You'd have bent me over that bench in church," she finishes.

I push into her, groaning as she squeezes me. It's been too long since we last fucked, and I can't restrain myself as I begin moving fast, slamming into her over and over. "I w-want you o-off the c-c-contraceptive pill," I mutter, nipping the skin on her neck. "We're g-g-gonna make a s-s-tart on f-f-filling you with b-babies."

"You're so romantic," she says, smirking. I slam harder, and she cries out, the smirk falling from her face as her orgasm rips through her. I kiss her hard to muffle her moans. I follow moments after, resting my head on her shoulder while I catch my breath.

I place her on the ground, and she straightens her dress. I'm fastening my trousers when my mobile rings. Pulling it from my pocket, my heart speeds up. "It's K-kat," I mutter, accepting the call.

"How is she?"

"W-where a-a-re you?"

"I called the hospital and they said she's been released. Is she with you?"

"Yes."

"Good," she whispers. "I'm sorry I ran like that. Honestly, things have been hard for me lately. I just couldn't take any more."

"S-social s-services are i-involved."

"I thought they might be. Look, I'm getting help for anger and depression. Would you keep August with you for now, until I'm feeling better?"

"Of c-course."

"It's not forever, Scar. I will come back for her. Tell her I'll call her every week, and tell her I'm sorry—" Her voice breaks with emotion. "I'm sorry for walking out when she needed me. I'll come back better and stronger."

"Do y-you n-need anything?" I ask.

"No. Just look after August until I can." She disconnects, and I stare at Gracie. I never expected that. I thought she'd turn up at the club screaming and shouting to take August back home.

Gracie smiles, she listened in. "She's gonna stay with us." I nod. "August will be so happy." I nod again. It's all August has wanted since I turned up to see her in hospital. "Last week, everything seemed such a mess. And today, everything's falling into place."

I kiss Gracie. She's right about that. "I l-love y-you."

"I love you. More than anything."

When I first met Gracie, she was a shadow of the woman she once was. She was scared and hurt. Looking at her now, it's amazing how much she's recovered. Her determination and strength have amazed me. Not only did she repair herself, but she repaired me too. Her light is so beautiful, it brought me from a dark place where I was barely existing. I will spend my life making her happy, so she never knows that sort of pain again.

I'll dedicate everything to support Mav in his fight to help women like Gracie, because he's right, everyone deserves to be safe and happy. If we can make that possible, then we should.

GRACIE
Six months later...

Hearing the guilty verdict is like music to my ears. Jen was the final trial to endure, and it was worth hearing every sordid detail of how her father begged her to set me up. Jen had been recruiting girls for years, even from school age, but she'd refused to hand me over. That was until she fell in love with Edward and realised I might get in her way. She drugged my drink and led me out the back of the bar, telling me I needed air. She then waited for me to pass out before letting Braydon and his friend take me away.

She told the judge she didn't think about me much after that because she felt guilty for what she'd done. My lawyer argued she wasn't that guilt-ridden because she sat with my family, planning search parties to find me, knowing they never would. She also went on to plan her wedding, thinking I'd never be seen again.

Edward came to the hearing and listened to the details, and the second her verdict was read out, he left. She called out to him from the dock, but he ignored her. I texted him shortly after to inform him of her ten-year prison sentence. The judge said she was no different to a people trafficker and, therefore, would get the same sentence. The police uncovered at least twenty girls with a connection to Jen who'd gone missing.

Scar spent the entire trial by my side. He's been amazing, juggling parenting and this. He's watched every sordid video, heard every single piece of evidence, and stood strong beside me even though I know it killed him inside. When the Chief Constable received a twenty-year sentence, I think he almost shed a tear. It was proof that my decision to prosecute and not kill was the right one. I feel like I have justice, but if he happens to die halfway through his sentence, I won't be upset.

I step outside the courthouse and feel the weight of the last few years lift. My mum squeezes my hand, and Scar rubs a hand over my very pregnant stomach. "I need ice cream," I announce, and they both laugh. My latest craving for strawberry ice cream is out of hand.

"We'll get August from school, then get ice cream," says Mum. It's the perfect end to a stressful few weeks.

I came through hell and found my perfect life. Without it, I wouldn't have met Scar, and I thank God for him every single day. He's everything I ever wanted and more. We helped each other overcome some of the worst times of our lives, and together, we're so happy. We'll soon be adding to our little family, and if he has his way, I'll constantly be pregnant. But that's okay . . . I like the way we get into this state.

THE END

A note from me to you

The Perished Riders series is my second MC series. If you haven't read the first, go check it out on Amazon.

For more books in this series, you'll find them here: https://linktr.ee/NicolaJaneUK

If you enjoyed this story, please consider leaving a rating or review on Amazon and Goodreads. It helps independent authors out.

I'm a UK author, based in Nottinghamshire. I live with my husband of many years, our two teenage boys and our four little dogs. I write MC and Mafia romance with plenty of drama and chaos. I also love to read similar books. My favourite author is Tillie Cole. Before I became a full-time author, I was a teaching assistant working in a primary school.

If you'd like to follow my writing journey, join my readers group on Facebook, the link is above. You can also use that link if you're a book blogger, I'd love you to sign up to my team.

Printed in Great Britain
by Amazon